# 2043 A.D.

# 2043 A.D.

Edward M Wolfe

This is a work of fiction. All of the characters, organizations, events and locations portrayed in this story are either products of the author's imagination or used fictitiously.

ISBN: 978-0692470619

Copyright © 2015 by Edward M Wolfe
Cover design by Shaelee Wolfe

All Rights Reserved

http://edwardmwolfe.com

Dedication:

*To dear friends, old and new.*
*And always, to Shaelee and Zachariah.*

Acknowledgments:

*Special thanks to my beta readers. Your input is more valuable than I can put into words. And being a writer, that says a lot.*

*Special thanks to John Zanetti, author of the brilliant sci-fi novel "Cantal's Revenge" for the idea of a news drone, which I'd somehow missed among all my other drones.*

# One

As soon as the small elderly Vietnamese man finished locking the front doors of his convenience store, one of the men in black handcuffed him while the other walked over to their patrol car. Equality Enforcement Corps was emblazoned on the vehicle's front doors, and abbreviated on their uniforms as EEC.

"How is this more fair when no one has convenience of convenience store?" he protested as he was led away from his store entrance. "I do not discriminate! I am minority! Why I would discriminate against minority?"

The agents ignored him, other than one of them pushing his head down as he guided the man into the back seat. They got into the front of the car and the driver backed up, turning it around toward the rising sun to exit the parking lot.

The two teenagers who had called in the "Eeks," as they were referred to on the street, smiled at the man as he was driven out of the parking lot and laughed at the results of their report.

"You know how much money this cost me? Everybody lose now. This is not more equality."

The agent in the passenger seat looked back at the prisoner.

"You can think about how much money you're losing while you complete your sensitivity training. And in the future, maybe you won't make the mistake of assuming young black men are going to rob you, just because they're black."

One of the teens who stood apart from the rest of the watching crowd frowned at what he was seeing and shook his head. The agent in the passenger seat noticed his expression of disapproval and quickly pointed his scanner at the kid. He then looked at the right half of the windshield and waited for the readout to display.

```
Chip I.D.: Null

RFID Failure. Attempting facial recognition.........

Target match found

Subject: Deron Michael Young
Age: 17
Race/Gender: Caucasian/Male
Mother: Kathleen Diane Young
Father: Unknown
No Arrests or complaints. Checking known
equality factors...
```

"I told you already! I do not think they thieves because black skin. They acting suspicious! Waiting for chance to steal. They looking around, careful, watching me, waiting for chance. I know thief when I see! I have business many years."

"That's enough. I need you to be quiet so I can write a report and call in your admission – so just can it for a while."

The tears welling in the old man's eyes finally spilled as he shook his head in disbelief.

"America bad place now. Worse than Vietnam."

```
Query Cont'd:

Social activity and reading habits indicate
high probability of unreported inequality
infractions and probability of anti-social
behavior.

Facial recognition search indicates association
with known felon convicted of distribution of
tobacco products to unregistered users.

Further examination recommended.

#End
```

The patrol car drove away with a silent hum from the electric motor. The old man looked back and wondered which one of the kids was Deron.

*You in big trouble now, kid.*

# Two

Several hours later, Deron sat alone at a school cafeteria table eating his lunch, lost in a novel, and almost oblivious to the sound of stupidity all around him. He could hear the other students talking, but it was just noise; a wall of sound that meant nothing to him and wasn't even noticeable after a while, like the smell of manure on a farm.

There were only a few pages until the end of his book. He suspected there was even less left to read than there appeared to be because there were always ads for other books in the back. He turned the page, and sure enough, that was the last page of the story. He felt something hit the back of his head, but he finished the last few paragraphs before closing the book and slowly turning around to look behind him.

As soon as he did so, several students two tables away started giggling. He knew it was them, but he didn't know which one. He looked down and saw a piece of an orange peel. He looked back at the giggling students and saw that one of the girls was eating an orange. It might have been thrown by the guy sitting on her right.

"Idiots." He stared at them and shook his head a little with a look of disgust. The giggling stopped, and was followed by forced attempts to ignore Deron and start a conversation.

"Did anyone watch *My Neighbor's Wife* last night?" one of them asked the other three.

Two of them nodded and one said, "Uh huh." They kept looking at Deron to see if he was still looking at them. He was, and they were all uncomfortable now. In fact, he had completely turned around on the bench and was now facing them, comfortably, just watching them as though he was watching television. The boldest of the group finally spoke up.

"Why don't you stare at some other shit, freak?"

Deron started laughing and said, "Some *other* shit? Apparently, you're not as dumb as you look." No one else joined in when Deron laughed again.

"Maybe I should just come over there and kick your ass, freak."

"Oh no! The angry Neanderthal is threatening to demonstrate physical superiority. Are you gonna beat on your chest too?"

"I'm about to beat on your head."

"If you touch me, I swear to the gods, you'll never play football again – if I let you live."

"What a psycho!" one of the girls exclaimed. "Just ignore him, Corey. He's like, totally mental, or something."

Corey continued to glare at Deron, who stared back at him calmly as if he were examining an exhibit in a museum. The other girl, the one eating the orange, waved her hand in the air.

"Can I ask you a question? What is your problem? Seriously."

Deron thought of a line from an old 2-D movie he'd watched at his grandfather's house, and answered, impersonating the villain, "It's the smell."

Both girls laughed. "Oh-em-gee, he is totally a freak!" one of them said.

Deron reached behind him for his book and stood up, facing the small group.

"I *am* a freak. A lethal freak. And I eat football players and cheerleaders for breakfast." He lowered his eyelids and looked into their eyes menacingly, one at a time, then walked away.

The other guy at their table, Brad, said, "You know, he really *is* crazy. It would probably be better to just stay off his radar. He might be crazy enough to actually kill someone."

Deron heard the remark and that was exactly the effect he was hoping for. The school had an anti-bullying policy, but Deron knew it was a joke. He was teased and taunted all the time, but there was little he could do about it. If he reported the behavior, he'd be treated worse by a greater number of people when the word spread that he had snitched. When the bullying first started shortly after he began attending high school, he decided the best defense was a feigned offense. If he could convince people he was crazy, then they might leave him alone.

His aggressive posturing and threats had taken place in view of lunch room security cams and were watched by a school safety officer monitoring the feeds. He made a note in Deron's file, reporting what'd he'd observed. "Student responding aggressively with threats of violence in response to playful teasing by other students." The safety officer attached a snippet of video to his note.

As Deron walked away, the bell rang, signaling the end of the lunch period. He left the cafeteria and entered the adjacent indoor quad, weaving in and out of increasing numbers of students filling the hall. He was only partially kidding when he had said the problem with other students was the smell.

Everyone he passed smelled strongly of something: perfume, cologne, body spray, hair-spray, hair gel, mousse, antiperspirant, dried sweat, flavored lip gloss, fabric softener, leave-in conditioner, e-cig vapor, and various body odors. Many of them just stood there talking; all of them interrupting each other and raising their voices to be heard over the sound of everyone else talking.

He was annoyed by them blocking the way, as if they weren't standing in front of their lockers for a reason. They just *had* to get in a few more words before going back to the dreadful silence and educational atmosphere of the classroom. And not one of them was saying anything of any importance. Just gabbing and blabbing and gossiping. Those who weren't talking were blasting their eardrums out with what passed for music through wireless earbuds as they rummaged in their lockers.

Deron went to his locker and retrieved his school-issued e-reader. Every book he could possibly need in any grade was pre-loaded on it, as well as all of the library books from the last twenty years. Few people read paper books anymore, except for the rare case when one was needed for research. Deron preferred reading paper books even though it contributed to his reputation of being weird. With his e-reader and paperback in hand, he closed his locker and headed toward his fifth period class: Independent Reading.

Most students who signed up for IR did so for the easily obtained high grade. Not that grades mattered anymore; everyone passed every class as long as they were present. But higher grade point averages translated to more bragging rights, as well as bonus credits in student bank accounts.

Reading entire books wasn't easy for them, but at least they didn't have to think or research or write a serious report. The only requirement in IR was to provide some basic information about the book in a small online form. They'd type the name of the book, the author, the number of pages, and the genre, then click Submit. The only thing some students got wrong was the genre, because it wasn't expressly stated anywhere in the book.

As easy as the IR class was, very few people signed up for it. The only elective class with less appeal than Independent Reading was Religious Studies, which wasn't going to be offered the following year. Despite laws against insulting people or being disrespectful, people still managed to get away with looking down on churchgoers without being charged with an equality infraction and loss of bank credits.

Deron exited the building on the far side of the quad, further from his next class than the side he'd started on. He deliberately took the long way around, walking on the grass to his next class. He stopped beside a large tree situated between two buildings, out of the view of the nearest security camera perched on the roof. He put his e-reader and his paperback in his backpack and reached into his pocket for a pack of real cigarettes. He took one out, looked around to make sure he was the only one out there, then lit it, blowing the smoke upward into the branches and leaves hoping to obscure it from anyone who might come along.

He pulled the paperback out and read the last page of the story again, enjoying it in silence this time. He found it easy to slip back into the feeling of being in the alien world. He closed the book and wished he could live on another planet, or have an exciting and adventurous life like the people in books always had. He'd even settle for peace and quiet somewhere on his own planet, away from all of the mindless zombies.

The bell rang. He was late for class, but didn't care. What difference did it make? If he just walked away from the school and never came back – what difference would it make? He wasn't really learning anything useful anyway. School seemed like nothing more than a way to warehouse kids while their parents were at work. It kept them busy and gave them a chance to practice being brainless robots before moving on to real life where being superficial, dispassionate, and up-to-date on everything that didn't matter could make or break your career.

He dropped his cigarette and snuffed it out under a black sneaker before finishing the long walk to his next class. Since he'd never make it to another planet, and was stuck on one populated mainly by stupid and useless people, all he could do was visit other planets in his mind. This served a dual purpose. It kept him entertained, and for much of the time, he was oblivious to his pointless real life.

# Three

Jameson Fielding, PhD and MD, sat in one his new offices staring at the fish swimming around on the far side of the room. He was anxiously awaiting the commencement of a program he had proposed and developed and been named the director of. It was his brilliant idea to not wait until young people developed criminal minds, but to spot them and treat them in advance. He thought of it as prehabilitation.

"Doctor Fielding?"

"Yes?" he responded to his administrative assistant who doubled as a security guard.

"Garrett is here to see you, sir."

"Excellent, Toby. Send him in."

The tall, handsome doctor swiveled his chair to face forward, eagerly turning away from the fish he'd been concentrating on as he waited for this moment. The door opened and Garrett entered the silent room. He stood just inside the doorway until the doctor gestured for him to sit on the couch. Fielding looked at him expectantly.

"Have you got them?"

"I believe I do, sir. I ran the revised algorithms again and a fourth name just came up. If you approve, we can start right away."

"Tell me about them."

"Subject number one was a lucky catch. He comes from a wealthy family and has a private home tutor but he attends a university class on business administration. His father is grooming him to start in the family business as soon as he graduates."

The doctor waved his hand, not interested in the family background. He wanted to hear the good stuff. How did this subject qualify as not a criminal yet, but with the potential to become one? He needed bad seeds that hadn't flowered yet.

"It was at college where most of the informative reports came in. He's been written up multiple times for behavior indicating a superiority-complex. He has no special skills to justify it — it's just based on his family's wealth and position, both pre and post-war."

"He continues to behave in a superior fashion even after the establishment of financial equality?"

"Yes, sir. I suspect the family has ingrained in him this idea of being better than those who had nothing before the war. According to the reports, you'd think we were still living in 2020. He has friends, so to speak, but he treats them as inferiors. Intellectually speaking, most of them are. He has a very high I.Q."

"Interesting. Who else?"

"Subject number two is a female. Also an only child of seventeen like subject one. She's adopted a retro look from the previous century involving strange hair styles and fashion associated with rebellion. When it first came about in the 1970s it was called 'punk'. She has no meaningful friendships and seems practically genderless in her behavior and activities."

"Why do you believe she has latent sociopathic tendencies?"

"Well, the punk sub-culture was against society in general, but strongly against the government. So naturally, that caught my attention. But in her case, she seems to hold animosity and resentment toward her peers. Complete lack of social integration."

"Another case of superiority complex?"

"Essentially, yes. She also has a higher than average I.Q. And that's something all four subjects have in common, which we may want to examine further. Perhaps they're unaffected by the fluoridation, or they're consuming less than average."

"We'll make a note of that and keep an eye out for other commonalities as we proceed with treatment. Number three?" The doctor went to take a drink of his tea and discovered that his cup was empty. Garrett continued as the doctor refilled his cup from the wall dispenser behind him. He did not offer anything to Garrett.

"Number three is in some ways a typical loner, but he's also an odd mix activity-wise."

"How so?" Fielding asked as he stirred sugar and cream into his tea with his back to Garrett.

"Well, he's very athletic, into exercise and weightlifting, but he's also very much into reading, *by choice*. That in itself is unusual since kids almost never read anything they're not required to read. But he not only spends leisure time reading fiction, he reads a variety of educational non-fiction. History, biographies, medical and nutritional books, and so on."

"Ebooks?" the doctor asked, raising his eyebrows.

"The fiction is digital. The other stuff is only available from libraries in paper form."

"Okay. And what brings him to our attention?"

"Aside from his unusual combination of activities, excessive reading, and the subject matter that he reads, he's a loner like subjects two and four. He also refrains from participation of any sort in classroom activities and a few of his teachers have red-flagged him just for being unusual and making them feel uncomfortable."

"In what way?"

"They don't come right out and say it, sir, but I suspect that with the amount of extra-curricular studying he does, they feel intimidated, as if he's making himself more educated than they are."

"That wouldn't be difficult. They're essentially babysitters. Tell me about the new one."

"Subject number four just came up, just before I asked to see you." Garrett eagerly consulted his printout to refresh his memory. The blinds on the wall behind the doctor cast horizontal shadow stripes on the page. "Two of his reports just came in today, actually. The most recent one from a school security officer. He was observed threatening and acting menacingly toward some athletes and cheerleaders."

The doctor leaned forward. This was interesting. Overt anti-social behavior. It might be too late to recondition him, but if it wasn't, and they succeeded, he could be a very valuable test subject. "Any history of actual violence?"

"No, sir. He's only threatened it, but his threats are rather vicious and unheard of since we began monitoring students. This morning, before school, he caught the attention of an Equality Enforcement Corp officer who was bringing in a citizen for racial sensitivity training."

"Was he cited?" the doctor interrupted.

"No, sir. He was only scanned. The officer reported that since they already had a citizen in custody, he just scanned the kid out of curiosity. As it turns out, he wasn't chipped, but facial-recognition came through.

The doctor opened his top desk drawer and removed his e-cig. He leaned back and begun puffing on it, contemplating the odd nature of this fourth subject. "And what did he have on file before today?"

"Miscellaneous but minor reports from teachers and security monitors about his unusual interest in reading, similar to subject two, but with four it's almost entirely fiction. Oh," Garret interrupted himself. "That's another thing. Almost everything he's ever read was written by Caucasian authors."

The doctor couldn't believe how complex this subject was becoming and he wondered how he hadn't already been cited and sent in for basic equality education.

"He sounds almost too good to be true. A virtual psychopath just waiting to break out of his shell. I wonder if it's not too late. I can't wait to see how he responds to treatment. Are you sure he has no record of being detained or cited?"

"There is one archival record of him being at the scene of a minor crime. A suburban drone has him on video purchasing illegal tobacco products."

"Why wasn't he arrested at that time?"

"The seller is on a Do Not Detain order so we can track him to his supplier. The kid got lucky."

The doctor set down his e-cig and said, "So did we. Is that all on the fourth subject?"

"There's one more thing that might be interesting. When his mother came to plea for religious exemption to keep the kid from getting chipped, the grandfather did all of the talking. And *he* has definitely been on our radar. He's a pre-war holdout with multiple citizen reports of outspoken condemnation of just about everything we've done to make life in Orange County better than anywhere in the country, if not the world."

"Interesting. He could be an argument for nurture instead of nature. He's perfect. When can we have all of them here and ready for treatment?"

"I can send eeks, I mean, E.E.C. officers for them as soon as you give the word."

"You have it," the doctor said and turned back to the fish that he found endlessly fascinating. "Thank you, Garrett."

Fielding's assistant walked to the door, thinking, then turned before leaving and said, "Doctor, do you think it's significant that all of the subjects are smarter than average? Are these kids just too smart for their own good?"

Fielding responded without turning his head. "They're too smart for the *greater* good, Garrett."

# Four

All six students in the classroom looked up as Deron opened the door. He thought it was funny how people always did that, as if something interesting was about to happen just because a door had opened. He did the same thing though, and didn't know why.

He went to his desk and logged in to the class via the computer embedded in the glass surface of his desk. Every time he did so, he wondered what point there was in having his body present in the classroom. Oh yeah. If he logged in from home, he'd miss out on the wonderful *socialization* that came from being there in person.

"14th Tardy" flew at him, blinked a few times, then shrunk away. *Whatever.* He quickly tapped the virtual keys to submit a new Completed Read, then thought about what he should read next. Classic twentieth century science fiction, or something completely different this time, but from the same era? Maybe some Stephen King for fast and light entertainment after the intense "Mote in God's Eye" he'd just completed.

He went up to the teacher's desk and asked, "Can I go to the library, Mr. Miller? I'd like to get another paper book."

"*May* I go to the library?" the teacher corrected.

"Yes, you may," Deron answered. "But no running in the hall."

The teacher smiled reluctantly as he typed up a digital pass which he beamed to Deron's communicator and made a print-out as well, just in case the comm malfunctioned. When the paper spat onto his desk, he handed it to Deron.

"Try not to take too long."

"Thanks." Deron took the paper and refrained from saying anything sarcastic about how he'd miss out on so much if he didn't get back right away. He felt that his thoughts about the pointlessness of so many things were also pointless. He had no reason to speak them. Besides, Mr. Miller was actually pretty cool. He didn't want to antagonize him.

He approached the door to the library, feeling the sun heating the back of his black tee shirt. The library windows were polarized and dark. He assumed there wouldn't be many students inside. There never were. The library was an unpopular place, except for when it provided a means of getting work credit for doing nothing.

He stepped through the door and welcomed the large drop in temperature. Outside was in the low 90s but felt hotter through his black shirt. Inside, the library felt like 65 degrees. He shivered and looked around. As he suspected, there were only a few students sitting at tables, talking and passing notes with open books sitting before them as if they were reading.

He headed toward the science fiction section to see what was available before checking with the librarian to see if "Lucifer's Hammer" had come in yet. He'd ordered it two months ago. It should be here by now. After browsing the same old limited selection of physical books, he headed toward the Check Out and Return counter that was adjacent to the librarian's desk. If he wanted to find something new, he'd have to browse the ebooks later, but that had never yielded anything good in the past. He suspected that computers wrote most of the new fiction books.

The librarian turned from the two EEC officers she had been talking to and looked right at him. Her eyes widened and she exclaimed in a surprisingly loud voice, "That's him!" as if he had snatched her purse earlier that day. Rather than charging him as he half expected them to do, they merely turned their heads and looked at him as he slowed down but continued heading toward them.

The three of them stood staring as he walked up to deposit his book in the slot labeled "RETURNS." The two men were in their mid to late 20's and dressed in the completely black uniform worn by all divisions of the Department of Equal Opportunity. Deron had no concerns about being guilty of any equality violations and didn't understand why they were looking at him as though he was. As he stepped up and dropped his paperback in the return slot, the librarian inched back and looked rapidly from Deron to the two officers. The man further from

Deron looked at a sheet of paper in his hand, then at Deron and asked, "Deron Michael Young?"

"Yeah. Are you looking for a serial killer?"

The men in black were confused by his question and looked to the librarian. She took another nervous step back and shook her head. She didn't understand him either.

"Excuse me," she muttered, and quickly let herself through the swinging, waist-high door to her left. Hurrying off toward the opposite side of the library, she started to look back once but thought better of it and kept her eyes straight ahead, looking toward the Library Administration office.

The man closest to Deron said, "We'd like to talk to you, Deron." He had an Asian accent that matched his features. Both of them had an air of command authority about them. Although he'd said they'd "like" to talk to him, it didn't sound like a choice was involved.

Deron knew they were similar to police, but they were different than ordinary cops. They didn't have the predatory look that Deron associated with police. Unlike the ones on TV, real cops seemed to be starving for crime or criminals so they'd have something to do. They scrutinized everyone in their line of sight for signs of criminality. It made no sense. The reported crime rate in the cities seemed to be constantly on the rise, although there didn't seem to be an increase in observable crime. And there were far more equality officers than there were police officers, so it seemed obvious to him they didn't need the police very much anymore.

They started to walk toward the exit fully expecting Deron to accompany them. He did, and he realized it was too late to hide the pack of cigarettes making a rectangular bulge in his shirt pocket. He assumed that the law to finally and completely ban smoking must've just been passed. Smoking was the only law he had ever broken. But he broke it consistently and in multiple ways. Being under twenty-one, he purchased his cigarettes illegally as many adults did. He had already decided he would not register as a controlled-substance addict and would not apply for a smoking license. He violated environmental laws every time he lit up outdoors within city limits, and inside his bathroom without an EPA approved indoor-air-filtration device. He probably violated another law when he smoked on school property like he had just done moments ago. *I'm busted*, he thought. *No doubt they can smell it on me. But it's not an equality crime, so why did they send eeks?*

After going through the doors, they headed north toward the main administration building. They continued without speaking as though they hadn't left the library's mandatory silence behind them. Deron thought about the insignia for the government department they worked for: D.E.O.

*It was just another useless part of the government. DEO might as well stand for Dimwits Engaged in Onanism.* He almost laughed out loud, but wondered again what the DEO could want with him. *Was the government using them to enforce a new smoking law?* Had he broken a new law that he hadn't heard of yet? New laws were announced every month. More and more citizens became criminals to some degree overnight. It was harder and harder for the average citizen to not inadvertently break the increasing number of laws.

He watched the pair of black pant legs in front of him as he walked along and thought about crime and being a criminal. He realized that there was only one pair of legs in front of him now and that the other man had positioned himself behind him. He suddenly felt apprehension. *Something's wrong with this picture. Possession of a pack of Marlboros was still a misdemeanor, wasn't it?* If they arrested him for it, it would surely cost his mother a lot of credits, but it would be his first offense. Maybe he should just ask them what the hell they wanted to talk about. For some reason, he couldn't. He pretended that it didn't matter and he didn't care. He continued to follow them right past the Admin building and now into the staff parking lot.

*Where the hell are we going?* he yelled inside his head. Now he was starting to feel panicky. An itch started in the center of his back, and regular breathing required effort. He imagined the tall, black man behind him pointing a gun at his back. His legs started to feel weak as blood rushed to his head, making him dizzy and flushed. Thoughts rapidly flashed through his mind. The librarian had pointed him out to these guys. Was his book *way* overdue? He laughed nervously at his internal monologue and tried to tell himself to relax. *There's nothing to get worked up over. This will end up being something completely mundane,* he told himself.

They stepped up to a white EEC four-door sedan with opaque tinted windows. Deron looked left and right, quickly debating if he should make a run for it without even knowing what he would be running from. The man in front turned sideways and faced Deron. "We're just going to take a short ride. This won't take long." The other man was still standing behind him.

"*What* won't take long?" he demanded to know, trying to sound aloof and unconcerned. But his voice came out sounding high-pitched and loud, like a scared kid was speaking through him. His ears burned at the sound of his own voice.

"Our job is just to transport you. Someone else will answer all your questions soon enough," said the man behind him as the man in front opened the back door and gestured for Deron to get inside.

"I'm not going anywhere with you until you tell me what this is about!"

His words came out in a rush and his voice sounded more like his own; confident and defiant. "I'm not about to be ordered around by two complete strangers and driven off to God knows where. If you expect me to get in that car and go with you, the least you're going to have to do is tell me why. "

The Asian looked at him for a second, not accustomed to non-compliance and said, "We're with the government. Get in."

Despite being a smoker, Deron was still a fast sprinter. He was sure he could outrun these two, even though they looked very healthy and in excellent shape. They'd beat him as far as stamina went, but he could lose them quickly by taking alleys and hopping fences into backyards, and zig-zagging his way through the neighborhood, or even the entire city if necessary. He had lived all of his seventeen years in various cities around Orange County. He knew Westminster and Garden Grove as well as he knew his own neighborhood. He knew he could get away and then find a place to hide if they were bent on pursuing him. His grandfather would give him money if it was an emergency.

He felt a hand on his back, nudging him toward the back seat. It felt surreal to him that he was about to be driven away from school in the middle of the day. He wasn't worried about being embarrassed. But he did feel like something was happening that would cause an irreversible change in his life.

He had no idea what he could've done to draw the attention of the eeks, but he sensed that whatever it was, it was going to require him to change something about his life that he wasn't going to agree with, then trouble was really going to start. He imagined that he'd end up being just like his grandfather.

Thinking of Charlie, Deron suddenly decided he wouldn't just go willingly into the arms of the government, and he took off running.

## Five

"No!" the old man yelled into the phone. He looked around his modest one-bedroom house with an expression of anger, fear, and exasperation. There was a softness in his eyes that contradicted his tone of voice and his flushed features. He stood there listening and shaking his head slowly like he was a camel being informed that the Straw-Placers were on their way to put another straw on his over-burdened back.

"Visitor," a female electronic voice called out, informing him that someone was ringing his doorbell.

"Honey. I've gotta go. Whatever happens, you know I always loved you and Deron more than anything. I just can't change, sweetheart. I'm sorry." He hung up the phone and wiped a tear from his eye.

"Visitor!" the voice cried a bit louder, having not sensed an auditory acknowledgement to its first announcement. *Just one more thing that isn't the same. One more robot to make life easier*, the old man thought as he leaned against the wall beside the phone.

Charlie had resisted every encroachment of what he still referred to as his "civil liberties" and "God-Given rights." He was an oddity long before the government had taken such a large interest in people's private lives. He had never licensed his pets and was outraged at the thought of having to get a license to have a four-legged companion. His dogs had always worn collars with their names and Charlie's phone number. What more was necessary?

"License" was a word that Charlie knew the real meaning of and he wasn't about to be brainwashed by any new-fangled definitions. He also refused to have his rights turned into privileges by strangers who granted themselves the power to control others. A man had a right to own and care for a dog. License meant "permission" and Charlie would be damned if he was ever going to ask another man, or a group of them, for permission to own a dog – to have a best friend.

Licenses for dogs, businesses, cars, and everything else were just for government agents to meddle in your business and keep track of what you were up to. Charlie used to try telling people that there were unlimited ways you could be tracked, monitored, and controlled, even before they'd started putting cameras everywhere and computer chips inside people "for their own good."

No one was a person anymore. They were files, numbers, statistics. Even before the war that led to this "great new society" they were allegedly living in now, employers were blatant about how they viewed the average working person. They'd referred to people as "human resources."

But nobody listened to Charlie then. His wife especially had little tolerance for his fanaticism and had threatened to leave him over it just before the war. Shortly after the reformed government took over, he'd finally given up on trying to share his opinion. Things were a hundred times worse with the new government and still, nobody seemed to care.

And now his daughter sounded just like the mother she'd only known as a young child, trying to convince him to just accept the way things were and to quit breaking so many laws all the time.

He now had a dog without a license, failed to register with the Senior Supplements Administration, smoked on occasion without a license, and worst of all he'd failed to turn in his weapons or check them in to a government sport-shooting facility which was the only way a person could "own" a firearm; and who knew what other host of smaller infractions he was guilty of on a regular basis. Charlie was waiting for the announcement that a county permit would now be required to scratch your balls.

And now he believed they'd finally come for him. They were at the door. He knew it was gonna happen sooner or later, and he'd always vowed that he would die on his feet before he'd live on his knees. He was actually surprised he'd gone this long without being taken in. He knew he set a "bad example," and in this new age where appearances and impressions were everything, he wouldn't be tolerated for very long.

Charlie insisted on using an old-fashioned handset. He had called the phone company shortly after moving into his house and requested a repairman to fix a problem that he would not give specifics about. When the repairman arrived, Charlie told him to disable all of the microphones in the house and to put in a regular phone that he could hold in his hand.

After some disagreement and squabbling, the repairman finally agreed to remove only the microphones that weren't legally required. He could take out the auxiliary mics that enabled hands-free communication from anywhere in the house, but the rest were required by the Orange County Homeland Security and Charlie couldn't pay him enough to mess with those.

Now he stood next to the counter where he kept his wireless handset charging cradle. He took deep breaths, trying to build up his resolve and courage to face what he believed was an inevitable confrontation. Every day he wondered if that would be the day they would come to take him away.

"A VISITOR IS AT THE DOOR!" the autohost sounded at a much higher volume. Sensors told the host that Charlie, or someone, was home, so it was determined to announce the visitor until it got a response. If it had not detected Charlie's body heat and motion it would've informed the visitor that no one was "available" and offered to take a message. If Charlie didn't answer very soon the autohost would call paramedics and police after one more announcement and an extremely loud alarm that might scare off intruders who were preventing him from answering. He had not given the house a Do Not Disturb request, and in the absence of a DND, it was assumed that the resident would want, and possibly need to be informed of visitors.

Charlie took a quick look at the phone and silently said goodbye again to his daughter. The moment had arrived and he was going to face it like a man. He went to the fridge and opened the door. He had removed all the shelves and drawers to make one large storage area. In the space where a crisper drawer had been, there sat a few cans of beer, a jar of mayonnaise, lunch meat, and a 12-gauge shotgun.

Charlie closed the fridge and opened the freezer door above. This was almost a ritual he had performed to calm his nerves whenever he was spooked or feared that the cops were on their way. Now he performed it one last time in preparation for the real thing. He took the lid off the box of shotgun shells and placed it next to the box and shut the door. He would invite the officers into the house and offer them a drink if they were going easy on him, or he'd beg to take his medication before being put in cuffs if they were playing hardball. And then he'd make his final stand for as long as it lasted. Reaching into the freezer for reloads, and maybe, if he lasted long enough, sipping a beer while waiting for re-enforcements to arrive.

Charlie took a deep breath and walked to the front door. He puffed up his 61 year-old chest and breathed life into his lean, old muscles. He was ready to die a free American. One of the last, he imagined. He put his hand on the doorknob and thought to himself, "Don't tread on me, you sons of bitches!" and pulled the door open just as the autohost blasted its klaxon alarm.

Charlie jumped and let out a small scream at the sound of the alarm. The boy on the porch also screamed and then ran away. Charlie watched him go down the street about a block and a half before he finally slowed to catch his breath and think about whether he wanted to sell any more candy bars this day.

"PLEASE RESPOND. YOU HAVE A VISITOR. PLEASE RESPOND NOW."

"Oh, Jesus," Charlie said with a sigh, and closed the door.

## Six

Kathleen Young got off the phone with her father and wondered where her son had disappeared to. If it wasn't one man in her life giving her worries, it was another. And of course her son had to be just as difficult and eccentric as her father. Deron took after Charlie in many ways. Not being where he was supposed to be at a certain time was just one of them.

If he'd had any friends, Kathleen would have assumed he was visiting with someone after school, but Deron almost always came directly home after school, went to his room and absorbed himself in a book. Kathleen would never understand her own son or what was wrong with him. She forgot to ask Charlie if he'd heard from Deron, but he probably would have mentioned it if Deron was coming over to visit.

She wasn't used to coming home to an empty house and the silence bothered her. She had always hated being alone. She spoke to the empty room. "Front blinds, open." The Venetian blinds turned sideways until they were completely perpendicular to the window, allowing as much light into the empty room as possible. She walked over and looked through the slats to see if anyone was walking down the street, working in their yards, or even driving by. She just wanted to see someone somewhere to break the feeling of loneliness.

It occurred to her that even if Deron had been home right now, the house would be just as silent with him in his room reading. She started to wonder why it mattered so much that he wasn't here when there'd be no noticeable difference anyway. Not wanting to be alone with her thoughts any longer, she turned on the television to clear her mind.

*"...is expected to meet with approval by the assembly and be signed by the County Administrator into law. Phil Harkner, a spokesman for the remnants of the American Tobacco Coalition says the measure will unfairly stigmatize adult smokers and cause a dramatic increase in crime if it becomes law. Assembly leader Nancy Nguyen said...."*

Kathleen picked up the remote control and changed the channel. If she knew what channel she wanted, she could have just told the TV, but she had never memorized the channels, and she didn't know what was on right now. Since it was on a 24 hour news channel, Deron must've been watching it before leaving for school.

She didn't think it was normal for a young boy to be so caught up in watching the news. She certainly had no interest in national or world events as a child, or even now, and she couldn't understand why her son did. It must be more of her father's influence on the boy.

She wondered what type of man Deron's father would have turned out to be and if he could have possibly been a better influence on her son than her own father had been. She supposed he probably wouldn't have been a good parent. After getting Kathleen pregnant at a party when she was fifteen, he offered to go with her to get an abortion. When she declined, he disappeared. The irony of the situation was that she had nothing against abortion – she had just thought that with a baby, she'd never be alone again. And now here she was, a young mother of a teenager who never wanted to do anything fun and preferred to be by himself.

She sat down on the couch and undid the loose knot she had tied her hair into for her job as a maid, and as she shook it out, letting it fall down her back in long blonde waves, she let her thoughts fall away from her as well. She resumed channel-surfing until she found a popular game show and relaxed in the more comfortable mental state she began to slip into as her mind focused on the smiling, woman spinning a large horizontal wheel.

She had one last thought about Deron's absence before she got completely caught up in the phrase-puzzle that three contestants were competing to solve.

## Seven

Deron dreamed that he and Michelle Granger were on the top of a tall building. Michelle was a junior at George Washington High and one of the few people with whom Deron associated. They had grown up as next-door neighbors, had been best friends throughout their childhood, and had almost become romantically involved at one time. Presently, Deron had mixed feelings about her, but those feelings were not present in his dream.

He looked over at her on the roof-top with the skyline behind her filled with the outlines of taller buildings contrasted against the setting sun and he was momentarily distracted by her stunning beauty. He wished they could just relax and talk and forget about the two young men who were chasing them.

"Go, Deron. You've got to hurry! They'll be here any minute."

"I know," he said. He suddenly felt an awful and overwhelming sadness. He loved her so much, and even now, with two strangers chasing him for some mysterious reason, and not knowing what his future held or if he'd ever see her again, he didn't feel safe telling her what he truly felt. He wanted to reach out and embrace her, knowing that his love for her was so strong and so intensely powerful that no words would be necessary. She would simply feel how he felt about her, and if the world were a sane and just place, she'd reciprocate his feelings.

He turned in a slow circle, scanning the rooftop for the best possible escape route. He had to address the more pressing problem just now. This wasn't the time or place to tell Michelle that he was in love with her.

He took her hand and rushed to the edge of the building. A three foot stucco wall lined the edge of the roof all the way around except for a gap where a metal ladder descended to the fire escape on the top floor. Deron and Michelle looked from this opening to the matching one on the next roof over, both of them thinking the same thing. Deron would have to jump across the seven foot span. It was his only chance for escape.

"You can do it. I know you can, Deron."

"I'm gonna need a running start. What will you tell them when they get here?" In the non-sense of dreams, he imagined her answering, "I'll tell them that I love you."

"That depends on what they ask me," she said with perfect, awake logic. "You better hurry or you'll be here when they arrive," she added. He took one last look at her face, her hair, her eyes. *God, she's beautiful*, he thought, then he turned and took several steps away from the edge of the roof. He mentally prepared himself for the jump. *If I don't make it I'll never see her again.*

He looked at her one more time as he readied himself to defy death.

"You're gonna be okay, Deron. You're gonna be just fine," she assured him.

He had seen her lips moving as she said this, but the voice wasn't hers. The incongruity instantly awoke him. He opened his eyes and saw a young blonde woman standing beside the bed he was lying on. "There you go, sweetheart. It was just a dream. You're okay. Are you hungry?"

His mind was swirling, rapidly sifting through various thoughts and images, trying to put reality back together. He didn't know where he was or what was real for a second as the pieces of the real world gradually fell into place. It was like a curtain had risen in a theater before the props and actors had gotten in their places and he was looking at the stage before it was ready.

Suddenly everything clicked and he recalled his last waking moments and what had happened and he asked, "Where am I?"

# Eight

It was the beginning of June and the sun was starting its late, summer descent. Drake Austin sat in his car across from the convenience store at an intersection of a residential and a commercial street. He looked to the west to gauge how much longer before darkness would fully set in so he could get to work.

He had just followed two young women from Westminster Community College until they turned onto this street. He pulled over to the curb and watched to see if they would pull into a driveway, or if they'd turn at the other end of the street, forcing him to try to catch up with them. His luck was in. They pulled into the seventh driveway on the right side. There was another car already in the driveway but it was a purple Mazda RoseZetta so he didn't think a boyfriend or husband lived with them. He was sure the RoseZetta belonged to the girl in the passenger seat.

Now he was just waiting for the sun to finish setting. The anticipation and excitement were driving him crazy. The day had been another hot one and he hoped the driver didn't go directly into the bath or shower. He hoped she would eat first or read her mail or something. He needed just a few more minutes until it would be dark enough for him to get into position.

He pocketed the slim camera that sat beside him on the seat and removed a spare battery and a memory card from the glove box. He would not risk taking these types of photos with his communicator's built-in camera. He didn't know what happened with the data on that device, but he suspected the authorities could scan it anytime they wanted since it was permanently on the city-provided Wi-Fi network. He pressed a button and the car windows went up. He got out and locked the car, then to waste a few more seconds, he put his left foot on the fender of his car and retied his shoelace. Then he did the same with the other shoe. He stood up straight and brushed imaginary dust from his pants as he surveyed the street. There was a woman walking her dog but she was heading in the opposite direction, so he didn't expect her to be a problem.

From force of habit he patted his right pant pocket and the breast pocket of his coat, confirming that he had both his e-cig and his spare battery. He looked at his reflection in the car window and wished again that he had kept a spare set of dark clothes in his car.

He'd been in the middle of a simple repair job on the college's wireless cable signal when he first spotted the brunette coming out of a class and heading to the parking lot. He stopped what he was doing and followed her as if he had no volition of his own. It would have been better to wait until he had scoped out her house, found out if she lived alone or not, and how frequently she had visitors, what her routine was, et cetera, but he was so stricken by her that he threw all his regular habits out the window and just followed her like an automaton.

When she reached her convertible Volkswagen, the other girl was already sitting in the passenger side waiting for her. The two girls talked, laughed, and looked around as they drove home, never looking at the gray sedan that followed them. Neither of them had any reason to notice the man with the dark gray hair behind the wheel. He was as anonymous and plain as his car. Both girls were young, healthy, and good-looking by anybody's standards. They wouldn't have noticed him even if they had been looking for single men.

Drake was forty-seven years old. He wore his gray hair unkempt and without any kind of part or style. It hung down on all sides at various lengths from a dirty baseball cap, more so in the back where it was the longest. His dress shirt was thin and old, translucent without a tee shirt beneath it, and it was permanently stained a light brownish-yellow below the armpits. The coat he wore looked like it came from a suit purchased long ago and had received little care or washing. His pants were a navy blue khaki that resembled the type that might've been worn by attendants who used to put gas in cars before he was born. His shoes were a nondescript black.

He definitely wouldn't attract the attention of two good-looking college freshman on their way home on a warm summer night. Drake knew he wasn't very attractive with his plain, featureless face. He was aware that his regular alcohol consumption was beginning to take its toll. His skin was looking a little bland lately; his nose always appearing as though he had just vigorously blown it. And failing to shave for a week didn't make him look at all rugged or sexy.

He'd never been married, and at this late stage didn't ever expect to be. In his more lucid moments he acknowledged that he was an ugly slob unlikely to ever have a real relationship with anyone - unlike the one he was about to begin five houses down on the north side of Maplewood street.

# Nine

The woman who might have been a nurse ignored Deron's question as she repeated her own, "Are you hungry, Deron?"

Deron didn't even know if he was hungry. It seemed that he couldn't recall having eaten for some time, but that hardly seemed important to him right now. Food was one of the last things on his mind.

"I'd like some ice water and some answers. Can you please tell me where I am, and why I'm here?"

"There's a pitcher of ice water on the table beside your bed. You're in an equality rehabilitation center, and I don't know exactly why you were brought here. My job is to make sure you're physically well-taken care of," she said, answering all of his questions to the best of her ability.

Deron rose up on one elbow and poured iced water into a paper cup and took notice of his surroundings for the first time. It looked pretty much like a hospital room to him. Sort of like a bare-bones motel room but with a tile floor.

"Why am I in an equality rehabilitation center?" he asked her after draining his first cup of water.

"I'm going to have to let someone else answer your questions. If you'd like some food, I can bring it to you now, or you can touch the call sensor when you're ready for it. Would you like anything to drink besides water?"

"No," he answered. She was nice but clearly wasn't going to give him the information he needed and wanted. "When can I speak to someone who can tell me what's going on?" He almost felt guilty for the tone he was taking with someone who was obviously only trying to do her job, but on the other hand, he felt he was doing a good job of holding back his temper under the circumstances.

"I'm sure the doctor will be in to talk to you as soon as I leave." She glanced up at a hidden camera, then looked around to make sure she wasn't leaving anything undone and then slowly headed for the door. She turned and faced Deron once more as she reached for the doorknob and said, "Don't forget. Just touch the call sensor and I'll bring your dinner." And then she was gone.

Deron quickly pulled the covers off and swung his feet onto the floor. He was wearing the boxer shorts he had put on this morning, or was it yesterday morning? He didn't know how long he'd been here or what day it was. The room had no windows or clock so he didn't even know if it was day or night. In the far corner of the room he saw a sliding wooden door and assumed he'd find his clothes behind it. He walked over, slid the closet door open and saw nothing but a white wall, an empty shelf, and a few bare hangers.

"Damn it! Where are my clothes?"

He turned to the right and yanked open the bathroom door. No clothes in there either. If he was going to escape, he'd have to do it in his underwear or try to find his clothes on the way out. He couldn't even guess how difficult either task might be.

*Screw it,* he said to himself. *I'll leave in my damned underwear.*

He walked to the door, put his hand on the doorknob, and as he began to turn it the door swung in at him before he'd even begun to pull on it.

\*\*\*

Kathleen Young awoke on the couch and looked around the room she was in. The game show had long since ended and the room was growing dark since the autohost turned off the TV after detecting no motion or sound in the room other than her soft, slow breathing. She was aware of being extremely hungry but not much else yet. She yawned and stretched and wondered what she should have for dinner. Thinking of dinner made her think of Deron. She sat up abruptly trying to recall something important.

"Deron!?" she called out. She stood up and felt a wave of dizziness pass over her as she headed toward Deron's room, thinking he was probably reading a book and didn't hear her. She glanced at her communicator. It was almost 8:30pm. Of course he was home by now, she thought, as she now recalled coming home to find that she was the first one there for a change. She stopped in front of Deron's door and knocked lightly, "Deron, honey?"

She waited a few seconds, then knocked louder. "Deron? Are you awake?" Still no answer. "Shit," she muttered and tried the knob. It was unlocked. She slowly opened the door, not wanting to wake him if he was asleep. The room was empty.

She was tempted to look around. Not to snoop exactly, but just to acquaint herself with her son a little more by looking through his possessions, noticing how he kept his room, and maybe by seeing what things he gave special placement to. If this had been her day off and Deron was at school, she would have done it, but right now she was hungry and starting to worry.

Kathleen went to the dining room after stopping in the bathroom on her way to the other side of the house. She looked at the fridge, then at the phone display, not sure which to start with. A loud rumbling in her stomach decided it for her. She would start printing something to eat first, then call Charlie and find out if Deron was visiting him.

***

Charlie was just getting up from his desk where he was writing in his journal when the phone rang. He picked up the phone and listened for a minute. His lips formed a straight line as he listened. "He's not here, Kathleen."

"Are you sure, Dad?"

"What kind of question is that? Do you think I might have overlooked him somewhere as I wandered through my palace?"

Kathleen ignored her father's quick temper. "You don't think he might be involved in unauthorized... drug use, do you?"

"No, Kathleen. Not Deron. That would almost require him to associate with people far below his cerebral level, and I doubt he'd find it worth the trouble."

Kathleen's mind registered the "no" part of his answer and the rest wafted by as she checked the progress on her lasagna dinner. She took some frozen garlic bread out of the freezer and put it in the mini-oven next to the food printer. She could've printed the bread, but she and Deron agreed that when it came to toast, the real thing was much better. She realized that Charlie had asked her something.

"What did you say, Dad?"

"I *said*, have you called the school?" Charlie grumbled, hating to repeat himself when he spoke clearly the first time.

"Why would I do that? School's been out for hours."

Charlie told himself to be patient with his only daughter. She wasn't actually stupid. He was sure of it. She just didn't *like* using her brain. "Because," he answered with forced patience, "if something happened to him at school, they'd surely know about it. In fact, have you checked your host thingy for messages?"

Kathleen glanced at the LED console on the wall. The door and phone symbols each had a glowing green 0 beside them. "No messages," she said, then she repeated Charlie's words in her mind, *"...if something happened to him,"* and she visualized Deron lying in the street, run over by an auto-car.

"Call me if you hear from him, Dad. Love you," she said, and hung up.

She tapped Deron's face on her comm's home screen. The call went straight to voicemail. She hit the off buttons on the food printer and the oven then quickly made her way out of the kitchen and out the front door. She looked up and down the street, hoping but not expecting to see Deron walking home with an open book held out in front of him, or better yet, talking to a pretty girl on her porch. She saw neither. She half-ran to her car, and was backing out of the driveway within seconds. She turned the wheel hard to the left, stopped, turned it back to the right, tapped the letter "D" and stepped on the gas.

Charlie squinted his eyes at the silent phone in his hand and wondered where the hell Kathleen had gone.

If asked, Kathleen couldn't have answered that question. She didn't know exactly where she was going.

\*\*\*

As far as Drake Austin could tell, it was time. He took another quick glance around and almost carelessly decided that there was no danger in heading down the street to where the two girls had parked. Drake left the illumination of the corner streetlight he was standing under beside his car and walked toward the darker part of Mayfair Street.

Although it was a summer evening, the street was quiet and no kids were about. As he approached the house, he saw that their large living room window had the blinds closed. At the adjacent house, nearer to him, there was a large willow tree with long branches hanging down all around forming a canopy. He ducked under the cover of the leaves and made his way diagonally across the yard to the ten foot wide stretch of grass that separated the two houses.

Lights were on in both houses, but so far his luck was in - windows were either blocked by drapes or blinds, and no one was in the rooms with an open view. In anticipation of what he was about to do, Drake's heart began beating faster; adrenaline surged through his veins and his sense perceptions were amplified. Foremost was the sense of smell. Summer grass was dominant. He could also make out the scent of the leaves twenty feet behind him in the neighbor's front yard. Somewhere down the street the smell of barbecued pork drifted to him. He could vaguely make out the sounds of children playing and laughing above the sound of his pulse thumping in his ears.

His visual perception also seemed heightened. The grass he stood on appeared starkly green, the stucco surface of the wall before him stood out in such detail it was as if he were looking at an aerial photograph of an alien white landscape. He reached out and pressed his hand to the stucco, feeling multiple pressure points push into his skin. He slowly slid his hand down and felt a ticklish scratching on his palm. He looked at his hand and saw traces of white powder left behind in the scratch lines.

He walked slowly, crouching to stay below the windows until he reached the redwood fence that formed a cul-de-sac in the space between the houses. The left side of the fence had a gate that led into the co-ed's backyard. Always keeping in mind the need for a possible quick escape, he noticed that the other side of the fence had no gate - it would be on the other side of the house. On his left there was a window a few feet from the gate. He glanced right and saw a matching window on the other house with Venetian blinds partially closed at a downward angle. The light was off and he assumed the room to be empty. On his left, the light was on.

He slowly straightened his posture enough to look into the young woman's room through the bottom slat of the fully opened blinds.

# Ten

Deron let go of the doorknob and stepped backwards when he felt the door opening. He saw a tall, well-dressed man smiling down at him. Deron wasn't at all embarrassed about standing there in his underwear. He was too angry to care about modesty.

The man with perfectly styled, short, blond hair continued to look at Deron with a self-assured politician's smile on his face. Deron glared back at him, grateful to have a better target for his rage than the pretty nurse lady. Neither of them was affected by the other's expression. Deron continued to glare, the man maintained his smile.

Deron saw something in his right hand and he seemed to have broken the spell he was under by glancing down at it. The man finally spoke in a rich, polished tenor, "Hello there, Mr. Young."

"Fuck you," Deron responded. But the man still didn't lose the smile that now appeared to be a permanent fixture on his face. Deron was angry at the man for staring at him, for smiling non-stop, for being in this place, for having his life mysteriously interfered with by strangers, and he was angry that the woman in his room earlier had been so nice and that only now did he have a chance to vent on someone.

"I understand that you're upset. Please, put this on and we can talk it over." The smiling man handed Deron a paper-thin hospital gown. Deron took it from his hand without saying a word and ripped open the thin wrapper. He deliberately put the gown on backward, tying the string in front.

"I believe you've got that on the wrong way, son." Deron thought of smacking the phony smile right off the man's face.

"I don't see that it really matters," he spat instead.

"As you wish. Come..." He turned back to face the door, apparently unconcerned that Deron might choose a physical outlet for the rage that was clearly visible on his face. Deron followed the man through the door and down an immaculate hallway. This was his first glimpse of anything outside the room he'd awoken in.

The walls were white with oak trim. Wooden doors appeared on either side of the hallway at ten to twenty foot intervals. Deron noticed his bare feet were walking on carpet, rather than the linoleum or tiled floor he would have expected. At the end of the hallway he saw a lobby with a round semi-circle of a desk, where two men sat in front of a switchboard, computer terminals, and various notebooks and office supplies. They were dressed in black uniforms like the men who'd taken him from his school.

No sounds came from any of the rooms Deron and the man passed on their approach to the lobby. "Good evening, gentleman," the man said to the two guards as they rounded the desk, heading for the reflective chrome elevator doors.

"Good evening, sir," they replied in unison.

"I'm taking Mr. Young up to my office for orientation. He's got a lot of spirit, but I don't anticipate any trouble."

"Yes, sir," the older of the guards replied.

The other made an entry into his terminal after checking the time.

Deron was looking around for escape routes. Not necessarily for the moment. The two guards were young and fit and were armed with something he couldn't identify. He'd looked closely at their holsters and noticed they carried the same strange weapons as the eeks on the street.

The blond man pulled a key from his waist out of a retraction device clipped to his belt and inserted it into a round lock on the wall below the call button. He removed the key and pressed the button. A voice emitted from an unseen speaker, "Seven seconds." He turned toward Deron, smiling as if he was satisfied with the short estimated time of the elevator's arrival.

"Forgive me. I forgot to introduce myself. My name is Doctor Fielding." He didn't bother to offer his hand. The doors opened silently and he gestured with his left hand for Deron to enter before him.

# Eleven

Kathleen departed quickly, accelerating down the street, then immediately realized that she needed to drive slower since she was hoping to find a pedestrian. She was eager to get closer to the school, but knew it was possible that Deron could be anywhere, so she slowed the car and looked all around as she drove. The vehicle computer system compared the route she was currently taking to previous destinations and offered hands-free driving to a short list of destinations. The school was not a place she usually drove to and was not on the list. She ignored the auto-drive options.

Her reasons for abruptly leaving the house and driving off in a rush were just now beginning to form in her mind. She just knew that something *had* to have happened to Deron. Maybe he was hit by a car on the way home from school. That was entirely possible. She could easily see him in her mind, crossing a street without looking, reading a book. If something like that *had* happened, and no one knew who he was, and they tried unsuccessfully to scan him, they wouldn't know to inform her that her son was injured. She knew she would one day regret not getting him chipped. But he was adamant that he would never be marked and tracked like an animal. *Thanks, Dad.* So she had applied for the religious exemption just to appease him and end the argument.

She followed along the route he normally walked from the school to their house, hoping she would not see evidence of an injury accident. She didn't know what form such evidence might take, but perhaps there would be crime-scene holo-tape somewhere, or maybe an officer taking pictures or digitizing an accident scene. Or, God forbid, she didn't want to think this, but she couldn't stop herself – it might come as blood on the highway and a medical examiner's vehicle on the side of the road.

She also knew that if he had been killed by a car many hours earlier, there might be no evidence of such a tragedy. It was dark and she'd surely miss small overlooked signs such as broken glass or shards of red or yellow plastic that weren't swept up during the accident clean-up. But she had to do something. It was supposed to be next to impossible for a car to hit a solid object, but that was technology she didn't understand, so she suspected it could still happen.

She slowed as she approached an intersection and turned on her left turn indicator. Something in her rear view mirror drew her attention and she saw a black car behind her that appeared to be speeding up when it should have been slowing down.

Shortly after she turned, the black sedan reappeared in her rear-view mirror. The driver flashed his lights and she wondered if he was signaling her or someone in the oncoming lane. But he stayed behind her, even as she began making random evasive turns and eventually deviating so far from the path to Deron's school that she became lost.

Finally she saw the flashing of blue and red lights inside her car and in her mirrors. She pulled over to the side of the road. As she did so, the flashing lights went off. The driver emerged from the car and approached her. The passenger stayed behind, occupying himself with the vehicle's computer.

"Mrs. Young. My name is Eric Harris. I'm with the Department of Equal Opportunity," the man said loudly so she would hear him through her closed window.

She looked at him, puzzled. Why would the DEO be following her and pulling her over? She hadn't done anything to oppress anyone, had she? She pushed a button to roll down the window.

"I tried calling your house and your comm but got no answer, so my partner and I came to visit you in person, but you were driving away as we were approaching, so we ended up following you. We didn't mean to startle you."

"You just want to talk to me? I can't imagine why. Have I done something wrong? Is there a problem at the hotel?"

"Oh no. Absolutely not. Can we go someplace to talk so I don't have to explain everything on the side of the road?" He smiled at her with charm.

"Oh, yes. But I, um... I'm not even sure where we are."

He quickly consulted his communicator and said, "There's a coffee shop not far from here. How about if we trade places and you follow *us* for a minute?"

"Okay. Sure." Kathleen felt sure that the man wasn't lying, and he was very attractive. She looked forward to finding out what the DEO wanted to talk to her about.

She followed the black car for about a mile until it pulled into the parking lot of a local restaurant specializing in breakfast. Within a minute the three of them were seated in a booth that the man asked for when he saw it was surrounded by empty tables.

The men sat on one side and Kathleen sat across from them. Eric introduced himself again. "I apologize again for inadvertently startling you. My name is Eric Harris, and this is my partner Johnny Tran."

"Pleased to meet you both," she said, mostly looking at Eric.

"Are you hungry? Dinner is on us if you are."

She *was* hungry, having abandoned her dinner. "No, thank you. Just coffee will be fine."

"Okay. Well, if you change your mind, just let me know."

"Thank you. I will. I'm more interested in what you wanted to talk to me about."

"Oh yes, of course. It's about Deron, but don't be alarmed. He's fine."

Kathleen's eyes widened at the mention of her son, then she relaxed when Eric told her that he was fine.

"Has he done something... unfair?"

"Actually, Kathleen, it's not so much what he *has* done as much as what he *might* do. There's a brand new program that aims to help people who are at risk of running afoul of the law, and as it turns out, Deron could very well be a good candidate for the program."

"Deron's at risk? I know he's different, but he treats everyone equally and he's completely law-abiding."

"Kathleen, do you remember when you were a teenager and you did things your parents didn't know about?"

She closed her eyes and nodded.

"Well, Deron is no different. He has done some things that I'm sure he hasn't shared with you. Maybe not enough yet to land him in jail, but enough to have gotten himself on our radar. The thing to focus on though is not what he's done wrong, but how much there is to be gained by being a program to iron out the wrinkles in young men like him. Get him back on the right path, and ensure a trouble-free future."

"It sounds pretty good when you put it that way. Like his misbehaving led to a blessing."

"That's a great way to look at it, Kathleen."

"How does this work? I'm sure he won't be interested if I suggest it to him. He's not much of a joiner. He's more of a spectator. He has very few friends, and the only person he spends time with is his grandfather – who is *not* a good influence on him."

"You don't need to worry about getting him started. We spoke to him at school today, and believe it or not, he's already joined the program!"

"Really? Deron joined something?"

"Yes. He did. And he started without delay."

"He didn't come home after school today. I was looking for him when you found me. Why didn't anyone talk to me about this before?"

"I apologize for that. It's a new program and things got a little disordered with different departments not communicating as well as they should have. But now you know where he is, and what he's doing. He started the program today, and since it's a residential program, he's at our facility. If things had been done in the correct sequence, we would've spoken to you first and gotten your consent."

Johnny opened his briefcase and extracted a manila folder.

"All we need now is for you to sign a few papers giving your consent for Deron to participate. If you'll do that, he'll be able to stay in the program and complete his orientation tonight and get acquainted with the other kids. It's a bit like summer camp with all of the youngsters having plenty of time for group activities when they're not in the special classes to teach them ideal behaviors."

Johnny slid some papers across the table and produced a pen.

"Is there anything I need to know? Is there medication involved?"

"That's up to the study participants. Sometimes the kids will request sleep-aids, or anti-anxiety meds. There are physicians on staff who deal with that type of thing. But unless they make such requests, medication is not part of the program."

"It sounds like it would be very good for Deron. This is just so sudden and unexpected."

"You're right. It is. And if Deron is going to become a model citizen and an example for others to look up to, the sooner, the better. Don't you think, Kathleen?"

After she signed the papers and Johnny returned them to his case, they finished their coffee and chatted briefly about the program in general. At some point Eric gave Johnny a signal Kathleen didn't see and he excused himself and went outside to wait in their patrol car.

"I hope you don't think this is too forward or inappropriate since I'm the one who talked to you about your son entering this program, but I was wondering if you'd like to attend the Quarterly Event with me?"

Kathleen blushed, looked down at the table for a few seconds, then looked up directly into Eric's eyes and said she'd love to.

## Twelve

One of the cool things about Jenny was that she not only had her own car, but she was allowed to drive it manually. Any kid could have one if they could get their parents to consent. And most parents were still hesitant to grant such autonomy to their teens, even with automated driving and the ability to know the car's location in real time and see inside the car via the rear-facing dashcam. But Jenny's parents were considered super cool, letting her do just about anything she wanted.

On this night, Jenny and Michelle headed to a club where age laws for alcohol consumption and any other mind-altering substance were not an issue. Its location was not advertised, but the right people knew where to find it. Hallucinogens were not legal for those under eighteen, but authorities merely monitored such parties as well as the kids' vital signs via their chips and allowed them to think they were getting away with something.

"Did you hear about the bust yesterday in the library?" Jenny asked, hoping Michelle hadn't so she could deliver the news.

"At school?"

"Yeah. In the library of all places!"

"No. What happened?" Michelle asked, instantly curious.

"Do you know Deron - that total bookworm guy that's actually kinda cute?" Jenny now had Michelle's complete attention.

Michelle thought Deron couldn't possibly have been arrested for anything other than possession of tobacco, but references to bookworm, library, and cute definitely sounded like "her" Deron. "You mean Deron Young?"

"I have no idea what his last name is," Jenny answered.

"I think I know who you mean. What happened?"

Jenny said, "Well, I wasn't there, but I heard that he must've done something really, really bad because the FBI was at school today and they arrested him – in the *library* of all places! Can you believe that??"

Michelle was concerned. She also felt guilt coming on strong. Surprisingly strong, and seemingly from out of nowhere.

"I wonder what he could've done," she said, hoping her curiosity sounded normal and that her voice didn't betray her rapidly beating heart and the unsettling fear she was now feeling.

Jenny swung the car into a diagonal parking space in front of what appeared to be an abandoned warehouse, turned off the car and said, "Maybe he killed his parents or something."

"Deron only has a mom," Michelle said, without thinking.

Deliberately, or not, Jenny didn't pick up on the fact that Michelle had more than a passing acquaintance with

Deron. She turned on the dome light and checked her make-up, hair, and lips in the rear view mirror.

"Are you ready to party?" Jenny asked with a mischievous smile.

Feeling less and less like partying with every passing second, Michelle exclaimed, "I can't wait!"

\*\*\*

The elevator doors opened to a very different looking lobby; no carpet or oak trim here. Marble and chrome were dominant. Deron noticed that even the security desk was different. Only one guy here at a simple desk, and if he was armed, it wasn't apparent.

Structurally, this floor was the same as the one they had started on. Again there was the desk in front of them, with a single narrow hallway beyond the desk with doors on either side of the hall. This lobby also had potted palm trees, giving it a more casual air.

Deron saw that the doors in the long hall had nameplates on them rather than numbers like the floor he had woken on. They were apparently in an administrative part of the building.

"This way, please," Doctor Fielding spoke. Deron followed wordlessly as they passed the security guard and went down a hallway to the farthest door on the left. The doctor extracted a key card, swiped it through the lock and opened the door to his office, motioning for Deron to enter.

The first thing Deron noticed as he stepped from the light colored marble floor onto the plush, carpeted floor was that on side of the room there was an enormous aquarium that spanned the entire length of the wall.

Deron knew as little about fish species as he knew about Indian cuisine or nano-technology but it was clear to him that this aquarium was filled with rare, exotic fish. He'd never seen anything like them. He recognized the sea horses and the manta rays, but the rest of the fish were an astonishing array of multicolored and unusual species that would've otherwise captured his attention completely were it not for the circumstances in which he found himself observing them.

"Have a seat," the doctor said. Deron remained standing for a few seconds then walked closer to the glass wall of the aquarium. The closer he got, the more he sensed something not quite right about this aquarium, but he couldn't identify what it was.

Doctor Fielding saw the combination of perplexity and admiration on Deron's face and said, "It's digital. Not an ounce of water or a single fish. Pretty nice, isn't it?"

Deron declined to answer as he continued to stare at the fish and their digital habitat. Knowing now that none of it was real, he visually sought out but couldn't discern any pixels or two-dimensionality in the entire aquatic display.

"Deron, I have a lot to go over with you. If you'd like, I can arrange another time for you to come up and view my eQuarium."

Deron spun around abruptly, feeling his anger return. "I'm underwhelmed by your hospitality. Let's forget the fish and get right to the point. You kidnapped me and now I'm being held prisoner. I want to know why."

Dr. Fielding laughed and said, "Now, Deron… I apologize for the manner in which you were admitted to the facility, but I can assure you that you were not kidnapped, nor are you a prisoner. Let me begin by…. Deron? Deron! Please! Hear me out…"

Deron had abruptly turned around and headed toward the door. As he opened it he turned to the doctor and said, "You said I'm not a prisoner, so I'm leaving." He shut the door behind him and walked toward the lobby.

## Thirteen

After his bizarre conversation with Kathleen, Charlie found it harder than ever to continue reading. He couldn't keep his mind focused on the written words. He'd begin to read a sentence, reach the middle of a paragraph, then he'd find himself wondering where Deron was and realize he had no idea what he'd just read. He decided he would try to take a nap and got up to turn off the light he had turned on when Kathleen called. He almost never used verbal commands with the house.

He knew that as soon as he turned off the lamp the house would turn on baseboard lights for a few minutes for his safety. It was almost impossible to experience total darkness anymore. When the house detected motion during a time of darkness, it would turn on the nearest lights that ran at twelve inch intervals along the baseboards in every room. These lights were designed to provide a minimal but sufficient amount of light with which to maneuver through the premises for brief nocturnal trips, such as to the bathroom or kitchen without imposing optical discomfort on the just awakened occupant. If Charlie's presence remained in the living room and continued to engage in detectable motion, then a lamp would come on, assuming that he was staying up regardless of the late hour and would thus need more light than that provided by the baseboards.

Technology made modern living easier, they said. But Charlie thought of it as one more way that control of your own life was taken away from you. What if he wanted to sit there and enjoy the fading light and just feel the night coming on? What if he wanted to read until it was too dark to see and then lapse into a nap? Or what if he fell asleep reading while there was still daylight, and wanted to stay asleep but got wakened by the lamp being turned on automatically, as had happened to him before?

"Ah, nuts!" he exclaimed as he turned off the lamp. Then he turned it on again and off again, repeating the sequence about five times with the childish hope that he'd cause the computer's brain to overload or short-circuit or something. After he stopped playing with the light switch, during which time the computer actually did nothing but wait, Charlie just stood there as if he didn't know where to go or what to do next.

Ordinarily, he would be reading or napping, or he would start to manually cook dinner at about this time. Or he might turn on the television, which he did less and less now, to watch the news and get caught up on how much more wretched the world had gotten. But right now, he wasn't hungry. He had tried and failed to read. The thought of the news broadcast filled him with a thick sense of frustration and dread. He hated the world he lived in now. He knew he was a relic; longing for a world that was dead and had no hope of ever returning.

He felt there was no place for him in this new world. Post-war rebuilding had given people a chance to rebuild their nation better than it was before, but in Charlie's opinion the government had reconstituted itself with an eye toward keeping the worst elements and with less good than ever.

If pressed, he would probably concede that his definitions of good and bad were not empirical. Yes, it was true that crimes against people were practically non-existent, and that was good. But the amount of ridiculous crime was through the roof. People were cited with infractions every day, all day. It wasn't safe to go outside anymore with the Equality Enforcement Corps everywhere you looked, and the fact that if you merely failed to wave to what Charlie referred to as a "BLTG" neighbor, they could report you as a possible bigot. At least before the war, you knew when you were doing something wrong.

Thinking of the war reminded him of his beloved dog, Feenix. He called her name and listened for the sound of her jumping down from his bed to join him in the living room. Charlie had found the German shepherd puppy in Phoenix, Arizona where he had taken his daughter and her young son to get them away from the corruption of California. When Charlie went to the police to tell them that his fifteen year old daughter had been impregnated by a thirty-seven year old man, the officer at the desk stared at him expectantly, then finally asked, "And...?"

Charlie concluded that his child and grandson were no longer safe in southern California, despite the burgeoning peace and prosperity. But Arizona was worse. If California had too much government that cared about all of the wrong things, Arizona had no government. It was like the old west, but without so much as a single sheriff. He reluctantly returned to Orange County and vowed to keep Kathleen locked up until she was an adult. That lasted about a week before she invoked her recently instituted Child's Rights and resumed her regular partying, leaving him to take care of Deron most of the time. Charlie didn't mind having to watch his grandson though. Raising the young boy and the dog gave him a new lease on life. He had been convinced he'd never love again after the death of his wife.

Charlie headed down the hall to his darkened bedroom to see if Feenix was asleep. He knew she didn't have a lot of time left, but each day he tried to avoid thinking that this could be her last.

He entered his room and said, "Light," instead of touching the wall plate as he normally did. The light came on in its gradual way – starting as a soft illumination, decorating the room with shadows and continuing to brighten until the occupant either said, "Stop" or it reached the full 50 watt illumination. Charlie let it reach full brightness as he stood there staring at Feenix on the bed, certain that she wasn't breathing.

"No," he whispered, straining to see if her chest was moving up and down, even a little bit. "Please don't be dead, Feenix." He walked to his bed and lowered himself to his knees. He reached out and gently laid his left hand on her ribcage. He felt soft fur and no movement at all.

She didn't suddenly wake up and look at him as she normally would've. Charlie buried his face in her fur and felt a pain in his heart that seemed stronger than a pain could possibly be in the absence of physical injury.

Feenix wasn't just Charlie's best friend. She was his only friend. All he had left now was family.

## Fourteen

The two girls stood in a line of more than forty people waiting to get in to the underground dance club. Jenny took a drag from the real clove cigarette she and Michelle were sharing, blew out half the smoke she had drawn from it and inhaled the rest before passing it back to Michelle. From where they stood, about ten people back in the line, they could feel bass sound thumping through the walls. The fast electronic beat filled Jenny with anticipation. They'd only been standing in line for about five minutes, but to Jenny it felt longer. She wanted In *now*. The whole line thing was a joke, she knew. The club was illegal to begin with so there was no need to monitor occupancy. Making people wait was just to make them feel really special for getting in at all. It was also a way to make extra cash on bribes. Some people were turned away by the doorman when they reached the head of the line. Others were motioned to bypass the line when the doorman felt so inclined.

Jenny had thought their matching sexy outfits would have gotten them right in without delay. Maybe they still would if she could manage to get the doorman's attention. Even with the outlandish costumes most of the people in line were wearing, Michelle and Jenny stood out in their black rabbit fur bikini tops and matching micro skirts. Michelle had at first rejected the outfit when Jenny presented it to her earlier in the evening, but after a while, she was talked into it when Jenny made a detailed list of things wrong with what Michelle had planned to wear.

Michelle finally relented and went into the bathroom to try on the few inches of furry clothing. She felt extremely exposed, even though her outfit covered more than Jenny's. As the two girls stood in front of the large mirror above Jenny's bureau, Michelle saw how the tiny top was insufficient to cover Jenny's breasts. Both outfits were the same size, but Jenny was more endowed, causing a half inch or so of the bottom of Jenny's breasts to be visible. Michelle tugged down on her top a little as if her own breasts were exposed. Then she pulled her skirt down a little as she noticed that Jenny's skirt also failed to entirely cover her ass.

"My god, we look hot!" Jenny had exclaimed, unable to take her eyes off her own reflection. Now, a few hours later, she decided to put her outfit to its first good use and see if she could get them moved to the head of the line. "Let me see that," she said to Michelle, indicating the clove cigarette. Michelle handed it to her and Jenny dropped it to the ground and stepped on it, twisting the front of her high-heeled shoe left and right, swiveling her ass as she did so.

Michelle looked at her, puzzled.

"Watch," Jenny said, then she stepped out of line and headed straight for the big, bald man guarding the door.

She had planned to use needing a light as her excuse for talking to the doorman, but ended up not needing to.

As she passed other people in line who were also provocatively dressed, she didn't doubt her ability to be more attention-getting than her competition. She saw a girl near the front of the line with tight black pants and a painted on top giving the appearance of a shirt where there wasn't one. *Less is more*, Jenny thought to herself. *Show 'em everything and they've got nothing left to be curious about.*

Zeke, the doorman would have agreed with her. He'd seen plenty of skin as a doorman/bouncer at underground clubs, and even more at his regular job at a strip club. Now he found himself more drawn to girls that were less exposed, leaving something to the imagination. When he saw Jenny approaching alongside the line of waiting people, she had his full attention. His eyes went straight to her top and the exposed flesh coming out the bottom of it. "Hey, baby. According to your tits, your top is too small."

Jenny, feigning ignorance of what he was talking about, glanced down at her chest and said, "Oops!" She smiled demurely at him and said, "I just painted my nails and they're not fully dry yet, could you help me with my top?" Zeke smiled and slid his fingers under the furry top and pulled it down to cover the bottom of her breasts. He pulled the top down so far that he fully covered the bottom of her breasts, and at the same time exposed her erect nipples.

"That's better," he said, laughing. "Looks like someone is a bit chilly." He stared at her nipples, smiling.

"Well, my outfit doesn't cover a lot," she said, glancing down at her chest. "As you can see," she added, looking up at him and defying him to make eye contact with her. "Is there any chance my friend and I can go inside where it's warmer?" They looked at each other and she asked, "And could you try to fix my top again, please?"

Zeke put the back of his fingers against Jenny's breasts, pinched her nipples between his fingers, then grabbed the top with his fingertips and pulled it up just enough to cover her nipples, revealing the bottom of her breasts again. "How's that?" he asked.

"I guess you're right. It is a little too small," she said, looking down at her breasts, then looking to the closed door, asking with her eyes if she could go inside. She pouted and said, "I guess I should go home and change if I can't get in where it's warm."

Zeke knew the type he was dealing with and figured he'd let her in after he played with her for a minute or two. The girl was smokin' hot and her outfit was tantalizing. The combination of the extremely soft, silky rabbit fur and her soft skin made him want to run his hands all over her.

"Go get your friend. I want see how well her clothes fit."

"Thank you!" she said as she flashed him a big, appreciative smile.

"Hey, I haven't made up my mind yet. Is your friend as hot as you are?"

"Hotter," Jenny replied, and spun around to go get Michelle.

Zeke watched her ass as she went and wondered if she was telling the truth. If she is, he thought, this is gonna be good.

## Fifteen

Drake looked in on an empty master bedroom. He glanced over to the open doorway to see what else was visible from his vantage point. He could just barely see a few feet of the hallway wall. That was it. He looked back at the room. Through another doorway he could see most of the left side shower door and the shower head, part of the toilet and the linoleum floor.

To the right, there was another window that faced the backyard. From that window, he'd be able to see straight down the hallway and into part of the living room or dining room. But if he moved to that window he wouldn't be able to see the bathroom at all. It frustrated him not being able to see or hear anything to indicate what the girls were doing. He also didn't know if there were better viewing possibilities on the other side of the house. Maybe from there he could see the dining room or another bedroom.

This was the price he paid for his impulsive decision to follow them home without doing his homework. So far the night was a wash. He hadn't seen them once since they'd entered the house.

***

Despite being told he wasn't a prisoner, Deron knew he wouldn't be allowed to just walk out. As he approached the lobby, not sure what he was going to do, he heard the phone at the reception desk beep and watched the security guard touch his earpiece.

"Yes, sir," the guard said. He touched his ear again, then swiveled his chair around to face Deron. "Let's not have any trouble," he said, getting up slowly with his eyes fixed on the teenager.

"Dr. Fielding said I could go." Deron stopped about ten feet from the guard and looked at him with a challenge in his eyes.

"Actually, he just asked me to bring you back to his office. So how's about we do that and then you guys can talk about when you can go?"

Deron took a deep breath and offered no resistance as the guard put his hand on Deron's shoulder and gently turned him around, like physically suggesting the direction Deron should go rather than bluntly forcing him. Deron took the suggestion and started walking, slowly. Dr. Fielding stood waiting just inside his doorway. He had finally lost his politician's smile and doctor's patience.

"Thank you," he said curtly to the guard and stepped aside to let Deron enter. Once Deron had done so, he pointed a remote control at the door, pushed a button on it and slipped the small device into his pocket. "Now, where were we?" he asked.

"You were just lying to me about how I wasn't a prisoner," Deron replied. "But I clearly am, since I'm not free to leave." Deron clenched his fists as anger flooded through him.

"I didn't *lie* to you, Deron. You simply didn't give me a chance to explain the nature of your presence here. You are *not* a prisoner. A better way of looking at it would be to say that you're an in-patient. And yes, I understand that your admission was involuntary, but that doesn't make you a prisoner. This is not a prison or a jail and you'll find that the accommodations are much closer to that of a very nice hotel than they are to a correctional facility."

"I see," Deron responded. "If we change the words, we can change the experience. I'm sorry, but when I'm not free, that means I'm a prisoner."

"Fine, Deron. You can choose to view your situation however you please. That is in fact the reason you're here. Your "viewpoint" or "perspective" is what brought you to us. You are a patient in an experimental rehabilitation facility. "

"What!?" Deron exclaimed. "You're going to experiment on me? Does my mother know about this?" Deron felt reality dissolving around him. He felt fear at the prospect of a suddenly bizarre and unknowable future. He felt extremely alone. Images of his grandfather and of Michelle went fleeting through his mind and before he knew what was happening, his eyes began to water and his throat constricted. To keep himself from crying, he focused on his feeling of anger instead. "What the fuck am I doing here?!" he demanded to know.

"Please, Deron. Have a seat. Drink some water." The doctor placed a glass of iced water onto the coffee table that sat between his desk and a leather couch where he gestured for Deron to sit. Although Deron wanted to accept nothing from this man whom he saw as his enemy, he did feel wobbly and his throat was dry with a small knot of pain that kept him from swallowing. He walked over to the couch, picked up the glass of water and sat down. He drained the glass, set it down hard on the table, then glared at the doctor, whom he now figured for a psychiatrist.

"I'm waiting," he said.

## Sixteen

Charlie didn't know what to do with Feenix. If he had grass in his backyard, he would have buried her in it. But it was all concrete. He wiped the tears from his eyes and pulled the comforter up from the foot of the bed and covered his beloved dog carefully as if he didn't want to disturb her final sleep. The loss of someone he loved so dearly brought to mind someone else that he feared losing. Deron was still missing and no one knew why.

He hadn't been overly concerned about his absence while talking to Kathleen, but now that Feenix was dead, his concern for Deron increased to the point of feeling almost urgent. It wasn't rational, he knew, but now he was afraid that something might be very wrong, and he needed to find out where Deron was.

He thought of trying to call Kathleen again to see if she and Deron had returned home, but he decided to drive over and find out in person. If they were both home, as he hoped they would be, he could do with some company right about now. Besides, he'd have to tell them about Feenix and that wasn't the sort of thing you told someone on the phone. At least Charlie would never do that. Others would probably send a text message with a picture of the dead dog and a sad face emoji. Deron was almost as fond of the German shepherd as Charlie was and he deserved to be told in person about her passing.

Without really thinking of what he was doing, Charlie took a blanket from the hall closet and used it to wrap his shotgun and box of shells, then carried the awkward bundle out to the backseat of his car. He had no reason for bringing it, but his mind was operating in crisis mode and he felt better having the shotgun with him - just in case. Somewhere in the back of his mind, he knew he could be jailed just for having it, and there'd be additional charges for having it loaded, and in a vehicle where he could reach it.

Deron was fairly predictable in his routines. If he wasn't home shortly after school let it out, it would only be because he had stopped at the public library or at a convenience store to purchase a paperback. He knew Deron could easily lose track of time when browsing through books and trying to make a choice, but he wouldn't fail to come home or at least call or text if he knew he was hours past the time he was expected.

Therefore, Charlie knew something wasn't right. He didn't know what or how bad it might be, but if there was trouble, he was going to be capable of confronting it. He couldn't imagine where Deron might be or in what circumstances his shotgun might be necessary, but he drove away from his house feeling a little bit better for having brought it.

Kathleen's house was just a few miles away, and within five minutes of leaving his place, he was slowing down to a stop in front of her house. All of the lights were out except for one dim lamp in the living room. It appeared as if the house computer had turned on one lamp in an empty house at dusk. Then he noticed the light flickering. It wasn't a lamp. It was the television. The rest of the house was dark. Then the flickering blueish light from main room went out and the house was fully dark.

Unbidden worst-case-scenarios flashed through his mind and he knew he had to look inside to make sure that nothing he was imagining had actually happened. He had never before thought of Deron as being depressed, but maybe he was, and maybe Deron had hung himself. Kathleen was not very stable emotionally and would lose her mind if she had found Deron hanging from a noose in the garage after she had ended their call earlier. Maybe upon finding such a scene she would go back inside and take an overdose instead of calling 911.

He told himself to knock it off with the suicide thoughts. Kathleen's car was not in the driveway and if it was in the garage, then Deron wouldn't be able to hang himself. Geez! What was wrong with his mind? He had to get a grip on himself and quit assuming terrible things. Deron had probably just met a girl - God knows it was about time he did so, and Kathleen probably ran out to get some groceries, or some of those creepy tubes for the food printer.

The house had probably just turned the TV off after some time because no one was watching it. Well, of course it didn't know if someone was watching the TV or staring at their navel, he told himself. But it knew from lack of heat and motion that the house was empty, and to conserve energy reserves, it minimized unnecessary electrical consumption, even though it was replenished daily by the sun and waste processing.

He tried the front door before knocking and when it opened, his mind went right back to imagining the worst. This was not right. Dark house. No one home. Door unlocked. Kathleen may not have been born with his I.Q. but she was no dummy. Just like her mother, she always felt safer with the door locked. Locking it whenever she entered or exited was automatic for her since she was a child. Charlie didn't know that the house had been instructed to grant him entry upon facial recognition.

He stepped inside and yelled, "Lights!"

His voice carried to every room in the house causing all the lights to come on and slowly reach maximum illumination. He looked to his right into the living room and saw that it was empty. "Kathleen! Deron! Anyone home?" He received no reply and headed left toward the bedrooms. He looked in Kathleen's master bedroom and found it clean and empty. He went through to the bathroom and it too was shining clean in the bright light, and empty.

He walked out, manually hitting light sensors on his way, turning off lights as he went down the hall and into Deron's room. As he expected, he found this room empty too. He looked at Deron's desk, half-expecting, half-fearing there might be a suicide note. He probably wouldn't have noticed the corner of paper sticking out from under a large photo-book if he hadn't been thinking of finding a note.

He walked over quickly and lifted the large, softcover book about a pre-war author named Stephen King. Charlie had bought the book for Deron on his last birthday. He picked up the unsealed envelope and saw that it was addressed to Deron's childhood best-friend, Michelle Granger. Deron hadn't mentioned her in quite a while. He wondered what had happened between them. He felt a little guilty as he removed the folded pages from the envelope, but he had to know if it was a suicide note. He began reading:

*Dear Michelle,*

*I don't know why I'm writing this because I'll probably never give you this letter. But I guess I have such strong feelings for you that I've kept bottled up for so long, I feel like I have to get them out in some way, or I'll just explode from the mounting emotional pressure. Even if you never see it, at least I will have let out some of the pressure that builds and builds every time I think of you. When I'm not thinking of you, I'm dreaming of you. My mind belongs to you whether I'm awake or asleep and the only time I don't think of you is when I'm reading. And even then, thoughts of you invade my mind and the world I'm visiting and the image of your face imposes on the fictional scenes I try to lose myself in.*

*I'm glad you'll never read this because if you did, you'd think I'm crazy and obsessed. In a way, I am. I'm crazy about you and obsessed with the thought of loving you* *and being with you forever. I know that someday we <u>will</u> be together again. I'm certain of it. Fate just hasn't let you in on its little secret yet. But I know. And I'll be patient as I wait for you to realize that being popular in school and hanging out with the "cool" people is just a temporary diversion.*

Charlie concluded that this wasn't a suicide note, and with Deron envisioning himself being with this girl forever, surely he had no plans of killing himself. In fact, this letter was not dated and Charlie wondered if Deron was with this girl right now. That would certainly explain why he'd been gone so long without notice. And what teenaged boy wouldn't lose track of time if he was with the girl of his dreams?

## Seventeen

Jenny came walking back to Michelle with a huge smile on her face. "I think we're going to get in! The doorman wants to meet you. All you have to do is be *really* sexy and he won't be able to say no." Jenny laughed and grabbed Michelle's hand, pulling her back toward Zeke. "Come on!"

Michelle forced a smile and began walking with Jenny. She didn't feel at all sexy. She was actually starting to feel sick to her stomach and she didn't know why. She only knew that nothing felt right. She didn't want to be here. She didn't want to dance. She didn't want to take Euphoria, the popular rave drug. She didn't want to be in the clothes she was in. And now here was a guy who must be Zeke, standing in front of the door with his arms crossed over his chest and staring at her like a pig as she approached.

"This is my friend. 'Chelle, say hi to Zeke. "

Michelle looked up at Zeke and muttered, "Hi."

Jenny nudged Michelle with her elbow, encouraging her to get closer and be a bit more persuasive about getting them inside.

Michelle just wanted to turn around and leave and be anywhere but here with this bald giant looking at her like he wanted to eat her for dessert.

"Come here, sweetheart. Convince me why I should let you in past that whole line of people. "

Jenny pushed Michelle gently forward until she was within Zeke's reach.

He reached out and put his hands on Michelle's bare waist then slid his hands upward, lifting her top. "Oh, baby. You are fine. Look at you!"

Several of the males waiting in line were watching and trying to see what Zeke was looking at but could only see the two girls from behind.

Zeke started fondling Michelle and the nausea she was already feeling became ten times worse. She hated Zeke. She suddenly realized that she hated Jenny too. She barely began to taste something sour in her mouth and before she knew it was going to happen, she vomited. She tried to turn away from Zeke, but still threw up on his right arm.

"You fucking bitch! What the fuck is wrong with you!" Zeke yelled. Everyone in line was now looking at them. Michelle heaved again and threw up more onto the pavement. Hot tears began streaming down her face. She was coughing and crying and just wanted to be at home, away from all of these people staring at her.

Jenny feared Michelle had just ruined their chance of getting into the club without waiting in line all night and she worked quickly to repair the damage and get them back in Zeke's good graces.

"Oh my god! I'm so sorry. Let me help you. There's water over here." She walked to a spigot sticking out of the wall a few feet away and Zeke reluctantly followed after giving a warning glare to the people in line. She turned on the water and as Zeke put his arm under the stream, Jenny wiped away the vomit and looked at him with her best seductive expression. "I totally can't believe she did that to you. Please let me make it up to you. I am like, so sorry!" With his arm now clean and Jenny still running her hand back and forth across it, he looked at her and his anger began to transform into something else.

"Yeah, you can make it up to me all right." He pulled his arm away from her and lowered the zipper on his fly.

"Right here? In front of everyone?" Jenny asked.

"Right here. Right now." He replied, looking at her with a mixture of lust and anger.

"Okay" Jenny said, greatly relieved that she wasn't barred from the club and her night wouldn't be ruined by Michelle after all.

***

Drake stood outside the window still peering in at an empty room, clenching his teeth in frustration. He couldn't believe he hadn't even gotten a glimpse of them in over two hours. Once, the blonde came back to go to the bathroom, but he barely saw her as she crossed the corner of the room. If they weren't so hot, and if he hadn't been so set on seeing them undress, he would've left by now. But he was determined to stick it out. The longer he waited, the more impatient he got and then the more impatient he got, the angrier he became. "Come on, you fuckin' bitches. Go to bed or take a fucking shower. Do something!" he muttered through his clenched teeth.

In the living room, the two girls sat watching television. Darla, the blonde was yawning and didn't think she'd be able to stay awake for the entire show. Gabriella was wide awake, but bored. They were watching a sit-com based on a romance between a tall woman and a short man. Gabriella thought it was stupid and the punch-lines were predictable and rarely deviated from quips based on the couple's height difference. Darla thought it was funny.

Seeing that Darla had fallen asleep, Gabriella turned the television off with the remote control, and picked up her eReader from the coffee table. She made herself more comfortable on the couch by bringing her feet up, and lying down, using the armrest to support her head. It wasn't as comfortable as using one of the couch pillows, but she didn't mind because it would keep her from falling asleep in the living room like Darla had done.

Drake saw the reflected light from the television stop flickering on the hallway walls and go dark. Finally, he thought. Bed-time. He thought they'd never leave the living room. He started to rub himself through his pants, anticipating the peep show that would begin as they came to their rooms and undressed for bed. He checked his position and moved away from the window a few steps. He backed into the wooden fence and stopped there, certain they wouldn't see him there in the dark.

The wall in the hallway only remained darkened for a few seconds and then it was illuminated again - this time by a very dim white light. *Jesus Christ! Would they ever come to bed!?*

He wished he was just a little gutsier than he was. Every time he watched someone, he got off not only on seeing nude women, but also on the fantasy of what he would do if he could work up the nerve to enter their homes and do what he really wanted. So far he'd been content to watch, but more and more he thought about taking the next step and actually touching his objects of desire. He had no moral objections to committing the greater crime of rape. The only thing that held him back was the fear of getting caught - not necessarily in the act, but perhaps afterward, once the victim reported the incident. They'd be able to describe him with ease, and eventually, he'd get pulled over for some stupid traffic violation and the cop would recognize him and his pathetic life would be over. If only he could come up with a fool-proof way of committing rape without getting caught and without having to kill anyone, he'd be all for it.

He'd thought of bringing mace with him, but he didn't think the effect would last long enough to keep a woman from being able to see him before he'd finished with her, and it would also probably affect him too since he'd more than likely have his face close to the victim's. He didn't know the range of mace, but he assumed that kissing someone who'd just been sprayed with it would be decidedly unpleasant, even if it didn't burn his own eyes.

He was confident that he could knock a woman out by hitting her over the head, but that ran the risk of accidentally killing her. And if that didn't happen, he still might end up injuring her, and a bloody unconscious woman was not on his fantasy list. He wanted his victim to be awake and aware of what was happening, but unable to see him and describe him to police afterwards.

If he'd had a solution to this problem, he'd use it right now. He'd sneak in through one of the bedroom windows and then he'd be more patient for one of them to enter a bedroom, knowing there was a much bigger payoff to be had. Then he'd show them what a man he was. He imagined himself on top of the brunette lying face-down on her bed, straddling her, entering her, pulling her ponytail and asking, "Do you still think you're too fucking good for me? Huh? Do you? Bitch. How do you like me now? How do you like having a real man inside you?"

Of the many women who had rejected Drake Austin and spurned his advances, these two were not among them. But he knew they were the same as all of the others. They were all the same; running around town without a care in the world. Flaunting their little bodies like they came down from heaven to where lowly mortals like Drake could look, but never touch. In fact, he wasn't even good enough to look at them. Whenever young women saw him eyeing them, they'd give him this look like they just bit into a lemon. The bolder, stuck-up bitches would glare at him as if asking how he dared look at the skin they so generously put on display. How dare

HE look at them? The display wasn't for him. It was for the sexy guys. The spoiled, pampered kids who had everything in life handed to them - including the most beautiful women in the world, all because of their social status and organic wealth before forced financial equality came along.

The fact that the government enabled all people to purchase anything and everything they wanted by subsidizing whatever anyone couldn't afford, creating the illusion of economic equality didn't really make a difference. People could tell if you were naturally rich, or just a subsidy case.

Drake was tempted to climb through the window in front of him right now. He'd show these bitches they weren't special. They were nothing but stupid sluts living a life of ease. But even if he did manage to get in undetected and grab one of the girls from behind and have his way with her without her seeing his face, there was too great a chance that the other would be awakened, and then he'd be screwed.

Nothing was going to happen tonight. Unless one of them ever went to bed. Then he'd at least get the pleasure of seeing more of them than he had at the college. At least. But he deserved a lot more than that. He had it coming to him.

Gabriella finished the chapter she was reading and yawned. She told herself she'd read one more chapter then go to bed.

## Eighteen

Deron stared at Dr. Fielding, waiting for him to respond. He was still thirsty after drinking a full glass of water but didn't want to pour another glass. "Deron, you're a smart, young man," the doctor said. "I believe that although you are angry now and may remain so for some time, you'll still be able to understand and appreciate our goals here, and eventually, you'll even be thankful for the changes we'll be making in you."

Deron was certain that the doctor could not be more mistaken, no matter what his goals were. He also wondered what sort of changes they wanted to make in him. He was trying to keep his mind from racing in multiple directions at once and just focus on what was being said to him.

"Someday you might even be proud that you were one of the first to help usher in a new age for mankind. This is actually quite an opportunity, which you'll understand shortly."

"Could you just actually tell me what "this" is instead of talking all around it without really saying anything?" Deron asked, and then decided he would have more water just to have something to do with his hands. He was trying to maintain control in the most out-of-control situation he'd ever found himself in.

"Of course. Forgive me. There's just so much that I wish to convey to you and I don't have a ready speech or prepared introduction to our program and how we intend to help you with it."

"And this is 'help' that I have no choice of opting out of. Is that right?"

"Well, for the time being, your participation is mandatory, but I'm hoping that as we progress you'll become more of a voluntary, and perhaps, even *proud* participant. But enough of our hopes and intentions. I'd like to tell you what you're waiting to hear, but I will have to start with a little bit of background. I'll try to be brief as I understand your current state of anxiety and impatience to learn your role in our program."

Deron took a deep breath, trying to keep himself as calm and as patient as he could manage. He wished he had a gun and imagined himself shooting this wordy bastard between the eyes, then shooting anyone else who came between him and an exit. He had never been so scared or angry before. He tried to will his heart to beat more mildly and to slow its pace.

Dr. Fielding stood up and walked toward the eQuarium, gathering his thoughts. He'd delivered this speech many times before in his mind, but hadn't considered the fact that young men and women suddenly torn from their familiar routines and loved ones wouldn't necessarily be in a receptive state of mind. He knew now that a modified approach was imperative, and that sedatives would be a must with future subjects. He looked at the fish, then turned around and faced Deron. He clasped his hands behind his back and said, "Deron, man's needs are simple. He needs nothing more than food and water to survive. Everything beyond those basic needs are choices. The choices we make are those that raise our existence from one of mere survival, to pleasure or happiness *while* surviving. And since man is a social creature, the choice is almost always made to congregate with others. This enhances our survival capability and leads to pleasure-producing interactions."

Deron felt like he was in sociology class and feared that this was going to be long and boring and maddening to listen to since he still could not conceive of how this had anything to do with him. If his mother had committed him to this place, he swore he wouldn't talk to her for at least a year. She always complained that he didn't socialize enough and now this Fielding guy was talking about mankind and socialization. Is that what this was about? Something his mother thought would help him become more like others - like the mindless zombies at school?

He wondered how long he would be stuck here. How long would it be until he saw Michelle again? And Charlie. And Feenix. Fuck! He hated being here already and wanted to cry.

Okay, he told himself. Calm down. For now, I'm stuck here and need to figure out what they want from me so I can appear to give it to them as quickly as possible and get the fuck out of here. But he was also determined to find a way to escape while going along with the program.

\*\*\*

Michelle walked away from the parking lot without saying a word to Jenny who was pre-occupied with Zeke and hadn't even noticed that she had left. Everything felt wrong to her right now. Walking down the sidewalk at night alone in an industrial area; wearing extremely revealing clothing; the sick feeling in her stomach that was less nausea now and more anxiety; and having Jenny as a friend.

Oh god, the thought of having to get on a bus and ride it home with the clothes she was wearing. She wished she could start this whole day over again. If she could, the first thing she'd do is find out what happened to Deron. If he had been arrested for something, she'd find out what for. She'd visit him in jail and give him money and talk with him and let him know he wasn't alone. Let him know he had friends.

As Michelle thought of herself as a friend to Deron she started to cry. What a great friend she'd been. She barely acknowledged his existence at school. She rarely talked to him even outside of school anymore. And yet, whenever she did "lower herself" to speak to Deron - who was not a card-carrying member of the popular crowd - she was brief with him, rushing their conversations to a speedy end – afraid that someone might see her with him.

Oh, Deron. Sweet, Deron. He hadn't changed. He was always happy to see her. He never seemed upset or angry with the way she acted toward him. Judging by his behavior and how he talked to her, one would think they were still best friends. Michelle began crying even more and felt an ache inside her chest as she thought of how she and Deron had been the best of friends most of their lives. They had grown up together and spent every weekend hanging out, watching movies, riding bikes, talking, and always laughing. Whatever else they were doing, they were always laughing. Deron made everything fun.

Wherever he was, Michelle knew he was not having fun or laughing now; sitting in a jail cell somewhere after being taken away by the cops. It didn't make any sense. Deron wasn't a criminal. He was a nice guy who never bothered anyone. During lunch break he ate quickly, by himself, then went off campus to smoke until fifth period. Was that it? Was he arrested for smoking without a license?

Michelle turned a corner onto a major boulevard and saw a bus stop just a few stores away. She looked around, feeling very self-conscious wearing Jenny's slutty clothes. There was moderate traffic in both directions, but no pedestrians. She could see people inside of a sandwich shop to her right, but their backs were to her. She walked quickly to the bus stop enclosure and pushed the Plexiglass door open, walked over to the bench and sat down.

She wished she had a coat to cover herself even though it would have made her uncomfortably warm inside the bus stop. She also wished it wasn't so well-lit. She thought it was ironic that she was put off by the amenities that made waiting for a bus much safer and comfortable than it was in the old days when there was merely a bench or a three-sided enclosure exposed to the elements.

Now that bus stops were fully enclosed and air-conditioned with bright lights, people felt safe and comfortable while waiting for a bus. But it made Michelle feel like a slutty mannequin on display for the passing traffic. On the far end of the bench, she saw a newspaper someone had left behind. She walked over to it, sat down and opened the paper, holding it in front of her like a shield. It was the sports section which she had no interest in, but she held it open, blocking the view from her head down to her waist. She waited for the bus that would take her back home to where she could get out of these awful clothes and start thinking about how she was going to make some serious changes to her social life.

When the bus finally came, Michelle boarded it feeling more embarrassed than she thought was possible. Women looked at her with jealousy. Their plastic surgery and other body enhancements couldn't compete with her youthful physique. They pursed their lips and squinted their eyes. Men looked at her differently. Licking their lips and opening their eyes wide, eyebrows involuntarily rising as they looked her up and down, then up again. Michelle opened the folded newspaper and again covered as much of her body as she could as she walked past the seated passengers.

A man who hadn't taken his eyes off of her since she got on moved over to the window seat and patted the seat he had just vacated, inviting Michelle to sit next to him. She quickly looked away and walked past him. She saw a girl a few seats down sitting by a window, chewing gum and staring absent-mindedly through the dirty glass. Michelle sat in the seat next to her and folded the newspaper, using it now to cover only her stomach and chest.

The girl in the window seat was wearing old-fashioned ear-buds. Michelle followed the white insulated wires flowing down from her ears to where they terminated inside of a small, purple purse. She was glad that the girl was absorbed in her music because it meant she would be unlikely to start a conversation.

"First time?"

Michelle was startled by the question. "Excuse me?"

"Is this your first time hooking?"

"What? No! I mean, I'm not. Hooking, I mean.

"You just like to dress like you are?"

Michelle blushed and looked away for a second, then turned back and said, "These aren't my clothes."

"Right. I suppose you're just wearing them for a friend," she said and laughed.

"Actually, I am. I know that sounds stupid, but they really do belong to a friend – an *ex*-friend."

"Is your friend working?"

Michelle looked at her blankly, not understanding the question.

"On the *street*. Is your friend a hooker?"

"No. She's just a bit..." Michelle was going to say "slutty" but then stopped, not wanting to insult the girl who was apparently a prostitute. "She kinda dresses like one."

"Well, if you ever decide you wanna work, you'll just need parental consent to get your license. With your looks, you could make a lot of money, girl. A *lot*."

"Thank you... um, but I don't think I ever will. Thanks." Again Michelle felt like she may have just insulted her seat-mate and didn't know if she should try to be diplomatic and assure the girl that she meant no offense, or if she should just shut up since she wasn't doing very well so far with her efforts at being social.

The girl was looking Michelle over with a clear view of her body behind the newspaper and finally said, "Yep. You'd do very good." She turned to her left and touched the sensor and said, "In fact, I'm getting off at the next stop where I'm gonna meet a client worth about $2,000 for thirty minutes. If you wanna come along, he'll probably pay you the same. You just have to promise not to steal him from me. I think you're a little cuter than me and he might like you more. Young ones get all the best customers."

"Thank you, but I just wanna get home. I haven't been feeling well. That's really nice of you to offer though."

Michelle felt like she was having a conversation in a bad dream or in a bizarre stage play. She just wanted this night to be over. She looked out the windows on the opposite side of the bus to see if they were near the next stop. She didn't know if she could handle much more of this conversation. All she could really see though was the interior of the bus reflected back at her on the Plexiglass windows.

"Around here, they spend way more time looking than fucking. It's way easier than you might think."

"They?"

"The Vietnamese. They like to look at your cooch. Well, pretty much most Asians are like that. All the ones I've been with, anyway. They'll gaze into your crotch like they're looking for the meaning of life to jump out at them. And half the time, they don't even fuck you – like they have some shame thing goin' on. Ya know? But it sure doesn't stop them from looking. I've actually thought of keeping magnifying glasses in my purse and selling them for an extra twenty bucks."

The bus began to decelerate and Michelle silently thanked God. She had absolutely no idea how to respond to the platinum blonde pixie and what she was saying. The bus came to a stop and the girl grabbed her little purse and got up.

"This is my stop. If you ever change your mind, you can usually find me around here." She squeezed past Michelle and stepped into the aisle. "Can I zing you my number?"

"Sure," Michelle said, pulling her communicator out of a boot. She pressed a few buttons, then the other girl pointed hers at Michelle's and they both chimed.

"Call me if you ever want to learn. My name is Sabrina. I'd be happy to work with you and show you the ropes. I'll even loan you the money to get your license. No subzies on licensing for some reason," she said, smiling.

"Thank you. That's very sweet," Michelle said.

The girl waved, flashing her brightly painted, purple fingernails. Everyone on the bus watched her every step to the front where she turned, smiled, and wiggled her fingers at Michelle, then descended the stairs into the night.

*One more mile, then I'm starting a whole new life. I swear to God. I think I'd rather be invisible than popular anymore.*

## Nineteen

Deron had gradually tuned out the droning sound of Dr. Fielding's voice. At first, he listened, because he wanted to know why he'd been brought here. He wanted to know what was going to be done with him. And he wanted to know how long they intended to keep him. Eventually, he realized the answer to the first question, even though it didn't make sense to him. And at the rate Dr. Fielding was going, he didn't expect to get solid answers to his other two questions any time soon.

Deron could sum up the first thirty minutes of the doctor's rambling in a few sentences: Man was entitled to happiness. The greatest barrier to man's happiness was man. So if people would stop being the way they were, we'd all be just fine. So Deron concluded that somehow, Dr. Fielding and the DEO had determined it was their job to make people better than they naturally were, and they'd identified Deron somehow as one of the bad guys.

This was just more evidence of how stupid the government was. Charlie had taught Deron that the government was comprised of stupid and dangerous people who should always be avoided, if at all possible. When occasions arose that required interaction with such people, they should be conducted sooner rather than later, quickly and efficiently, and the less one said during the interaction, the better off one would be at the end of it.

Charlie told Deron about a time before the war when he was adding a room to his house. He went to the city planner's office to get the necessary permit, which really made Charlie mad. He owned the land and the house – why in God's name did he need permission to add a room? He could understand that they'd want to check the electrical installation and make sure Charlie didn't fry his nuts off when he flipped on a light switch, but *permission* to build in the first place? Even if he did wire the place like a deathtrap, that should be his own problem and no one else's, but he consented based on the fact that he didn't want some idiot neighbor of his creating a fire hazard, setting his house on fire and then burning down Charlie's along with it. So he went for the permit.

In the interest of getting all of the facts out up front, Charlie told the clerk what he intended to build, what materials he was going to use and who would be doing the labor. After answering questions for fifteen minutes, he was given multiple applications, wage forms, inspection requests, material safety data sheets, pesticide requirements, Social Security withholding forms, an environmental impact questionnaire, immigration affidavits, and so on, until he finally just said to hell with it and stormed out.

"It's a special kind of shithead that wants to be a government employee, son. There are builders in life, and there are destroyers. There are artists and there are vandals. There are people who add to the world and people who take away from it. People who make you feel good when they walk into a room, and people that just make you want to leave when they show up. Every single shithead who works for the government belongs in the latter of those groups. And they all dream of being bigger and badder tyrants than they are in their current position. They want to rule over people – impose their will, and stop dreamers from achieving anything because they themselves are incapable of creating anything and they despise those who can and do."

Unlike listening to Dr. Fielding, when Charlie went off on a rant, Deron felt like he was in for a treat. Charlie told the truth. He was smart and he'd been around for a long time and Deron trusted that everything Charlie said was the absolute truth. And unlike most people, Charlie would even state that he could be wrong. Charlie told Deron to beware of government employees – including everyone employed at his school. Not the laborers like the janitors or lunchroom employees and landscapers, but anyone in teaching or administration – watch out for them. Especially administration. Every petty tyrant in government started somewhere, and schools were government institutions that attracted shitheads just like any other government institution.

Deron thought about the fact that when he was taken by the DEO officers, the librarian certainly had no problem pointing him out and watching him be led away. And for those men to have been on the school grounds, they had to have checked in at the admin building, so that meant the school officials were aware of and approved of what they were doing.

"Shit, by its nature, will stick to other shit, and it doesn't mind the smell," Charlie had said. Deron laughed out loud when he recalled this, and Dr. Fielding abruptly stopped what he was saying.

"Do you find this amusing, Deron? Does the idea of making the world better for everyone sound foolish to you? Would we be better served by just letting the civilized amongst us fall victim to the sociopaths as we've done all throughout history? Or better yet, you can explain to me in your own words just what it is about our goals that makes you chuckle."

"I was just remembering something," Deron responded. "But now that you're actually asking for my input – I think it's fine if you want to make the world a better place and you want to eliminate crime and all that – but what does any of this have to do with me? I still have no *fucking* clue what I'm doing here."

Dr. Fielding winced at Deron's profanity. He stood up and walked toward the eQuarium as he formulated an answer to Deron's question. "Well, as I was saying, behaviors are learned. And though the age-old question of nature vs. nurture has never been scientifically resolved, it has been proven that even if a person *is* born a sociopath, which I doubt, by the way, that doesn't mean they can't be made worse through experience.

Conversely, and more importantly for our purposes here, that doesn't mean they can't be made better.

"The key is in modifying their thought processes as well as their internal reward system early enough - before they reach the point of no return. And that's precisely where you come in, Deron. There is *still hope for you*." With that, Dr. Fielding turned and beamed his brightest smile at Deron.

"Are you out of your fucking mind? Is that what this is about? You think I'm a sociopath and you're gonna *cure* me? What the hell makes you think—"

"Slow down, Deron. Let me explain."

"I'm not a criminal and I don't get off on hurting people. If anyone here is psychotic, it's you!"

"Deron, please listen to me. I'm not saying you're psychotic. What we have managed to do here is identify precipitation markers that give us the ability to identify those who are *at risk* of becoming anti-social to a criminal degree, but who have not *yet* become criminal. You are *not* a criminal, Deron – and with experimental treatment, psychological reconditioning, and behavior modification therapy, we can keep you from ever *becoming* one."

Dr. Fielding stood there smiling and looking at Deron, waiting for Deron to see how wonderful this was going to be. Deron was momentarily speechless now that he knew why they had taken him, and what they were going to do to him. And since they were wrong about him being pre-sociopathic or whatever, he could conceivably be here forever as they tried to change him from something he wasn't into what he already was – a normal, non-criminal, teenaged boy.

Now he needed to think. He had to figure out a way to escape from here, and since they would undoubtedly come looking for him, he'd have to hide and stay hidden or get very far away. He couldn't believe this day.

He controlled his outrage and anger. He wanted to scream and curse and smash the eQuarium since there were no windows, but he knew at the instant he felt these urges, acting on them would merely prove Dr. Fielding right. Any anti-social behavior on his part would confirm the doctor's suspicions about him, so he was determined to be as social as possible until he exited this building.

He tried to think fast in terms of cooperation. How would Dr. Fielding want him to respond? What's the best he might be hoping for? Dr. Fielding was still looking at Deron with the unspoken question "Well?" still on his face. Deron decided he'd start off with something truthful.

"I don't know what to say. This is so... unexpected, and I guess it actually is a good thing, and I'm... relieved. Yeah. It's such a *relief* after not knowing all this time what was going on and what I was doing here, and now I see that all along you were only planning on helping me."

"Yes! That's right, Deron! We have nothing but the best of intentions for you – and ultimately, for all of society." Looking at the time, he saw that he'd missed a meeting, but it was worth it. He was actually making progress with Deron.

"I see that now. I apologize for the way I was earlier. I just... didn't know."

"Of course not, Deron, and no one would hold that against you. It is a bit of a shock to be abruptly removed from one's normal routine and environment. Our experiences, and dare I say *mistakes* today will go a long way toward improving our procedure with subsequent candidates. Forgive us for learning as we go. You are, after all, part of our first group of candidates."

"So, my mom knows about this? Can I call her? I'd like to see her and my grandfather and let them know I'm okay and everything is going to be fine."

Dr. Fielding glanced away at the mention of Deron's mom. His permanent smile finally seemed to have lost its adhesion for a moment. The DEO committee who approved the rehabilitation program had decided that the interests of society were greater than the interests of a single parent and had deemed parental approval to be a mere formality.

"Yes, yes, Deron, we'll get to that. We still have much to do to get you settled in, oriented, and prepared for your treatment. It would be a bit premature and unproductive to worry about scheduling visits at this early stage."

"Right. I forgot. I haven't even been here that long. But my mom does know I'm here, right? Otherwise, she'll be expecting me home from school and will think something has happened to me."

"We've had people in contact with your mother today, Deron. I assure you she will not be worrying. Not in the least."

Dr. Fielding didn't know yet if the parents of the first group of teens had consented, or if they'd been deemed criminals for failure to consent, and thus been shipped to the penal island. Once again, he lost his purchase on his game-show host smile for just a second or two and quickly restored it. He was not as successful though at restoring eye contact with Deron and kept looking over at the digital fish.

Deron knew he was being lied to, but didn't know exactly how. He could only guess that maybe they lied to his mom and told her he'd been arrested or that he was mentally ill and had been committed. Deron felt a new surge of anger well up inside of him at the thought of his mother relaying to Charlie that Deron was in jail or in a mental hospital. It would break Charlie's heart. Charlie was the one person who really loved Deron and cared about him. Deron had never had a father, but he had Charlie, and Charlie was better than his father ever could have been.

He realized that his plan of acting like a perfect citizen with no anti-social issues wasn't going to work for the long term. After all, wasn't that one of the characteristics of the anti-social personality – the chameleon-like ability to charm and schmooze and get along with anybody?

Deron suddenly knew that the longer he was here, the harder it would be to get out, or to prove that he wasn't anti-social.

Dr. Fielding turned to the eQuarium again with his hands behind his back, fingers interlaced as if he had just shown a child *'This is the church and this is the steeple. Open it up and see all the people.'* "Well, Deron. Now that you see the goal of our institution and realize we're not in the business of—"

Dr. Fielding heard the shattering of glass before he felt the impact of the water pitcher against the back of his head. Semi-conscious, he dropped to the ground and his blood quickly seeped into the plush beige carpet. He stared up at the digital fish with his glassy eyes and his mouth opening and closing, trying to form a word – unaware that at that moment he looked very much like the fish did.

Deron felt his whole body shaking with adrenaline. His mind raced. What to do next? Keys. He needed Fielding's keys. Or key card. Whatever it was. He also needed to come up with a plan for getting past the guard in the lobby. He hadn't thought that far ahead. When he had seen Fielding standing with his back to him, he looked at the glass pitcher and it was like the idea suggested itself to Deron, and Deron executed it. He didn't really have a plan at all.

He was surprised the guard hadn't come bursting through the door already. The office must be soundproofed. Well, that gave him an idea. Get the guard to come rushing through the door. He'd look down at Fielding and then Deron could hit him in the back of the head too. He looked around the office for another weapon. There was a stone paperweight on the desk, but if the guard looked at Deron's hands, that would be too obvious.

He thought of a better idea. He opened the door and started screaming. "Help! Help! You've got to help the doctor! I think he's having a heart attack!" He stood in front of the doorway blocking the view to Fielding's body behind him. He heard the guard running toward him. Deron tried to sound scared and frantic. "You've got to help him. He just fell down and dropped the pitcher he was holding! Help him, please!"

"Step aside!" Deron did so and the guard went past him and looked down at the doctor. He bent down and reached his hand toward the doctor's neck to check for a pulse since the doctor was not moving and didn't appear to be breathing. As soon as he bent over, Deron put his right foot low on the guard's back pushed forward as hard as he could. He immediately thought that maybe he shoved too hard. The guard went toppling forward, tripping over the doctor's body, hitting his head on the wall and dropping to the floor.

With the door unlocked now and the guard on the ground, Deron grabbed the doctor's elevator key and ran out the door, and down the hall. He went around the security desk and over to the elevator. He touched the letter G on the panel.

The elevator doors opened on the much larger ground floor lobby. This one had a fountain in the center and miniature palm trees like the first lobby he'd seen. There was also a crescent shaped counter like the one on the ninth floor, only much larger. There were chairs for three people behind this one, but only one was occupied.

Deron burst out of the elevator and ran to the counter, shouting, "You've got to help. Dr. Fielding needs you on the ninth floor. He and the guard were fighting. The doctor told me to find help and call the police. Quick! You've got to go up there and help him. I'll call the police!"

The guard looked frozen in disbelief. He stared at Deron then looked at the elevator, then at his security console to see if there were any alerts. There weren't. He asked, "What did you say?"

"We don't have time! The doctor needs you, dammit! Get to the ninth floor as fast as you can, and take your gun out. The guard up there went crazy and the doctor needs help before that guard kills him. The ninth floor. Go!!"

The guard looked unsure of what to do. He'd never had any problems in the short time he'd been employed here, and now this. He decided that it would be easier to explain why he left his station than why he failed to help the doctor if what this kid was saying was true. He got up and ran to the elevator. Deron said into the phone. "I have an emergency. Please send an ambulance and police to the address I'm calling from."

The guard heard Deron talking and realized this was actually happening. He pushed a button and the elevator doors closed.

Deron dropped the handset and ran through the lobby, around the fountain and toward the glass doors. He pushed one, then the other, but neither one opened.

As he fumbled again through Dr. Fielding's keys, he heard the ding of the elevator open behind him. He turned around to see who would emerge. The guard he'd thought had just went to the ninth floor came back out and pointed something black at Deron as he walked toward him. At first, Deron thought he was just aiming a strange gun at him, but the closer the guard got, the more sick and dizzy Deron felt.

By the time the guard reached within ten feet of him, Deron collapsed to his knees and began drooling. The guard continued pointing the weapon at Deron until he passed out.

## Twenty

Charlie refolded the note and put the envelope back under the Stephen King book with the corner just barely sticking out the way he had found it. He thought of young love and he smiled. Just finding Deron's letter to Michelle eased Charlie's fears. He wasn't certain that Deron was with the girl who had stolen his heart, but it was possible so Charlie stopped imagining worst-case scenarios as he left Deron's room and headed back to the living room.

He decided he'd wait here a while to see if Deron would come home soon. He sat down on the living room couch, swiveled to the left and lifted his feet up onto it. If Kathleen came home first, she'd gripe about him lying on the couch with his shoes on so he kicked them off.

He adjusted a fluff pillow behind his head and closed his eyes. With his mind on budding romance, he recalled the girl who had once owned his heart. He shut out a momentary flash of heart-ache as he inevitably recalled her murder during the early stages of The War. He pushed past that memory to a much better time and place when he had first met Elizabeth, and drifted off to sleep.

***

After the bus stopped at what seemed like every possible place that it could on the way to her own stop, Michelle couldn't believe it when her turn finally came. She touched the stop request sensor and wished she could wrap herself in the newspaper. It would make more sense to hold it behind her as she walked to the front of the bus since that's the direction all of the passengers were facing, but she felt stupid enough already and didn't want to look ridiculous as well as slutty.

The bus slowed and Michelle stood up and started to grab for the overhead rail to steady herself as it came to a stop, but her top rose along with her arm so she quickly brought her arm back down and tried to tug her top down to the least embarrassing position.

She mentally cursed herself and Jenny for the hundredth time. How could Jenny go places dressed like this on a regular basis? The bus stopped and now Michelle thought of how she was a magnet for the attention of every hetero man around, and she was almost afraid to get off the bus. But her neighborhood was much safer than where she'd already been, and she reminded herself that violent crime statistics were at their lowest point ever. She took a deep breath and stepped into the aisle, telling herself that the pervert who wanted her to sit next to him was going to be undressing her with his eyes as she passed him, but it was a million times better than doing it with his hands.

She made it to the front of the bus and saw that the door wasn't open yet. *Now what!?* The driver always opened the door as soon as the bus came to a stop. She was standing and looking at the closed door, three steps down from where she stood. She expected it to open right now. It didn't. She turned around and looked at the bus driver. He raised his eyes from where they had been looking at her too short shorts and spoke to her.

"Um, pardon me for saying so, miss, but you might not be safe walking around at night dressed like that." His eyes flicked from hers to her chest and back. He licked his lips.

"Can I just go, please?" Michelle nearly whined. She wanted this night to be over. She wanted to be off of this bus and in her house and wearing clothes that covered her entire body.

"Do you need me to walk you somewhere?"

"Don't you need to stay with the bus? *Please* just open the door."

He reached for the handle that opened the door without taking his eyes off her chest, and then as she turned at the sound of the door opening, he dropped them again to her shorts. She quickly descended the steps and started running when she hit the street.

"Have a good night!" the bus driver said after her, and watched her run past the front of the bus as she crossed the street.

Michelle heard the airbrake release behind her and was grateful to finally be off the bus and close to home. There was much less traffic here than where she started. This street intersected with her own just a few blocks up. She was thirsty, but there was no way she would stop in the convenience store at the corner of her street with the clothes she had on. She could easily wait until she reached her house a mere block from the store.

She held the newspaper in front of her chest while she half-jogged down the sidewalk. As she cut the corner to her street, she came close to the front of the convenience store, drawing the attention of the cashier and another man who was apparently just hanging out with him. They both stopped talking and watched her pass. The man on the customer side of the counter stepped outside to watch her round the corner of the store. He wolf whistled as he watched her run diagonally across the street and then continue down the sidewalk.

Finally, she was almost home. Safety, sanctuary and sanity. Only thirty yards away. Oh great. A man came walking from her front yard out onto the sidewalk, heading right toward her. He stared at her like a sex fiend as he approached but she wasn't afraid of him, being just yards from her house. They passed by each other without incident and she was glad to be on the other side of him, but she could still feel his eyes on her.

She reached her house with the big willow tree in the front, intending to go inside and never come back out again.

## Twenty-one

Charlie was sitting in the driver's seat of a Model-T Ford that was on top of a parade float. Deron was sitting next to him and they were both waving at the people who dotted the sidewalks on each side of the street. Not much of a turn-out, Charlie thought. Theirs was the only float. It was pretty pathetic as far as parades went. He was waving like a prom queen to the few people on the right side of the street and turned his head to the people on the left and he could swear that there were fewer people now than there were just seconds ago. He looked back to the right and saw that one of the three people he had just waved to over there was now gone.

He jerked his head back to the left and now the sidewalk on that side was empty. He looked back to the right and the two remaining people were still there, but he felt that something else was missing. He tried to think of what it was, but all he could think of was that the people on the sidewalks were disappearing. He wanted to ask Deron if he had noticed it too and he realized that's what was missing. Deron was no longer sitting in the passenger seat. He too had vanished.

Fear squeezed his heart and he shouted, "No!" and woke up on Kathleen's living room couch. He looked around, wondering where he was for a moment, and then it came back to him. He had been looking for Deron and decided to lie down and wait a while to see if he would show up. It didn't appear that anyone had come home while he'd been napping, but he got up to walk around and make sure. Maybe someone had come home and just didn't want to wake him.

A quick tour of the house confirmed that it was as empty as it sounded. Charlie would've ordinarily looked at his communicator to get the time, but made an exception and called out to the house unit, "Time?"

The unit responded, "Seven forty seven, pee em."

"Damn it." Charlie started toward the front door, then stopped, went back to Deron's room and looked once again at the address Deron had written on the unsent letter to Michelle, committing it to memory. That's the only place he knew to look, so he was going to go there with the hope of finding him. If Deron wasn't there, Charlie would be more certain than ever that something bad had happened. For now though, he was holding on to hope that once he got to Michelle's everything would turn out to be okay.

When he went outside, Kathleen's car pulled into the driveway. Charlie was disappointed to see that the passenger seat was empty. Kathleen got out of the car and crossed the driveway, surprised to see Charlie was at her house.

"Dad. What are you doing here?" She pressed a button on her car fob and the garage door rose silently.

"I came over to see if Deron had come home, but he's not here. And he's not with you either, so I'm going to go look for him."

"You won't find him." The headlights of her car flashed and she moved out of the way, allowing it to move forward into the garage.

"Just what is that supposed to mean?

"Come inside. I'll explain." After the car parked itself the garage door beeped a warning as it closed.

She'd explain? Charlie really didn't like the sound of that. Deron was somewhere, and Kathleen knew where that was, and yet she hadn't known earlier on the phone. Or, she had lied to him. He took a deep breath and followed his daughter into the house.

"I need to finish making dinner. Are you hungry, Dad?"

"I don't know. Where is Deron?"

"Just a minute. Let me get us some coffee, then we'll talk."

Charlie refrained from saying anything. As usual, Kathleen was engaging in her uncanny ability to drive him crazy. His fingernails tapped a staccato rhythm on the marble table top. After what seemed like a long time, Kathleen came to the table carrying two cups of coffee.

"It's instant, but it's all I have."

"Thank you," he said, looking at her sternly. He didn't appreciate being kept in the dark about Deron's whereabouts, even if it was only for a few minutes. "Now will you tell me where my grandson is, or would it be quicker if I searched the city for him?"

Kathleen told herself to be patient with her father. He had a short temper on top of everything else he had working against him.

"Deron is in a special program that is going to help him with his problems. He just started it today, and he'll be there for at least a few months."

"What do you mean a special program, and his problems?" Charlie was ready to blow his top already and she'd just barely started explaining what was going on.

"I know you're not going to like this, but it's a *government* program. But it's not anything to get upset about. It's entirely for his benefit."

"You have got to be kidding me. You enlisted my grandson in a government program? To do what, exactly?"

Kathleen didn't want to tell Charlie what she had been told by Eric. She needed to lighten it up a little so Charlie wouldn't go ballistic.

"It's to help him with his social skills," she said, feeling like she wasn't even lying really.

"Deron doesn't have a problem with his social skills. He's one of the most capable youngsters I've ever known!"

"Now, Dad, you know that Deron doesn't socialize very much. He never spends any time with kids his own age."

"By choice, Kathleen! He *chooses* who he wants to spend time with. That isn't a problem. Have you spent five minutes talking to the average teenager lately? Not that *you'd* notice anything wrong with them, but Deron is a little more discriminating in his tastes. Kids today are mindless fools. If Deron wants nothing to do with them, that *isn't* a problem!"

"Dad, calm down. Deron was given an opportunity to be part of a special program, and *he* is the one who chose to do it. So if you want to be mad at someone, you can just save it for him."

"I don't believe that for a second. Did Deron tell you he wanted to do this of his own free will, with no coercion or threats?"

"He didn't tell me himself, no, but he—."

"That's what I thought," Charlie growled, getting up from the table and leaving without another word.

## Twenty-two

For the second time that day, Deron awoke in a strange bed without knowing how he'd gotten there. But this time, the room wasn't as nice and there wasn't a pretty nurse-like woman attending to him. He tried to move and found that his arms were restrained.

"Hey!" he shouted.

He looked around and saw that there wasn't much to see. Lime green walls and a toilet right out in the open. No bathroom this time and no closet and no nightstand next to the bed with a pitcher of water.

"Can anybody here me!?"

"I can hear you just fine. There's no need to yell," a voice sounded from a speaker he couldn't see.

"Let me out of here!"

"Not gonna happen, obviously. So just calm down. If you behave yourself, we'll take the restraints off, and maybe even provide you with some reading material."

"Fuck you! I'm not going to calm down. Let me out of this—" Deron suddenly felt incredibly drowsy. He looked down at his left wrist were he felt a funny heat traveling up his arm. There was a remote controlled I.V. bracelet on his wrist.

"You fuckers..." he said, and drifted off to sleep.

The next morning he awoke knowing that resistance was futile. It was time to employ his original plan of going along with the program – whatever it was. He would cooperate and earn his way out through completion of their program, or he'd escape. Whichever came first. He hoped it would be escape.

"If you can still hear me, I could really use something to eat. I haven't eaten since lunch at school yesterday."

"We'll bring you something shortly."

A few minutes later he heard a door open. He looked to his right and there was Dr. Fielding with a bandaged head.

"Good morning, Deron."

Deron sighed in embarrassment. He didn't know what to say.

"Can you give me your assurance that if we remove the restraints you will show your appreciation by simply eating and not attempting to use your dishes or utensils as weapons?"

"I'm sorry about that. I didn't mean to hurt you."

"I believe you certainly *did* intend to hurt me. What other outcome could there have been from smashing a glass pitcher on the back of my head?"

"Okay, yeah. I mean, I did, but my intention wasn't about you personally. It was just to get away. I'm really sorry. And yes, I promise it won't happen again. You can remove the restraints. I'll even sit on my hands."

The doctor looked up at a hidden camera, nodded, and the restraints fell away.

"I've released your arms and legs. You can sit up. But if I even suspect you're about to become violent, you will immediately be rendered unconscious."

"I understand. Thank you."

"Throughout the day you will be monitored. The longer your behavior remains appropriate, the more liberties and privileges you will regain. Misbehave, and you'll find yourself strapped to the cot, fully restrained again. You control your own destiny."

Deron nodded, wondering what type of liberty he could have while he was imprisoned. He was determined to be a model prisoner though, or model patient, and gain as much liberty as possible. He couldn't stand being restrained or drugged. And he really didn't want to use that toilet in the middle of the room.

The doctor must've signaled someone because the door opened again and an orderly pushed a cart into the room and over to the cot. He turned around and left without a word.

Deron lifted a large metal lid and revealed a plate with bacon, scrambled eggs, and hash browns; all of it cooked well-done. He couldn't believe it. Real food. He lifted a smaller lid and found four pieces of sourdough toast and a small cup of whipped butter.

"This is exactly the way I like my breakfast!"

"We know," Dr. Fielding replied.

"But how?"

"Just because you aren't chipped yet doesn't mean we can't track your purchases in stores and restaurants. But it will be easier once the chip is in you, that's for sure. Much more instantaneous than the weekly uploads we receive on the few people like yourself who aren't chipped. But we'll be taking care of that soon."

That answered how they knew *what* he liked, but not *how* he liked it. His mom is the one who bought the groceries and print tubes, and did the cooking. This had to mean there were cameras in his kitchen, despite the government claiming that the only domestic cameras were the ones that were built in to televisions for interactive purposes, and the exterior security cams.

Deron ate while the doctor told him he would be showering after breakfast and then having his first therapy session, followed by social time, assuming he behaved himself through each activity. When the doctor finished, he left the room, closing and presumably locking the door behind him.

Deron didn't see any cameras in the room, but there had to be at least one somewhere because the same person who brought the food cart came back to remove it as soon as Deron finished eating.

When that guy left, two more came in with someone who was probably a nurse. But this one was nothing like the last one he'd had. This one looked big and mean.

"I'm removing your I.V. so you can go to the showers, but any funny business out of you and you'll regret it." She glanced at the two guards, each of whom held a black device that Deron recalled could make him feel extremely sick, very quickly.

With the I.V. bracelet off, they led him out of the room. The nurse went one way and the guards indicated for him to go the other way. One walked in front of him and one stayed behind. They took him to a room that looked like the gym locker room and showers at school, only smaller.

When they entered, both men stood still by the door, crossing their arms in front of their chests. One of them nodded toward the showers. Deron wondered why they hadn't spoken a word yet. He undressed and showered, and when he came back toward the men at the door, one of them threw him a towel. After he dried himself, the other man threw him a package with a paper gown in it.

*Great. I guess I have to earn the right to wear real clothes.*

The men escorted him away from the showers, down the hall and into a room with a desk and a long horizontal metal cylinder. After Deron entered the room, the men left without giving him any instructions.

\*\*\*

When Charlie got up he decided to bury Feenix after all. So what if he didn't have a backyard? He got his old army shovel from his closet and went to his front yard and started digging. It wasn't easy to dig with a two-foot long shovel, but Charlie was determined to do it to bury his best friend.

He had no idea what the punishment would be if he was spotted, either by surveillance cameras on his street, a neighborhood patrol drone, or if someone reported him. At this point, he was so disgusted he didn't care. Without Deron or Feenix in his life, he felt he had nothing else to lose. At least Deron was only gone temporarily, but for how long, he had no way of knowing. So he wouldn't make matters worse by shooting the cameras or the street lights. As long as Deron would be returning, he had something to live for.

Shortly after he had finished filling in the grave, while Charlie was sitting on the grass and thinking about Feenix a blue and white EEC patrol car pulled up partially blocking his driveway as well as the next-door neighbor's. Charlie figured he was busted, and it hadn't taken long at all.

The officer in the passenger side of the car looked at him, the shovel, and the small rectangle of fresh soil amidst the perfectly groomed lawn and wondered what the hell Charlie had been doing. Then he and his partner got out and walked up the neighbor's driveway and over to the front door.

They knocked, then spoke to someone, then returned to their patrol car with the man next-door following them. The two black officers and the white man stopped when they reached the patrol car. Charlie could clearly hear their conversation.

"Am I under arrest? I haven't done anything. I swear."

"No, Mr. Johnson. You're only receiving a citation and a training order." The officer read over the report on his slate computer. The other one stood there looking around, frequently glancing at Charlie inquisitively.

"I honestly don't know what I've done wrong," the man said.

"It's come to our attention that there's some inequity in your physical relationship with your wife. A small matter of only one of you regularly reaching full satisfaction." The officer looked at the man to see if he understood now why they were there.

The man closed his eyes, sighed, and nodded.

"Do you think that's fair, Mr. Johnson?"

"I...um..."

"Are you a racist, Mr. Johnson?"

"Me? I'm married to a black woman! How could you accuse me of racism?"

"I'm just observing the signs of inequality that I see and asking a question. Marrying a black woman does not serve as automatic proof that you're not a racist. Men have historically treated their wives as the inferior people they believed them to be. Perhaps you're doing the same.

"I can't believe you're accusing me of racism," the man cried out, looking around to see if there was anyone else on the block to witness this outrage.

"Are you resisting a lawful equity intervention, Mr. Johnson?" The officer looked down the street and spotted a patrol drone. He pressed a few buttons on his communicator and the drone immediately changed its course.

"I'm just trying to make sense of this. I'm not resisting anything. I still don't know what our races have to do with our sex life, or why that's any of the government's business."

"Okay, I'm going to ask you to lie face down on the ground," the nearest officer said, while drawing his weapon and backing up toward his partner.

The drone arrived and hovered ten feet above the three of them, positioned so that its camera and frequency weapon was pointed at the man who was obeying the order but shaking his head as he did so.

Charlie got up, picked up his shovel and went into his garage. He was relieved they hadn't asked him what he had been doing in his yard, and he felt sorry his neighbor.

\*\*\*

After Michelle made it home, she had found the house empty, as usual, so she didn't have to explain to her parents why she was dressed the way she was. She figured they probably wouldn't have noticed even if they had seen her. And if they did notice, they wouldn't have cared. She suspected they were swingers, but she couldn't say why. Maybe her mother just liked dressing provocatively no matter where they went. Sometimes they told her they were going to dinner or to a show. Most times, they just said they were going out. No matter how late they were gone, they were usually back in the morning, unless they went away for longer than a day, as her mother was telling her they planned to do now.

"We'd take you with us, but you have school, of course."

"Of course," Michelle said. But there was only a week of school left until summer break. They had obviously planned their trip to Paris before school let out precisely so they wouldn't have to take her. Not that she'd want to go with them anyway.

"Do you have enough money in your account to last you a week?"

"Probably."

"Just let us know if you need more. In fact, I'm going to give you 500 credits right now just to make sure."

Barbara tapped on her communicator for a moment, concentrating on the screen.

"There. If you spend all that, which you shouldn't unless you buy clothes this weekend, let us know. You do need more clothes, you know. I do not want you wearing my clothes while we're away. And if you have friends over, please do not allow them into your father's and my room."

"Of course not."

Michelle wanted to say, "He's not my father," but there was no point. She'd lost that battle long ago. Just then, Stan entered the dining room.

"What's this about our room?"

"Just making sure Michelle knows the rules while we're gone."

"Nobody goes in our room. Is that clear?" he asked, looking at Michelle with his eyebrows raised.

*No, it's all sort of muddled and confusing. I'll need time to piece it together.* "Yes, Stan. It's clear," she said.

"Good. You have our numbers, so just call us if you need anything. We're only a phone call away, even though we'll be in France."

*God, can they be any stupider?* Of course she had their phone numbers, and she knew that phones worked across great distances. Did they think she was five?

"I know," she said. "I'll call if I need anything or if I run out of money, and I won't go in your room, or let anyone else go in there."

"Good girl," Stan said.

"Okay, I guess we're off then. I love you, sweetheart," her mother said, bending down to give Michelle an air-kiss by each check, apparently feeling European already. Stan winked at her.

Michelle poured cereal into her bowl, relieved that she could finally eat in peace.

## Twenty-three

Deron was tempted to look around and see what he could discover about this place while he was alone in the room, but figuring there would be cameras, he just stood patiently and waited.

A minute later the door opened and a man dressed in business casual slacks and a polo shirt came in. He was younger than Dr. Fielding and looked like he spent more time outdoors than in.

"Deron! Hi. My name is Gerald. It's nice to meet you," he said, extending a tanned and muscled arm toward Deron. He shook Deron's hand with a strong grip. "Have a seat." He gestured to a chair facing the desk which he went around and sat behind.

"I understand you got off to a rough start here, but I won't hold it against you." He smiled like a happy actor for a toothpaste commercial. "You and I have a clean slate, and I'll treat you just like I would anyone else. Do you have any questions before I explain how our session here works?"

Deron shook his head.

"Okay then. Let's get right to it. There's no time like the present! That strange looking metal tube you see over there is an isolation chamber. Your first assignment is going to be a tough one. You ready? You just need to lie down and float in warm water. How does that sound?"

"That sounds pretty easy, Gerald. Is that it?"

"That's it for your part. For our part, we'll be a little more busy, but you don't need to worry about that."

"I'd like to know what you'll be doing while I'm hard at work floating."

"Right, right. Of course. You're no dummy. Of course there's more to it than you just floating. On our end, we'll be monitoring your vitals and your brainwaves, and we'll be playing some entrainment music, watching realtime images of your brain, and make adjustments here and there as needed to get everything just right."

"What does entrainment mean?"

"Mostly it means you'll be listening to music. But on a sub-conscious level, a part of your mind will be listening to signals that you won't be able to hear or isolate from the sound of the music."

"You mean you'll be programming my mind to think the way you want me to think?"

"I wouldn't say that. I'd we'll be teaching your mind to process information more effectively and come up with results and decisions that are advantageous to both you and to society as a whole, rather than to just one individual."

*As I thought – brainwashing.* Deron knew he needed to stop verbalizing his rebellious thoughts, and try to appear as though he was going along with the program. "Will this help me get along better with others?" he asked.

"That's just the tip of the iceberg, Deron. You have a lot to look forward to. We can talk more about all of that after you've had a few sessions and start to see the benefits. I know you're going to be very pleased."

"I can't wait," Deron replied, trying as hard as he could to not sound sarcastic.

"Great. Then let's get started. You can undress over there behind the partition next to the chamber and then hop right in."

As Deron changed, Gerald tapped virtual keys on the glass surface of his desk and checked various monitoring systems in the inlaid display and confirmed that everything was ready to go.

Deron climbed the steps and slowly entered the chamber. After he was floating on his back, Gerald confirmed he was in position with the camera feed aimed down at the chamber and tapped one more key.

The lid of the chamber slowly descended. Deron started to feel claustrophobic and forced himself to relax. They hadn't gone through all this trouble just to kill him, so he told himself he had nothing to worry about; nothing but losing his mind, and his identity.

*** 

Drake pulled up at an apartment complex and parked his truck. It was his third appointment of the day; a routine call for a new installation of basic cable in two rooms. Arriving at a house or apartment and finding an attractive customer wasn't uncommon, but when the door swung open after he knocked, Drake was momentarily speechless.

The young lady standing in the doorway was wearing a big smile and little else. She was twenty-two years old, with dirty-blonde hair, a dark tan and wearing a very skimpy two-piece string bikini. "Hi!" she said. "Cable guy?" she asked, still smiling.

"Uh... um. Yeah," Drake said, struggling to direct his gaze at her eyes and not be so obvious about looking at the rest of her mostly exposed flesh.

"Come on in. Would you like something to drink? I don't care if you drink while you're on duty," she said with a mischievous grin.

Drake said he'd take whatever she was offering, and after he said it, he realized it could be taken two ways. He was glad he accidently did because if he'd thought of saying something with a double-meaning, he wouldn't have had the nerve to actually say it.

The girl, whose name was Mitzi, also got the double-entendre and said, "Well for now, I'm serving Heineken. Will that cool you down a bit?" It sounded like she was playing her own word game. He told her that would be great and waited just inside the doorway as she rounded a corner to the left. Drake was pleased and hopeful. He could feel the familiar buzz of sexual excitement beginning low in his brain.

This might be his best day yet as a cable guy. In fact, it almost was already just in terms of her being the sexiest customer he'd had yet in his six months on the job. His best previous day in terms of sexual excitement was when a hot, thirty-five year old lawyer was walking around cleaning on her day off and wore a loose tank top with no bra. For forty-five minutes Drake's brain had buzzed with electricity and he could barely keep his mind on the installation.

And now here he was in the apartment of a co-ed who was totally deliberate and open in her sexuality. The lawyer woman had been hot, but apparently unmindful of her exposures. She hadn't been unfriendly, but neither was she at all flirtatious like Mitzi was being now. She handed him a Heineken in a frosty green bottle.

"Come," she said, as she turned around and began walking down the entry hall to a doorway up ahead on the right.

Drake had a better and longer look at her backside than when she went to get their beers. From her shoulders to her bare feet, Mitzi had a dark, golden-brown tan. She was slim without any extra padding anywhere. She looked like she worked out, but not to the point of body-building. She had great muscle tone everywhere and Drake found himself taking just as much pleasure at watching her hair swish back and forth at her shoulder blades as he did looking at her superbly firm buttocks. That was where Drake's attention returned after each glance at the rest of her. Mitzi was wearing a thong bathing suit bottom and only a small amount of flesh was covered by a thin hot pink triangle of fabric that extended into two thin strips that wrapped around to the front from each side.

She had to know Drake was enjoying the view. With a body like that, barely covered, and the way she was walking, swishing her ass just a little more than seemed natural. Then to confirm his suspicions, she stopped suddenly and said, "What's this?" as she bent down to pick something up from the carpet that Drake couldn't even see. He'd almost bumped into her, and the thought of doing that caused him to get aroused, imagining what it would feel like if he had kept going until his crotch bumped into her ass. Mitzi looked at the piece of black string she had picked up and said "Hmm" and turned into the open doorway of the living room.

"Here it is," she announced, extending her hand, palm up like a game show beauty presenting a prize to a panel of contestants.

Drake cleared his throat and thanked her. He didn't know if he was thanking her for showing him the television, for the beer, or for putting herself on such an exquisite display.

"I bet you know exactly what to do, so I'll leave you to play with your toys. If you need anything, I'll be out back working on my tan. I have just got to get rid of this tanline. See?" She pulled part of her bikini top away from her breast, exposing too much for just a second before moving it partly back in place. "Oops," she giggled. Pulling the fabric to the side more carefully, she asked, "Can you see the difference?"

"Yeah. A little," Drake said.

She let go of that side and then more carefully pulled back the other side of her top to check the tan differential on the other breast. Drake continued to stare. After all, he was invited to and she was obviously putting on a show, so he didn't feel nervous about it.

"Almost there," she said. "Well, the patio is just outside the dining room. You know, where I went to get the beer?"

Drake made eye contact with Mitzi and nodded. He didn't even want to try speaking. His mouth was dry and his head was buzzing and a bulge was growing in his pants which was embarrassing him even though he felt she was totally responsible for it and she should be okay with seeing what she'd done.

"I'm sure you'll be able to find me... if you need anything." With another flash of perfect white teeth, she turned and walked out, swaying even more than before.

Definitely putting on a show, Drake thought. Once she was out of the room, he took a long drink of the beer he was holding. He needed to think and his brain felt devoid of blood. It had all gone south. He was already trying to think of a reason to go speak to her on the patio where she as much as told him she would be lying topless, and practically invited him to come speak to her there.

Just to get on some kind of solid mental ground, he looked over at the TV. It was a UHD crystalline screen mounted on the wall just a few feet from her signal transmitter a few feet to the right. There was already a green light indicating it had connectivity with the local access point, so this would be a cinch.

He knew he'd have to go talk to her when he was done if she hadn't returned by then, but he wanted a reason to go to the patio before then and see how she'd respond to him looking at her topless. Would she cover herself with an arm or a hand-bra? Would she just lay there with no modesty concerns at all like the suburban nudists he always hoped to get a service call for? Or would she be lying on her chest? Drake frowned at that thought, thinking what a shame it would be if she were lying face down and merely turned her head in his direction to talk to him. But then he remembered that she wanted to even out the tan on her chest and that there was no tanline on her back.

Having reassured himself that good things were in store, he quickly accessed the wi-fi network settings on her TV to sync it with the cable feed while still trying to think of an excuse to talk to her. And who knew? Maybe before this appointment was over, he'd end up doing a lot more than just looking. He smiled. Mitzi seemed to actually like him.

## Twenty-four

Michelle took her bowl of cereal to the living room and sat on the couch where she was not allowed to eat anything; especially not cereal since it could be spilled. She told the television to turn on, and then she said, "Internet. Search. Deron Young."

The top search results were for an NAFL quarterback.

"Modify query: Orange County."

The same quarterback had played in the Orange Bowl.

"*Minus* football," she said, frustrated.

Now the first result was for a doctor named Deron Younger with an office in Tustin. She thought for a second.

"New search: Deron *Michael* Young, plus Orange County."

*"Did you mean: Deron Michael Younger?"* the voice of the search assistant asked.

"No!"

*"No results for Deron Michael Young and Orange County. Would you like to broaden your search?"*

"No. TV off."

The screen went black and the room fell silent. Too silent.

"TV on. Music. KLOS."

The screen came back on and displayed information about the modern rock song flowing from the speakers.

Michelle leaned back on the couch and sighed, wondering where Deron was. She thought she would have at least found an arrest report. But there was nothing.

***

Floating in the warm water in complete darkness with soothing music made Deron feel like there was nothing at all to be concerned about. And that scared the hell out of him.

Whatever they were doing to his mind, it was happening in such a way that he was completely unaware of it. He tried to focus on his own thoughts to see if they were changing in any way. Was he still thinking like himself?

He concluded that he was because he was worried about the fact that there didn't seem to be anything to worry about. He wasn't just enjoying his time in the chamber without fretting, so whatever they were doing to his mind, he still seemed to be himself.

He feared though that the process might take effect later. Or maybe it would build up gradually without him even noticing it. And one day he wouldn't even remember the Deron that he was today. This had to stop.

He had no idea how long he'd been in the chamber before the music ended and the lid began to rise. When it did, he felt like he was in an alternate reality, and looking out into the room as he sat up was like looking at another world. He felt spaced out, but very relaxed and calm. Gerald was sitting at the desk looking as perky as ever. He looked like he might have only been sitting there for only a minute or so.

"How long was I in there?"

"Just two hours. How did you like it?" Gerald got up and handed Deron a towel.

"It was nice. Very relaxing." He wasn't making that up. Under different circumstances, he could enjoy it.

"Great. Great. So you see now there's nothing to worry about. Each day, you'll spend two hours in the same type of session. You'll probably even start looking forward to it."

"Cool. I'm *already* looking forward to it."

"Great! Go ahead and get dressed and I'll walk you to your next session. You get to keep your clothes on for this one." Gerald laughed.

"Can I have my own clothes?"

"Umm, let me find out. Just a sec..." Gerald put a wireless bud in his ear and tapped a few buttons on his desk console. Dr. Fielding answered.

"Yes?"

"Would it be okay for Deron to wear his own clothes? He's doing very well and he's ready for his social group. Everyone else will be dressed there."

"I suppose that would be best – although he certainly doesn't deserve them yet."

"Thank you, Doctor."

Fielding said he'd send someone with the clothes and Gerald tapped a button and removed the earbud.

A short while later, after Deron was dressed, Gerald walked him down several halls until they came to a door. Deron heard a click in the door, then Gerald opened it and gestured for him to enter.

This room looked like a recreation center. It was long and rectangular with partial dividers separating the area into multiple sections. The left side looked like a cafeteria. Gerald walked Deron to the center of the right side of the room from which they could see into each smaller section.

"Your job for the next few hours is to have fun. How do you like that? After a while, someone will bring lunch in."

Gerald left the room and Deron looked around. Three of the four quadrants were occupied. He walked toward the empty one which was furnished with couches, floor pillows, lamps, a large bookshelf, and a small stack of slate computers.

One of the other quads had a large screen TV and a young male playing a virtual racing game, the partial race car tilting and bouncing. Another quad was populated by a young female watching a romantic comedy. The last quad had another male running on a treadmill.

Although Deron was naturally drawn toward the books, he had no intention of reading. It was one of the few times he didn't want to read. Neither was he inclined to walk up to any of the three strangers.

He sat on the couch and relaxed for a moment, then he realized that this wasn't just recreational time. Their interactions would be monitored for their progress with socialization. He knew he needed to talk to someone, but he was also afraid of playing the part of a happy, well-adjusted teen too well, or too soon. They'd know he was faking it. So he decided to act a little bit interested in talking to someone, but not overly so.

He got up and slowly walked through the center of the room. It was easy to ignore the girl watching the movie. Who'd want to sit down mid-way through a movie they knew nothing about? Besides, a person watching a movie probably wouldn't appreciate someone trying to strike up a conversation.

He went into the room with exercise equipment and looked around at his options. If he hadn't just gotten out of the isolation tube and fully dried himself, he would've been inclined to use the Swimulator, but instead, he grabbed some free weights and started curling.

The guy on the treadmill looked at him but didn't say anything. After a few minutes, he turned off the machine and introduced himself.

"Hey. I'm Michael."

"Deron."

"What they'd get you for?" Michael asked.

"Isn't it the same for everyone? Candidates for Future Sociopaths of America?"

"I guess it is. That's what they said to me too. But it's total bullshit. I'd rather not even deal with anyone at all, and that includes not wanting to be anti-social toward anyone."

Deron laughed.

"What?"

"It just sounds funny. Not wanting to deal with people *and* not wanting to be anti-social toward them," Deron answered.

"Oh. I see what you mean." Michael chuckled. "I meant I don't want to be anti-social in a sociopathic way. Ya know? I'm not out to fuck anyone over or anything. I just value my time and like to do what I want to do, rather than what other people want me to do. I'm very purpose-oriented and most people aren't. That annoys me."

"What do you most like to do with your time?"

"I play piano and I compose. I also like to read, work out and go hiking. I just prefer doing all of those things alone, so I guess that makes them think I'm going to turn into a psycho someday. If anyone is mental, it's the people who decided we need to be here."

"I think they have good intentions, but they probably could've picked people who were at greater risk of posing a threat to society than us." Deron was in total agreement with Michael, but he was aware that along with video surveillance, there would be audio as well.

"No kidding. I know some seriously fucked up people and I don't see any of them in here."

"I think that's the thing. They're looking to keep us from becoming seriously fucked up. So maybe it won't be that bad. Besides, the food is great, and this is a pretty nice place to chill for a few hours."

Michael looked at Deron like he was a kiss-ass. "Do you really like it here? You're not pissed off at being locked up without even committing a crime first?"

"I'm totally not happy about the way I was brought here, but so far, it's not so bad. The isolation chamber was pretty cool. I love to read and there's a library here with real books, so I figure I'm pretty lucky as far as that goes." Deron put the weights down. "I'm gonna see if I can get in on that racing sim."

"Good luck," Michael said, and lowered himself onto one of the floor mats and began doing sit-ups.


Dr. Fielding turned to Gerald and said, "Not bad, after only one session. I think he's showing promise already. Go ahead with Level 2 entrainment. And double his sessions."

"After just one day? Are you sure?"

"Yes. I think Deron might advance faster than the others and the risks will be minimal."

"You're the boss," Gerald said, but suspected that there was a vindictive motivation for Fielding's decision.

## Twenty-five

After recreation, food was wheeled in and placed on one of the several tables. The teens, now gathered in one place, introduced themselves while they ate.

"I'm Chad," the short guy who had been playing the racing game said. "Don't think that just because I'm in here, I'm some kind of fuck-up like you guys. They made a mistake with me."

"Right," Michael said. "Astute of you to notice though that *we* definitely *are* fuck-ups. No mistakes when it came to us, fuck you, very much."

"We'll see who's a fuck-up when my dad gets me out of this place. He has a whole team of lawyers. I'll be gone by tomorrow. Watch."

"I'm really happy for you," the girl said.

"I'm Deron. What's your name?"

"Jacey," she replied, leaning back in her chair and biting into an apple.

Chad looked annoyed. "J.C. as in Jesus Christ?"

Jacey glanced at him without responding then resumed eating her apple.

"Nice to meet you, Jacey. How long have you guys been here?"

Chad said, "Since yesterday."

"Me too," Michael added.

Deron looked at Jacey and she nodded.

"I wonder if we're the start of a new group, or if the program is new and we're the first," Deron said.

"Who cares?" said Chad.

"Right. I guess it doesn't matter to you because you'll be gone tomorrow."

"You got that right. I'm getting the fuck out of here. I don't care what these jerks say, I'm not a fucking sociopath. I come from a very wealthy family with a lot of influence. They're going to seriously regret dragging me in here."

"I'm sure the government is quaking in its figurative boots," Jacey said. "And in case you didn't notice, everyone is wealthy now, so you're not special anymore."

Chad scowled at her, then grabbed a banana and moved to another table on the other side of the room.

"Hi Jacey. I'm Michael."

"Hey," she said.

"I'd ask what you did, but since this isn't jail, that would sound funny. Any idea what it is about your personality or behavior that caused them to select you?" Michael asked, looking at Jacey.

Jacey thought while she chewed, then said, "Maybe because I speak my mind without worrying about whether some special snowflake is gonna get their precious little feelings hurt. I have no tolerance for political correctness, which is actually social censorship. It has nothing to do with politics or being correct about anything."

"Maybe it's because of your hair," Chad said loudly.

"Fuck you," Jacey replied. "If they had a problem with purple, spiked hair, they could've just taken me to a stylist, or passed another law, like usual. They wouldn't put someone in a rehabilitation program just to change their fucking hairstyle, genius."

"But they might, to make you *want* to change it," Deron said.

Jacey glared at Deron.

"I was kidding. I think Chad's just as stupid as you do."

"You know, I can hear you assholes loud and clear over here."

"Pretend you're deaf and dumb and shut the fuck up?" Jacey said.

Michael and Deron laughed. Chad turned his back to them and pushed his food tray away, muttering to himself.

After a while, Dr. Fielding arrived with two guards in tow. Chad looked up as though he expected they had come to get him to let him go home. He started to get up.

"Please remain seated," Dr. Fielding ordered.

Chad sat back down.

"Each of you will have a two hour therapy session with your counselors. Please wash up and return to your therapist's office. Thank you." He left the room but the guards stayed behind.

Three of them got up and headed toward the guards. Deron piled his refuse on his tray and carried it over to a trash bin, discarded the trash and put the tray on top along with other trays, then joined the others.

"Follow me," one of the guards said, and both of them began walking toward the door.

"What if I follow him?" Jacey asked, pointing at the other guard.

The guard didn't respond and continued walking until they reached an office. They stopped and Michael went inside. They continued down the hall, turning at the first corner. When they reached the next office, all of them stood there.

"Chad Parker, this is your stop."

Chad sneered at the guard as he walked past him and opened the door to the office. Deron recognized the next office they came to as Gerald's.

"See ya later," he said to Jacey.

"Yeah. Later," she replied, and resumed following the guards down the hall.

Deron entered and found Gerald waiting at his desk, patient and smiling.

"So... make any friends?"

"Not really," Deron replied, "but they seem okay. Except for Chad. He's kind of a dick."

"He'll get better. It's only been one day. We don't anticipate improvement in attitudes until at least a week. Although I must say, you're doing very well, Deron."

"Thanks, I guess. But I don't feel like I'm doing anything other than just being here."

"And how do you feel about that? About being here?"

Deron thought fast, then replied. "I resent the way it was done – dragging me out of school like that, and drugging me, or whatever they did to knock me out, but now that I'm here, I look forward to improving myself."

"Good. That's really good, Deron. And you know, the only reason they incapacitated you was because you attempted to flee. It would've been tragically ironic if you had gone from borderline antisocial to *actively* antisocial due to the act of intervention. We couldn't risk adding a criminal to the population while trying to prevent one. Does that make sense?"

"I guess, but couldn't they have just come to my house and spoken with me and my mom? Talk about being antisocial – these guys came to my school, knocked me out, then locked me up – and all of this with no explanation of what was going on at all. So yeah, I resent that, and I think your recruitment methods are pretty fucking Neanderthal."

"You have valid points, Deron. There's definitely room for improvement, and I apologize for the rough approach." Gerald looked at Deron for a moment, giving him a chance to respond before moving on to the next item on his agenda. He opened a drawer and pulled out a slate computer. He turned it on, tapped some keys, waited a few seconds, then handed it to Deron. "Here. I need you to answer some survey questions."

Deron took the device and rested it on his lap.

"If you'd like external display, hit the icon near the top left corner that looks like sun rays beaming up to a rectangle."

Deron tapped the key and activated the holographic screen that projected out to where a laptop screen would've been, only larger.

"If you touch the same icon and slide your finger upwards—"

"I know. The holo-screen gets bigger. My teacher has one of these."

"Okay. Great. Go ahead and go through those questions for me, and just answer spontaneously. No need to consider them for very long."

Deron read the first question:

*1. Is violence by civilians ever justified when it's not an act of self-defense?*

## Twenty-six

Drake cursed as he followed the curving onramp onto the freeway. "Stupid little cocktease. I oughta turn around, go back to your house, and show you what happens when you lead someone on like that. You're playing with fire, you little bitch."

He looked down at the slate computer sitting on the passenger seat with the work order displayed. He looked at Mitzi's address. "When I find a way, I'm coming back for you."

After he had finished setting up the TV in the living room, he went to the back patio to ask about the bedroom TV. He could have found it himself in the small apartment, but it was the only excuse he could come up with to go check out Mitzi on the patio.

He opened the sliding glass door, stepped out and saw her lying face down on a chaise lounge. He asked where the second TV was that she requested service on, and without moving or even turning her head to look at him, she just said, "It's at the end of the hall. You can't miss it."

He setup the second TV quickly, eager to get back to her. She had completely ignored him, but he considered that might have been because she knew he was still busy. Maybe she'd act differently once the work was done. But when he went back to tell her that everything was finished, she just said, "Thank you, very much" without even turning to face him.

Trying to draw her out and delay leaving, he asked if she needed any help with the remote control, or channel guide navigation or setting up facial recognition or anything. She said she was very familiar with it, and thanked him again. It sounded like she was trying to go to sleep and he was just an annoyance, keeping her awake.

He drove home angry and aroused. The combination was powerful and disturbing. He was determined to do something about it.

When he got home, he turned on his TV and browsed to Adult Services, subcategory Intimate Companions. He drilled down through the categories, selecting body type, hair color, and so on, finally selecting the girl who most appealed to him. She had a platinum blonde pixie hairstyle and looked small and frail, almost like an elf.

He had thought of doing this many times, but had never been able to follow through. He wasn't too shy to schedule a session with a prostitute, but he was embarrassed to do so with his Adult Benefits Transfer card. It was humiliating to not be able to afford a sex worker with his own income and having to rely on government welfare. But he had the presence of mind to realize he was in the exact situation that the service was intended for.

He was single, unattractive, lacked social skills, not interesting, and in desperate need of adult companionship. He was also angry. The legislators who introduced the program argued that if people could hire sex workers, then the crime of rape could be eliminated. They further reasoned that merely legalizing prostitution was insufficient. Not everyone could afford it. And so the ABT was tacked on as an additional measure to reduce crime and increase equality.

Drake highlighted the word *Schedule* and chose the time option *Next Available.* Text appeared on the screen informing him that the estimated time of arrival was less than two hours. He was then prompted to make a deposit, with accompanying text informing him that this would cover the minimum fee, and that patrons were encouraged to show their appreciation at the conclusion of their visit with a gratuity that was not payable with ABI funds.

Drake told himself that with the government picking up the main tab, his embarrassment would be lessened by paying the tip himself. Since he had time, and he was hungry, he browsed to Restaurants and ordered a pizza and beer for delivery. He wondered for a second if he should shower while waiting for the food and sex he'd just ordered. But he said to himself, "Screw it. She's just a whore."

\*\*\*

Michelle got bored with having the entire house to herself and nothing to do. She'd routinely be at Jenny's on a Saturday or have Jenny over to her house; especially with her parents out of the country. It was an ideal time for a teen to have a friend over, if not a full-blown party.

Thoughts of Jenny led to thoughts of clothes, and that led to thinking about her wardrobe. She decided that some change was in order. Since she wasn't going to be hanging around Jenny and her entourage anymore, she wanted to get some sensible clothing. She was sticking to her decision to change her friends, her life, and her lifestyle. What better way to start than with a new wardrobe?

Riding the bus in normal clothing was a completely different experience. Men still noticed her, as they always did, but at least now they weren't looking at her as if she was a piece of flame-broiled meat they were eager to consume. They were paying more attention to the video ads in the back of the seats in front of them. The print and video ads on the bus were very provocative and Michelle was relieved that she wasn't in competition with them as she had been last night.

Michelle's phone rang and for the third time that day she selected Ignore. She knew she'd have to face Jenny eventually, but she didn't have to do it right now. Last night she was ready to call Jenny a slut and tell her she wanted nothing to do with her or her friends, but now, after having some time to think about it, she realized it would be better to just distance herself from Jenny gradually without burning her social bridges and incurring Jenny's wrath. She didn't want to hang out with the popular girls or even be one anymore, but neither did she want to be ostracized and shunned by everyone in the school, which is what would happen if she became Jenny's enemy.

She sent Jenny a plain text message with no video: *Still sick. Talk later...*

\*\*\*

Charlie could not get into a deep sleep the night before. He would fall into a light sleep, then wake up at the slightest sound. Every time he woke, he was painfully aware that Feenix wasn't there. He kept expecting to see her lying beside his bed. The empty space on the carpet was a jab to his heart every time he saw it. He finally got up and went outside, wrinkling his nose at the faint odor of burnt grass. He hated the laser mower that popped up on the edge of the lawn twice a week at 3am, shooting out its low-powered beam and rolling down the width of the square yard, cutting it to a height of exactly 1.5 inches.

He sat in a folding chair that he kept on the porch and looked at his perfectly groomed lawn. Then he looked over at where he'd buried Feenix and just stared. He heard the low-pitched hum of a neighborhood drone before he saw it. When it was even with Charlie's house, it stopped and turned toward him. Charlie waved and it took a picture and then continued on down the street. Charlie shook his head.

The drone reminded him of the government, and that reminded him of Deron. He didn't buy Kathleen's story that Deron was in a residential therapy program. His daughter was lying to him. This wasn't the first time, but it was the worst.

He knew she was lying because it never would've occurred to her to seek out such a program for Deron. She'd complained about his unwillingness to get involved in sports or any afterschool activities, and his lack of a social circle, but she never once said she thought he needed mental help because of those things. This was definitely someone else's idea. So either someone put her up to it, or someone else decided on it and she just went along with it.

Maybe it was the Child & Family Services people. The same idiots who had come to his house after he'd reported that Kathleen was pregnant. They came and explained to him that his daughter had a right to discover and explore her sexual identity regardless of her age. He could easily imagine them deciding that someone wasn't as actively involved with their peers as they deemed normal. Or maybe it was the school that was behind it. They were in a position to see Deron not socializing every day, always sitting with his nose buried in a book.

Whoever did it, it wasn't right. Deron had a right to be exactly how he was. If he wasn't hurting anyone, what gave anyone the right to meddle in his affairs and try to make him into someone he wasn't?

He didn't understand how Kathleen could fail to see the simplicity of that. Actually, he did understand. She'd always been superficial and she fit right in with the rest of society in thinking that your social activities defined you.

She was a social butterfly, and completely undeveloped mentally. She never thought about anything more complex than fashion, make-up, or the latest ridiculous show on television.

She probably jumped at the chance to hand Deron over to the government to make him more social. Maybe he'd come out of the program and join a football team, then he could finally be considered to have value to the school and to society. *Idiots.*

Then he'd graduate high school and find out that all of the popularity in school vanished like fog the day after you graduated. You were suddenly nobody. No one in the adult world cared if you were the quarterback or the homecoming king. School is just a big playground and social get-together, and once it's over, the only thing you take away from it is the education you were supposed to have gotten. And that's the one thing Deron did well – the one thing he was supposed to be doing. He was learning and getting good grades. But apparently that wasn't good enough.

Charlie decided he would go to this facility Deron was in and find out everything he could about their program and what rights Deron had as a citizen.

# Twenty-seven

Deron looked at the question and thought about how he should answer it. He wasn't supposed to give the questions any thought, but he had to. His first thought was, of course violence was okay when it wasn't in self-defense. What if you were defending someone else? Duh. But if he answered it that way, would they think that he wasn't law-abiding? The law said that if you saw a crime being committed, you were to call the police. No exceptions. But Deron thought that was stupid. What if the police couldn't possibly get there in time to save someone? What if violence was the only way you could save someone else from harm, or even death? What you did should be the important thing – not how you did it.

But the DEO counselors were not looking for rational responses. They were profiling him; gauging whether he was socially maligned. He was surprised they hadn't done the questionnaire before his treatment had begun. It would seem they'd want a benchmark for comparison and to measure his progress, or lack of it.

"Remember what I said?" Gerald asked.

"Yeah. I was just thinking about something. Sorry."

Deron typed "No" without delay, as if that was the answer he'd intended all along but had just been distracted. He continued through the questions, automatically answering in the way he assumed a "normal" person would answer; someone who trusted the government to always do the right thing and who wanted to get along and be liked above all else.

As he sat trying to not over-think any of the questions, Gerald was typing away on his personal communicator, apparently involved in a fast-paced text conversation with someone. Every time he stopped typing, a few seconds later, his comm chimed with an incoming message. After he received the last message, he looked at Deron and appeared to be weighing something in his mind.

"Deron, I need to make a call. I'll only be a minute. I'm going to trust you to stay here and not try to run off. Can I do that?"

"Sure. Isn't the door locked anyway?"

"Right. You couldn't leave if you wanted to. I'll be right back. I'm just going to duck into the bathroom."

Gerald got up and went through a door at the far back end of his office. As soon as the door closed behind him, Deron got up and tip-toed over to Gerald's desk. The screen was unlocked with Deron's treatment plan sitting in plain view. He couldn't believe it. Gerald had to be talking to a girl.

Deron read over the plan, unable to understand much of what he was reading. There were references in the beginning to his therapy and entrainment sessions; he understood some of that, but then there was a list of what must've been medications that he'd never heard of before that he was apparently taking without knowing it. Were they drugging his food?

He recognized one of the names in the list of drugs. Fluoride. Why would they be giving him fluoride? It was already in the water, wasn't it?

He skipped past the list to where normal text resumed and read as fast as he could. He could hear Gerald laughing and talking in a different tone of voice than he normally used. Definitely a girl. He read the last paragraph: *If corrective therapy fails, subject will be transferred to legacy rehabilitation studies to improve leucotomy and cingulotomy procedures, followed by aptitude testing to assess remaining potential for meaningful contributions to society.*

Deron wasn't sure if he really understood what he was reading, but it sounded pretty much like they intended to fix him if possible, and dispose of him if they couldn't. He needed to find out what those two strange words meant. He assumed they couldn't be good.

He quietly got back to his seat, picked up the slate computer and resumed answering questions. A few minutes later, Gerald returned to his desk, smiling as he sat down.

"Hey, Gerald. Have you got a dictionary I can use to be sure of the meaning of some of the words in the questions?"

"Just tap on a word you don't know and a definition will pop up."

"Oh yeah. Thanks."

The questions were worded in simple terms. Deron felt that he'd given Gerald the impression that he wasn't very bright. But it didn't matter. It might even work to his advantage later. He went through the questions more quickly now, unconcerned about what the results would say about him. He wasn't going to stay around to find out.

When he finished, he handed the slate to Gerald and asked, "Now what?"

"Um... back in the water."

"Again?"

"Yep. You like it, don't you?"

"It's relaxing, but I don't know how much I want to keep getting relaxed in one day. It would make more sense if I did it once, right before bedtime. Don't you think?"

"That does sound like a practical approach, yes. But we're aiming for therapeutic goals – not just to help you get to asleep." Gerald smiled as he said this. "Come on. In you go..."

Deron disrobed and entered the chamber feeling very ill at ease. He didn't want to be here, didn't want anyone messing with his mind and he absolutely did not want to find out what was going to happen to him if he failed to make progress. This time as he lay floating on his back, he felt anxious and restless, and when the lid came down, he had greater difficulty getting past the feeling of claustrophobia.

# Twenty-eight

As Michelle looked around the clothing boutique she and Jenny had always shopped in, she found herself mentally putting all of the outfits she observed into two categories: Slutty and Very Slutty. Whenever she looked at a top that was too skimpy or shorts that were too short, she could just imagine Jenny gravitating straight to those items.

She couldn't believe she'd never seen this before. Her best friend was a total slut and she'd been blind to it. Actually, she'd been blind to a lot of things. She decided this store had too little to offer now and she exited, thinking about other things she hadn't been seeing, but should have. Jenny wasn't the only slut she'd been hanging out with. Everyone in Jenny's group was just as bad as she was, if not worse in their efforts to compete with her.

She glanced at the stores on either side of her, some featuring 3-D posters, some with barely clothed androids, and one with live models. All of them attempting to lure shoppers with provocative imagery that spoke of sex and being sexually attractive. She wondered where she could go to find some plain old normal clothes. What if she didn't want to be a sex object?

She needed to stop for a few minutes and just think. Ahead of her, before the entrance to the food court, there was a fountain ringed with benches. Michelle walked over to it and sat facing the marble figures in the fountain display. In the center was a bronze statue of a nude man looking like an Olympian god. Rising up from the water in various places around him were topless mermaids.

Michelle blurted, "Does everyone have to be naked?"

No one thought it was odd that she was sitting by herself and talking out loud. Most people were seen talking by themselves and everyone knew or assumed that they were on the phone with either Bluetooth or subdermal devices. The procedure to have an earpiece and microphone surgically implanted was relatively inexpensive and many people had done the quick out-patient procedure.

A few feet away from Michelle, a man sat looking straight ahead with his eyes glazed. His right thumb continuously moved around on the side of his index finger just below the knuckle, occasionally pressing on the flesh there. Michelle recognized the creepy behavior. He had the new micro touchpad-mouse embedded in his finger and was looking at a display that was projected onto his retinas from what appeared to be sunglasses.

That was another thing Michelle thought was out of control. Talking to friends or being on the internet was not important enough to her to ever have computer parts put in her body. Did people really need to be online twenty-four hours a day? This guy had come to the mall for a reason, right? So why didn't he do what he came to do and then get on the web or go to the digital dens after he was finished?

The man started rubbing his crotch with his left hand and Michelle had seen enough. She looked around for a mall security drone and spotted one hovering just twenty feet away. She waved at it and it flew close to her. She pointed at the guy. The drone turned slightly, presumably examining him. It detected no crimes or signs of distress, then returned to its previous position.

Michelle decided she'd had enough of the mall. She'd find somewhere else to buy clothes. It was stupid to have come here in the first place. She knew it would be filled with sex-obsessed people, sexual ads everywhere, semi-nude shoppers, girls with spray-on tops, men with colored saran-wrap pants, and of course, the nude statues and nude models and nude mannequins. She really needed to start using her brain and making conscious choices instead of operating on autopilot like everyone else.

Michelle got up and started walking toward the end of the mall, ignoring the stores and their advertisements as she passed them. She walked fast and also ignored anyone who spoke to her, whether they wanted to sell her something or hook up with her. She decided that the mall and those who shopped in it had nothing to offer her and she had no reason to ever come back.

Outside, the fresh air and sunlight were a welcome relief. She headed toward the bus stop and tram terminal, but walked past it without even consciously deciding that she was going to walk home instead. She just walked, trying to clear her mind and feeling like she was missing a lifestyle that she hadn't really ever had. She wasn't sure what it was she was trying to put her mind on until she thought of the word innocence. That led to other words. Natural. Honesty. Security. Fun. Safety. These words crystalized in her mind to form a conceptual thought. She just wanted to be a normal teenager, living and acting naturally, being honest with herself and others, able to have fun, and enjoy the comfort and security of feeling safe in her daily life.

Was that too much to ask?

## Twenty-nine

When Drake's pizza arrived, he took it without thanking or tipping the delivery man. There was already a tip and delivery fee built in to the price, so why should he? He just shut the door, took the box to his couch and began stuffing pizza into his mouth, barely even noticing the taste as he watched a reality show called "You Almost GotRape'd!"

In the show, a hidden camera crew filmed a man who would be stalking a woman until he found an appropriate time and place to begin his attack. Footage from the cameras was edited to include jerky motion from body cams worn by the attacker. After the woman was taken down, the producer and a cameraman would come out of hiding, approach the pair and suddenly aim bright lights at them, announcing, "You almost got raped!"

Invariably, the women were relieved that the attack wasn't real, and they looked around in delight to see other hidden cameramen come out of hiding, and then they blushed in embarrassment, wondering how they looked, knowing now that they were on TV; adjusting their hair and clothes and hoping their makeup looked good. They laughed and smiled and hugged their almost-rapist. Off-screen they always wanted to know when the episode would air so they could tell their friends they were going to be on TV.

Drake got an adrenaline rush every time he watched the show and fantasized about raping someone for real. He looked at the time to see how much longer it would be before his adult companion would be there. He was ready for her now. He wondered if acting out a rape fantasy was allowed.

He recalled the prostitute's image from the website and imagined raping her. The thought of this pretty blonde coming to his house specifically for the purpose of having sex with him was exhilarating and he couldn't wait. He couldn't believe he hadn't done this before. Why had he always been too embarrassed about it? It was her job. It was how she made a living. And besides, no one would know. His neighbors weren't likely to recognize the woman when she knocked at his door – and if they did, then it was only because they'd used her services, or at least seen her on the Adult Companion pages themselves. So who were they to criticize him?

Drake was working his way through his past fears and simultaneously getting aroused as his thoughts went back and forth from why he'd never done this to what it was going to be like now that he was actually doing it. He stuffed the last of the pizza into his mouth and stood up to take the empty box to the recycler when his autohost announced a visitor.

For just a second, Drake was afraid to answer the door because he had an erection. But he quickly realized that it was perfectly okay for once to answer the door with a large bulge in his pants. In fact, it might even be a compliment. He laughed and wiped his greasy fingers on his pants as he went to open the door. He waited a second to finish swallowing the pizza in his mouth, then brushed his hair out of his eyes and pulled the door open.

"Hi! Mr. Austin?"

"Yeah. Come in."

Drake couldn't believe it. She looked way better in person than she did in her online photo. He feared it would be the opposite, like the time he'd tried online dating. She was tiny in a purple mini-skirt with a see-through top; bright blue eyes made up to look big and innocent like one of those Japanese cartoon characters, and had short platinum blonde hair with a hint of violet shading.

She came through the door and Drake felt like she was his for the next hour. Not just as his guest, but as if she were something he owned, or at least rented, and could do whatever he pleased with her. At least for a while. And goddamn, she was cute.

"Where would you like me?" she asked with a smile.

Drake was struck dumb. This was almost surreal.

"I guess in the bedroom," he said, and pointed toward the hall that led to his room.

"Great!" she replied. "Do you want to go straight there, or do you want to talk first? Some guys like to talk for a few minutes. But just remember, time is ticking..." She tapped her wrist as if she were wearing a watch.

"Go on in. I'll be there in just a second."

She said okay and walked down the hall. Drake admired her tiny ass as it swayed in the shiny purple material of her skirt. But then he realized that as visually pleasing as it was, he wasn't getting turned on by it. In fact, he could feel himself going soft.

It must've been that remark about the time. Damn her. Why'd she have to say that? She brought the fact that he was *paying* and had a time limit into the forefront of his mind. He didn't mind seeing her as an object he could purchase, but at the same time, he didn't want her seeing him as just another meaningless customer. Couldn't she have just kept her damned mouth shut and let this play out like it was real? Let a guy have a little bit of fucking dignity?

He looked up at the ceiling and took a deep breath and tried to flush the angry thoughts out of his head. He turned to the front door and said, "Do not disturb. Two hours." He saw the availability status light on his autohost turn to red. He took another deep breath and walked to his bedroom, thinking, "You ruined it, you stupid whore."

## Thirty

When the isolation chamber hissed and the door began to rise, Deron was much more disoriented than he was the first time. He knew it was time to get out of the thing, but he just laid there in a daze of mental static. It's as if his mind was saying, "Let's get out now," and he was responding, "Okay. Yeah. Let's do that," but he made no move to get up and had no desire or inclination to move. He was aware of the strangeness of it too. He knew he wanted to get out, and felt his lack of desire to do so.

He moved his right hand, wiggling his fingers in the water, just to demonstrate to himself that he could; that he wasn't paralyzed; because that's what it started to feel like. He was afraid he *couldn't* get out, despite wanting to. Since he was able to move his hand, he willed himself to sit up.

*Okay, so I'm not paralyzed, but I don't feel right at all.*

He slowly climbed out and went behind the partition to dry off and put on his clothes.

"Welcome back, Deron! How are you doing?"

Deron thought of saying, "Fine," but just like getting out of the chamber, he didn't feel like saying it, although he wanted to. As he put on his clothes, he became more aware of how dull his mind felt, like he was a brainless robot putting clothes on a body that had little to do with him. He wondered if they were drugging him in the chamber. If there was a drug in the water, could he absorb it through his skin? His mind felt wooden, and it took great effort to even form these questions. He was trying very hard to have awareness of what he was feeling mentally and physically. But it was hard. He just wanted to sleep. Or sit down and be still and quiet.

"Deron? You alright back there?"

Could Gerald just shut up and leave him alone? He was getting dressed for god's sake. Isn't that what he was supposed to be doing?

"Yes," he managed to say in a dull, lifeless tone.

*Was that me? That didn't sound like me.*

"Okay. Great! Just checkin' on ya."

*Yeah. Whatever.* He didn't care that Gerald was just checking on him. He didn't really care about anything right now. Once he was fully dressed, he just stood there behind the partition, staring at it like a complete moron. He knew he should walk around it and perhaps sit down where he usually sat on the opposite side of Gerald's desk, but, whatever. Standing there seemed perfectly okay too.

After a minute of standing still, Gerald poked his head around the partition.

"Good, you're dressed. Why don't you come on out and have a seat?"

*I don't know why not,* Deron thought. *But okay. Since you say so.*

He followed Gerald around the partition and back to the main part of the office. He sat in his usual chair and sighed. It seemed to take all of his energy to have gotten dressed and then to have walked all the way over to the chair. Like maybe ten steps.

"How are you feeling, Deron?"

Deron turned his head toward Gerald and stared at him as if he didn't know who, or even what, Gerald was. He let the words echo once in his mind. *How are you feeling, Deron?* He knew all of the words, and therefore he was able to identify the question for what it was. He mentally understood that this person across from him was inquiring as to the state of the entity called Deron, which was him.

His mental response to the query was, *whatever*, and he looked away without saying anything. Gerald clapped his hands together one time making a sharp sound that bounced off the walls. Deron could visualize the sound wave bouncing off the wall. He looked at Gerald, annoyed.

"What?"

"How are you feeling, Deron? Are you okay?"

"I'm fine."

"Hmm. I'm not convinced. How was your session in the chamber?"

Deron took a deep breath. He felt like it would take a lot of energy to answer Gerald's question.

"I think I'm gonna throw up."

Gerald quickly got up and helped Deron out of his chair and down the hall to the restroom where he vomited. Deron found it interesting that he wasn't distraught about vomiting like he normally was. It was more like it was happening to someone else and he was just a guest in their body. Like it had nothing to do with him at all.

## Thirty-one

When Charlie arrived at Kathleen's, he was in a huff. He had really worked himself up on the drive over, determined to tell his daughter his thoughts without his usual regard for sparing her feelings. Deron meant a lot to Charlie, and the fact that Kathleen had casually thrown him to the wolves was intolerable.

He pulled up to the curb with the driver's door facing the house. He got out and walked across the lawn, neglecting to use the driveway and sidewalk in subconscious protest of his daughter's preferences. He rapped his knuckles on the door three times and breathed through his nose with his teeth clenched while he waited. He was prepared to argue if necessary, but hoped he wouldn't have to.

"Dad! What are you doing here? I was just about to go out."

"That's fine. I just need the address to where they're holding Deron and I'll be on my way."

"No one is *holding* him." She turned and walked further into the house, leaving the door open behind her as a passive invitation for Charlie to come inside.

"I'm not here to argue the semantics of it with you. Just tell me where the place is. I want to see my grandson."

He followed Kathleen down the hall and stood outside the bathroom she had entered to resume the application of her makeup.

"They haven't informed me that he can have visitors yet, so it won't do you any good to try to see him."

"How can this place be for therapeutic rehabilitation without allowing visitors? Even prisons have visiting hours. This is just one more reason I don't like this. Not at all, Kathleen. Just tell me where he is and I'll deal with their stupid policy when I get there."

Kathleen dropped the eyeliner pencil on the bathroom counter, turned to Charlie and said, "You are not going to go over there and make a scene, Dad. In fact, since they're trying to help Deron integrate with society, you're probably the *last* person who should be visiting him right now."

"Just what is that supposed to mean?

"If you want to know the truth, you may be a big part of the problems Deron has." She walked out and squeezed past her father on her way toward the dining room. "You're anti-government, anti-people, anti-progress... you're anti-everything, including society!"

Charlie shook his head as he followed her. This was going worse than he had expected. He knew she'd resist and argue, but he didn't think she'd come out with a complete indictment of him. Of the many times he had momentarily felt like turning his back on his daughter, he wondered if this would be the time he finally did it.

Maybe they'd let him take Deron out for dinner and he'd just never bring him back. They could disappear somewhere.

"I am not anti-everything, and you know it. Just because I speak up against things that are wrong does not mean I'm against all things. That's ridiculous, Kathleen."

She passed the dining room table and turned into the kitchen. "It is not ridiculous. It's the truth. Do you want some goddamned coffee?"

"I thought you were on your way out."

"I was, but for some reason I'm not in the mood for fun right now. I'll see how I feel about it when I'm done fighting with my father."

"We are not fighting. You're just being unreasonable and hypercritical. Tell me where Deron is and you can go get drunk and stupid with your friends. I don't want to keep you from the things that really matter in your life."

"Dad, that is so unfair. Having friends and wanting to spend time with them does not mean I don't care about my son. In fact, it's because I care about him so much that he's in the place where he is. I want him to have a real life. A meaningful life with his own fun and friends. If you had your way, he'd be a shut-in, cursing the world and hating his life."

"It's amazing that you've managed to know me for thirty-four years and still haven't gotten a clue about who I am."

"I know exactly who and what you are. You're a holdout, Dad. You want the world to be the way it was before. I'll never understand why though. How could anyone prefer racism and crime and poverty? Just what is it that you find so appealing about the way things were? Why do you hate modern society and modern technology so much anyway? What do you have against progress?"

Even as she railed against her father's preference for the past, she indulged him by making coffee the old-fashioned way with a coffee-maker she kept just for him. But she was not going to grind the beans she'd purchased earlier for a possible special guest. She took two cups from the cabinet and set them next to the coffee pot.

"Kathleen, you're not old enough to know what it was like before. It wasn't all crime and poverty. And we had plenty of technology. Where do you think it all came from? Everything you enjoy today came from the advances in technology from before the war. We just didn't let it run everything in our lives back then. It was a tool."

"It must've been great to have to mow your lawn all the time," she said, scoffing as she poured the coffee. "Technology frees us from menial tasks. We have more time to live now, Dad. That's not a bad thing."

"Like I said, you don't know what it was like before. You have nothing to compare to."

"I know that people were killed and raped all the time, and I don't need to experience that to know life is better now. Would you really like it if things were the way they used to be? Drunk drivers, child abuse, serial killers? Everyone running around with guns. How could anyone *want* that?"

"Obviously, I don't want the worst of the way things were. That's a pathetic way to make a point and you should know better. But yes, there were bad things that needed to be addressed and the government at the time did a piss-poor job of it. But that doesn't mean the way they're going about it now is right."

"Have you looked at recent crime statistics, Dad? Crimes against people are practically non-existent in the redeveloped areas. So I definitely vote for the way things are now. I'm happy. And you could be too if you weren't so stuck in the past. And I want my son to be happy like me. Not bitter and hateful like you. And that's why he is where he is. If they can help Deron have a happier life, I *want* that for him, Dad. Don't you?"

"Of course I do. But not like this. Did you ever wonder where all of the criminals went, Kathleen? They didn't just reform. They disappeared."

"What's so bad about that?"

"I guess it depends on what is defined as a crime, and who gets to do the defining. And now look what they're doing. They're taking people who aren't even criminals and they're trying to reform them. Shouldn't Deron be free to be who he wants without someone judging him and trying to change him before he's even become who he's going to be? And what happens to him if he doesn't turn out the way they want? Have you thought about that? Maybe he'll just disappear one day because there's no place for people like him in this modern fucking paradise."

"Dad, this is a voluntary program he's in, designed to help him. The jackbooted thugs of your nightmares didn't come and take him. It's voluntary!"

"It wasn't voluntary for Deron. What choice did he have in this? You see, Kathleen, we don't have freedom today. Everything we do is regulated, monitored, controlled, recorded, automated, and mandated. We're like lab rats and we don't even know it. As long as we have plenty of useless luxuries and meaningless sex, what more do we need, right? Life is grand!"

"You just have a general mistrust of government. No matter what good they do, you'll find something wrong with it."

"You're goddamned right. Because to them, we're just objects to be controlled. I'll take my freedom with risks over being a rat in a shiny lab. Deron should have the same choice. Are you going to tell me where he is or not?"

Kathleen opened a drawer and took out a seldom used notepad. She uncapped a pen and tried to start writing, but the ball-point was dry. She shook the pen and scribbled for a few seconds, then, looking at her communicator, she copied down an address and handed the paper to Charlie.

"Here. Go see him, and try to be civil. And try not to get yourself arrested. You'll be in a government facility, surrounded by government employees. I'm sure that's your worst nightmare."

"No. My worst nightmare was when jack-booted government thugs killed your mother."

Charlie slipped the paper into his pocket and left.

## Thirty-two

While Deron was cleaning himself up in the bathroom, Gerald summoned a medical doctor to have a look at him. He went over Deron's treatment plan and then the log of his actual treatments. He swiped his finger one way, then the other, comparing the two documents.

"This doesn't match up. If this log is correct, he's spending too much time in the chamber and getting double-dosed on his medications."

"That's correct," Gerald said. "Dr. Fielding verbally ordered the increase but hasn't updated the treatment plan yet."

Dr. Carson scrunched his eyebrows and examined Gerald as if trying to make sense of what he'd said. "But that is an utter deviance of the accepted and *safe* protocols."

"I know," Gerald said, feeling guilty and wanting to say that he was just following orders.

"We spent months on these protocols until we'd determined maximum efficiency with the least adverse impact on the mental and physical health of the subjects."

"I know."

Dr. Carson stared at Gerald, expecting an explanation.

Gerald just looked away, not offering one.

"Is there a reason why?"

Gerald glanced at the glass display in the surface of his desk, reassuring himself that there was no open communication line or recording software running. He spoke quietly.

He spoke quietly, just above a whisper. "I can't say for sure, but I think Dr. Fielding is pushing Deron out of personal animosity. Deron assaulted him, and I think the doctor is sort of—well, this will sound petty, but I think he's getting revenge. He's personally angry at Deron."

"That's untenable. He shouldn't even be involved in Deron's treatment after that incident. In fact, I argued against him being both an administrator and a practitioner at the same time."

"But what can we do? He's the director."

"That's exactly my point. That makes him his own supervisor in terms of medical practice. And we obviously can't report him to himself. But this needs to stop before this kid overdoses or has a mental breakdown."

"But I have to follow Fielding's orders. He's my superior."

Deron entered the room looking much better than he had left it. Dr. Carson saw him and smiled, then turned to Gerald.

"We'll come back to that later." He turned to Deron. "Hello. I'm Dr. Carson." He extended his hand and Deron shook it. The doctor asked Deron how he was feeling, then proceeded to check his vital signs and peered into his eyes and ears.

"Just a little spot-check. You seem to be okay. You're probably going to be very hungry, but I'm going to recommend that you try to eat a light dinner. Let your stomach get settled. We might have a bug going around."

"Is he okay for counseling, or should he get bedrest?" Gerald asked.

"He'll be fine for a short counseling session. I'll talk to you more later."

Dr. Carson left and Gerald asked Deron how he was feeling.

"A little better." He plopped down in his chair and yawned.

"You're supposed to have a two-hour counseling session, but I'm thinking one hour sounds good for now with an hour of unofficial free time for you to do whatever you want before dinner. But you'll have to stay in here so it looks like you're having a two-hour session. I've got some video games on my slate you can play."

As far as Deron knew, Gerald was being extra nice because he'd thrown up. He didn't feel sick, but if he was going to get some free time, he didn't mind Gerald thinking he was still sick. He leaned back, slouching in his chair.

"Okay," he said. "Now what?"

"Now we have just a normal counseling session. Have you ever seen a counselor before, or a psychologist or anything?"

"No."

"This will be really easy and you might even like it."

"Okay."

"What I'd like to do is have you identify something in your life that makes you unhappy. Something that has perhaps bothered you for a long time. The kind of thing that comes up over and over again in your thoughts. Then when you identify something, we'll just talk about it a little. As simple as that sounds, it can be very therapeutic."

"Do you mean like something from my childhood?"

"It could be, but it doesn't have to be. We're not necessarily looking for blood and gore." Gerald smiled. "It can be as simple as something that regularly makes you sad or unhappy when you think about it."

Something immediately sprang to Deron's mind, but it was personal and he didn't want to talk about that with Gerald. He tried to think of something else.

He was able to think of a few other things that bothered him like the way his mother and his grandfather often didn't get along, and how much he hated school, but his mind kept returning to his first thought. Maybe it wouldn't be so bad to tell someone about it, he told himself. After all, he'd be out of here soon and it's not like he'd ever see Gerald again after he left.

"Well, there is one thing," he said.

"Great. Take your time and tell me about it whenever you're ready."

"There's this girl..." Deron started.

"Isn't there always?" Gerald laughed. "Tell me about her."

"Her name is Michelle. And she's really sweet and unlike anyone else I've ever known. At least, she used to be sweet. And that's the problem. I think deep inside, she still is, but she's like, out of touch with her real feelings, you know?"

"I think I know what you mean. That happens to a lot of people, unfortunately."

"The thing is, we used to be best friends. We grew up together and we were really close. And then…I started to feel something more than just friendship after a while. And I know she did too. And the whole time we were friends—best friends, actually, we prioritized each other, sorta. Do you know what I mean?"

"Each of you came first with the other?"

"Yeah, but even more than that. Not only was she the most important person to me, but she came first even when maybe she shouldn't have. Like boys and girls can be friends up until a certain age, but then they usually have same-sex best friends. I had male friends, but I didn't ever really connect with them the way I did with Michelle. And so I'd get teased and called names for always hanging out with her, but I didn't let that affect our friendship. I guess what I'm trying to say is, I took my friendship and my feelings for her seriously, and I didn't treat her differently, or dismiss her just to gain the acceptance of others, or like, bow to peer pressure or whatever, like most people would've. I stayed true to my best friend, no matter the consequences."

"That's very admirable. You sound like a great friend."

"But not great enough apparently."

"Did she not reciprocate with the same degree of loyalty?"

"Yeah, but it's even worse, and that's what I don't get, and so that's why it's like you said – something that really bothers me. I didn't just imagine that we felt the same toward each other, like from when we were friends to when things started to change toward being almost romantic, or however you want to put it."

Deron bit the skin on his bottom lip as he stared into the past at images Gerald could only imagine. He could see the pain in the boy's eyes and he genuinely felt for him. He spoke softly.

"So, what happened?"

"Well, one day we were at Mile Square Park by the lake. We were just sitting and talking and goofing off. You know. Nothing special. Just hanging out like usual. Some friends of mine came by and told me they were going to ride their bikes to the beach and they wanted me to go with them. I declined. Whenever I had a choice between doing something with the guys I knew or spending time with Michelle, I always chose Michelle. She'd always been the one friend that I really cared about and the one I related to more than anyone, but now, there was something even more to it. Like some kind of magical new element that was just getting ready to blossom. I could feel it changing. We'd both reached puberty and our interest in each other was developing a new and exciting layer on top of our friendship.

"And I swear, if things had gone the way they should have, we would've ended up like those old stories of people who fell in love and stayed together for like eighty years or something."

"But?" Gerald asked, hoping the story wasn't about to turn tragic.

"Usually when I turned down an invitation from my 'friends,' they'd give me some shit about it but they didn't didn't get all bent out of shape. But this time they did. I don't know why. It was like a do or die kinda thing. Maybe they were tired of having me as a friend who always turned them down, so like I had to make a choice once and for all. It was a no-brainer for me. I'd never turn my back on Michelle."

Deron shook his head slowly, thinking of something that would come later in the story.

"Anyway, things got ugly. They called me worse names than usual and it was like they really meant it this time. There was this one guy, Billy, who said to let him know when my period started. Then they left." Deron just sat there, remembering.

"And then?"

"Then the most amazing thing happened," Deron said, smiling for the first time that Gerald had seen. "After they rode off on their bikes, she kissed me." The smile grew until it morphed into a grimace.

"It sounds like you two were off to a great start. It's unusual to see that level of commitment at such a young age. Peer pressure can be a very powerful influence."

"You're absolutely right. It was. For her. But after that day, she started acting different. She got distant. I'd reach her voicemail more than I'd reach her. We hardly ever saw each other anymore, and when we did, she didn't have time to hang out. She acted like... what's the word? Cordial. Like I was someone she knew and who she was required to be nice to or something.

"It didn't make any sense. At first I thought it was because we kissed and now she didn't know how to act around me. But the new school year started the Monday after we kissed and I found out later that she was immediately drafted into this group of super popular girls who everyone thinks are the hottest girls on earth. But if you ask me, they're so empty inside they might as well be dead."

"I take it girls like that are required to have boyfriends who are equally popular and vapid?"

"Exactly! And that's part of what's so messed up about this. Michelle isn't like them."

Deron got animated now as he spoke, sitting up in his chair and looking at Gerald with newfound respect because he seemed to really understand.

"This girl I'd known all my life suddenly became a stranger. She became one of them – a hot zombie. And now I suddenly wasn't good enough for her. She gave up everything we had between us, and even more that we would've had, just so she would be liked by girls whose opinions she never would've even given a damn about. Girls she wouldn't have even liked because they're so shallow and stupid. I just don't get it."

"It's even more than that, isn't it, Deron?"

"What do you mean?"

"She didn't just change and start acting out of character, turning her back on you, but to make it even worse, you had just sacrificed your social standing and invoked the wrath of your peers as you declared your loyalty to her."

"Right," Deron said, facing another painful aspect of the situation. "It's like I stood up to everyone for her, and brought on whatever hell that was going to put me through for her sake. But when she was faced with a fraction of the same thing, she caved without a second thought like I meant nothing to her." Deron noticed his eyes had begun to water, but he didn't care.

"I wouldn't assume it was without a second thought though, Deron. She probably gave it a lot of thought and made a painful decision that she believed was in her best interest."

"How? Didn't I count for anything?"

"Of course, you did. You were her best friend."

"Then how could she do that? I never would've done such a thing to her. I cared about her too much to ever treat her that way."

"Socially, you two were entering a new world, and something about that world scared her. But apparently, right from the start, she was offered a chance to be with an in-crowd. Automatic acceptance, adoration, envy. Parties, cheerleading, and so on. That meant being put on a pedestal from which she was safe from all of the things she feared. If this group rejected you as her potential boyfriend and they imposed some set of standards on her, she didn't have the inner strength to throw away all of that security and face her fears with just you to support her from a distance. Have you tried looking at things from her point of view?"

"I thought I had." Deron shifted uncomfortably in his chair, thinking. "But I guess I really didn't. I never thought of her as being afraid of anything. It kinda makes sense when I look at it that way. I mean, it's still fucked up, what she did and all, but I can kinda see it differently."

"Most people learn to mask their fears, and when we don't factor them in to our considerations, much of their motivations seem mysterious. We try to understand why people do things based on what we see on the outside, and from our own different viewpoint. But it's what we don't see, the things that people hide that can be their strongest motivating factors. Fear is viewed as a weakness, so we all hide it."

"But why would she be so afraid? It doesn't make sense."

"That probably has a lot to do with her family and possibly a lack of love and grounding, but that's a deep subject for another day."

Deron was surprised to find that he actually liked talking with Gerald. He even thought he might miss him.

# Thirty-three

Drake had already felt that the situation with the prostitute was ruined by her comment about time ticking away, but then it got worse when he walked into his room and found her lying on his bed with her clothes off already.

*How sexy is that? Oh yeah, this isn't a date. This is an appointment. What was I thinking?*

When she saw Drake, she smiled and patted the sheet beside her. He wasn't feeling at all in the mood for sex now, but he thought maybe the mood would develop if he went through the motions. He actually wanted to ask her if it was too late to cancel, but with her lying there naked, he assumed that would be a stupid question. Plus, what kind of douche-bag would she think he was if he did that? He didn't want some common whore looking down on him.

He took off his clothes without fanfare and lay on the bed next to her.

"So, what's your name?"

"Trixie."

"Really? I guess you guys have to use a fake name for security, right?"

"If I tell you my real name, will you promise not to tell anyone?"

*Who the fuck would I tell?* "Okay. I promise."

"My real name is Sabrina."

"That's much nicer. It doesn't sound like such a…" He was going to say "whore name," then stopped himself. "Doesn't sound like such a fake name. I like it."

"Thanks! Are you ready? Is there anything you need me to do to get you… prepared?" She glanced down at his flaccid penis, then looked back up at him and smiled.

"Um… no, I just like to kinda get to know someone first. Ya know?"

"Sure. What would you like to know?"

*Not like that*, he thought. Not like a fucking formality. Couldn't she even pretend to have a real conversation?

"Do you wanna know where I'm from, and what a girl like me is doing in a job like this?"

She wasn't actually trying to be flippant and insulting, but Drake didn't know that and he got angry at her. He got up and straddled her and roughly grabbed one of her breasts and squeezed it hard.

"Hey! Take it easy. I don't do rough stuff."

He leaned down to try to kiss her and she turned her head.

"Do you think you're too good for me or somethin'?"

"Just get off of me. I'm cancelling this appointment."

"Oh no you're not! I'm gonna get what I paid for."

"You didn't pay for shit, asshole. And I don't put up with creeps who get rough. Especially welfare cases."

Drake tried to slap her but she blocked him with one hand and brought her other hand toward him in a blur of motion and jabbed his chest with something black.

When he woke up later, he saw the two marks left on his skin by her taser.

***

When Michelle saw the small boutique called Sara's Vintage Clothing, she decided to check it out, partly just to cool down after walking in the sun for so long, and she still needed some new clothes. The sun was beginning to set, but the temperature was still in the 80s and air-conditioning would feel great.

She'd never seen this place before but was intrigued by the idea of vintage clothing and wondered how far back it went. She heard a real bell jingle as she opened the door and she smiled. Vintage security. Then she stood still and let the cool air wash over her.

"You look like you could use some cold water."

Michelle turned toward the voice and saw a lady behind a counter sitting on a tall cushioned stool. She had long grey hair in braids that hung down on the sides of her face and a friendly smile.

"That would be great. Thank you so much."

As Michelle walked over to the counter, the lady got off her stool, ducked down out of view, then popped back up with a cold bottle of water which she placed on the counter top. Michelle opened the bottle, thanked the lady again, then looked around her as she took a long drink, feeling the coldness travel down her throat and come to rest in her stomach.

She'd never seen clothes like these except for in movies. Everywhere she looked she saw explosions of colors. She was really glad that she'd come in.

"These clothes are amazing! Where do you get them?"

"A few I pick up from estate sales. The rest, I make myself. I'm Sara, by the way."

"Hi Sara. I'm Michelle. It's nice to meet you. You must be the one on the sign."

"That's me. In the flesh!"

"And you make these clothes yourself?"

"Most of them, yes. I'm tickled that you like them so much. If there were more like you, I wouldn't have to close down."

"Oh no! Really? But I just found you, and I love your stuff." Michelle put the bottle down and drifted to the nearest display, lifting a sleeve from a deep purple top and admiring the feel of the texture. "This is beautiful."

"Thank you, sweetheart. And I mean that. You're very sweet. Maybe if you share your enthusiasm with your friends, I might be able to keep this place running a little longer. I don't even make new stuff anymore since I'm not selling what I've got. Do you think your friends would like my clothes?"

"That's actually why I'm here. We totally disagree on clothing styles, and I don't want to dress like them anymore. In fact, they're not even going to be my friends anymore. I'm going to try to make new ones."

"That sounds like a positive attitude. I'm sorry to hear things didn't work with your old friends though. What style of clothes are they into?"

"The slutty kind. And I don't mean 'sexy,' I mean like totally trashy. They dress like prostitutes."

"That's a very popular style today," Sara said with a small shake of her head. "But styles come and go, and this one will fade out too, eventually."

"I wonder. It seems like the only thing that can come next is everyone just going around naked. Without any paint even."

Sara burst out in unexpected laughter. Michelle found herself laughing too. She hadn't meant to be funny though. She was serious.

"I know what you mean, dear. People are getting a bit overboard with their sexuality and they're overly focused on their appearance. It's nothing new of course, but I don't know if there's ever been a time like this exactly. Sexuality should be one of many aspects to a woman's attractiveness, not the sole focus."

Michelle nodded. "That's kind of how I feel. I like feeling attractive, but geez, I'd also like to be looked at like I'm a person too. You know?"

"Yes, I do. People are putting the greatest value on the least valuable part of you – the exterior, that honestly, when you think about it, has very little to do with who you are. It's just your genetic makeup that gives you your appearance. A lucky roll of the DNA dice."

"Hmm," Michelle said, thinking for a minute about what Sara had said. "You're right. I didn't make me look the way I do. I can only take credit for how I fix my hair and how I style my makeup and stuff, but I was born with my face and body."

"That's right," Sara replied. "And yet everyone looks at you on the outside as if your appearance was some kind of personal accomplishment, or a sign of your inner quality. Then they judge what kind of a person they think you are before they've even gotten to know you. And since people do that, we try to make our outside more and more appealing, thus obscuring who we really are even more. And so it goes."

"Well, I think it's stupid, and I'm not going to be a part of it anymore," Michelle declared proudly and defiantly.

"Good for you! I wish more people thought the way you do."

"Cuz you'd make more money?" Michelle teased.

"Yes, but also because the world would be more sane and relationships would be based on something real. As it is now, they're based entirely on sexual attraction, which is just silly. You don't have a relationship with a body. You have it with a soul and a mind."

Michelle found herself wishing that Sara was her own age. She would love to have a friend she could talk with like this.

"How come you're so cool?" she asked the older woman.

They both laughed, then Sara said, "I don't know. How come men my age don't think I'm so cool?"

Michelle looked at Sara's left hand and noticed the bare ring finger. "I can't believe you're not married. You're the coolest lady ever."

"Talking to you makes me wish I was forty years younger, and a lesbian." The two of them cracked up again. "I almost got married once, but in the end, I decided that I'd rather be true to myself instead of doing what others expected of me. And that meant waiting to meet a truly good guy. I'm not sure if there are any left though, because here I am, fifty-seven years old and still single."

Michelle looked down at the floor, took a deep breath, and sighed.

"Oh no. You must think if I haven't found a man in all these years of waiting for Mr. Right, then there's no hope for you. I'm sorry, dear. I didn't mean to make things look bleak. I'm sure you'll meet someone just perfect for you. You're very intelligent, insightful, honorable, and I do have to say it, unbelievably gorgeous. Just make sure you give yourself some time and don't just go with the first guy who acts nice to get you in bed."

"Actually, I wasn't thinking so much of the future. I'm pretty sure I already know the perfect guy for me."

"Wow. I don't think I've ever heard someone say something so wonderful with such a terribly sad face. How is that possible? Where is this young man, and why isn't he with you?"

"That's the problem. I have no idea where he is. And if I manage to find him, I doubt he'll want anything to do with me."

Michelle began to cry and Sara came around the counter and held her, whispering that everything was going to be all right.

## Thirty-four

Jacey only picked at her food while the guys ate everything on their plates. Chad complained about the inferior quality of the food but also wondered aloud if they could get seconds. Jacey stood up and walked toward the exit door.

"All I need is a cigarette and I'll be happy," she said.

She reached the door and looked through the tall thin rectangle of glass and spotted the guard standing to the right of it.

"Have you got a cigarette?" she asked him loudly.

He turned to look at her and she smiled at him. He held up a finger and spoke into his lapel mic. She couldn't hear what he had said, nor the reply he'd gotten. With one hand still on the mic, he gestured toward the others at the tables with his other hand and raised his eyebrows.

"Hey! Anybody else want a smoke?" Deron was the only one who did. Jacey indicated as much to the guard. He nodded. A few minutes later someone who looked like an orderly appeared and handed something to the guard. He opened the door and handed her two e-cigs.

"You're only allowed to have these."

"Is there nicotine?"

"I don't know. Doubt it."

"Shit. I mean, thank you. I appreciate it. Anything is better than nothing. I'm going crazy in here."

"You know what they say," the guard smiled at her. "Anyone who isn't crazy when they go into a mental hospital will be crazy by the time they leave."

Jacey smiled back and said, "At least I have that to look forward to."

She walked back to the table and handed one of the e-cigs to Deron. They removed them from the plastic containers and started puffing away, still sitting at the dining table. A voice sounded from the ceiling.

"Vaping is only permitted in the designated area next to the wall with the ventilator label."

They looked around, spotted the ventilator and the sign and made their way over to it. Once there, they resumed vaping, dutifully exhaling toward the wall vent which promptly sucked the clouds out of the room.

"Shit. These *do* have nicotine," Jacey said.

"Yeah. I'm actually getting a head rush. I don't remember the last time I had a cigarette," Deron replied. They smoked for a few minutes then he asked, "Have you ever heard of the word leucotomy?"

Jacey looked at him suspiciously, wondering where he was going with this. "Yeah. Why do you ask?"

"It's just something I read recently and I don't know what it means."

"It's another word for lobotomy."

"Really?"

"Yeah. Really."

"How about cingulotomy? Do you know what that is?"

"What the hell were you reading? A manual on fucked up mental health treatments?"

"Something like that. What's it mean?"

"It's when they burn holes in your fucking brain."

"Why would they do that? It doesn't sound at all therapeutic."

"But an ice-pick through the eye socket does? They're both totally freaking barbaric, and they should be banned, but they're not. In fact, they're doing them more now than they did a hundred years ago."

"How do you know this stuff?"

Jacey took a deep drag and turned to the wall, slowly exhaling the smoke-like vapor. Then she replied, still facing the wall. "Stupid doctors did that shit to my mom."

"What happened to her? I mean, after they did that?"

"You ever watch those old zombie movies from before the war?"

"I'm sorry I brought this up. I didn't know."

"Of course you didn't," she said. "How could you?"

"Thanks for gettin' me the cig. That was nice of you.

Jacey looked at him for a second, weighing something in her mind. She took another hit, then asked, "Can I trust you with a secret? You seem like an okay guy, and I need help with something."

"Sure. What is it?"

"I'm getting out of here tonight. But I need help. If you're willing, you don't have to risk getting in trouble by actually trying to escape with me, but I need someone to help me get out."

"I already tried once and they shot me with something that made me totally sick."

"What was your plan?"

"I tricked the guard on the ground floor lobby into leaving his post, then made a run for the front door."

"Too bad your brain isn't as big as your balls. That wasn't very smart."

"I know that – now. What's *your* idea?"

Jacey looked around the room and said, "Let's go to the TV room."

When they got there, she sat on the couch and gestured for him to sit next to her. She turned on the TV, raised the volume, then leaned in close to him as if they were a couple and whispered to him.

It didn't take Deron very long to make a decision. His choices were to either be brainwashed and drugged into oblivion and then possibly be allowed to go home, or fail in his treatment and have holes burned in his brain, possibly with the frontal lobe scrambled as well. Yeah. He'd help Jacey, and go with her, regardless of the danger involved.

He told her he'd do it, and they remained on the couch, watching a movie together and continuing the charade that they were a couple, sitting close together with Jacey resting her head on his shoulder.

When group recreation time was over, a guard entered and called the teens to the exit door. He ordered them to line up behind him, single file, hands at their sides and to not get out of line until they arrived at their rooms.

They reached Chad's room first, then Deron's, then Michael's. When the guard reached Jacey's door, he unlocked and opened it.

She asked in the sweetest voice she could muster, "Don't I get a kiss goodnight?"

"Don't be ridiculous," the guard replied.

Jacey took one backward step into her room and undid the top button of her shirt. She pouted and asked, "You think I'm ridiculous? I was hoping you'd find me just a little bit sexy. At least enough for one little kiss."

The guard looked down the hall to his right where there was a surveillance camera affixed to the ceiling. He got an idea and bent down to tie his shoelace, positioning his head just inside Jacey's doorway, out of view of the camera.

"Okay. One quick kiss," he said.

She smiled and said, "You look really sexy in that position." Then she wolf-whistled and leaned down to kiss him, immediately slipping her tongue into his mouth and moaning in pleasure.

When Deron heard the whistle he pulled open his door which he'd been holding onto since he'd entered his room, preventing the latch from catching. He ran up behind the guard who was caught up in the thrill of the forbidden kiss and grabbed his head, quickly swinging it into the wall as hard as he could.

The guard went down, but he didn't go out. He reached for something on his belt and Jacey quickly stomped on his arm and kicked at his head with the other foot. Deron also kicked him once and saw that he was unconscious with his hand twitching as it lay on his belt.

Jacey removed his keycard and said, "Let's go," and ran down the hall back toward the dining and recreation room. Deron grabbed the guard's unusual gun and ran after her. When they reached the end of the hall, she turned left toward a part of the facility he hadn't been to.

"Do you know where we're going?"

"Mostly," she replied.

Halfway down this hall she passed a door, then stopped and backtracked to it. It was unmarked, but she decided it had to be the one she was looking for. She swiped the guard's keycard and pushed the door open. Deron followed right behind her and shut the door as soon as he was in the room which looked like a large cleaning supply closet. He turned around and saw Jacey already making her way up some shelves against the side wall.

She stopped climbing and started sweeping away the items on the top shelf, sending stacks of garbage can liners to the floor, then she climbed up and lay on her back, positioning herself so she could get her feet beneath the A/C vent. She kicked as hard as she could and dented the panel.

"Try to put some shit in front of the door in case they find us," she said, panting.

Deron began moving mop buckets over to the door, turning them upside down. There wasn't anything else large that he could use so he started throwing everything he could into the area in front of the door. Brooms, mops, gallon containers of liquid cleaner, packs of toilet paper, paper towels. None of it would keep anyone from opening the door, but it would slow them down a little as they tried to get past it all. As he was considering whether or not he should pour out some cleaning solvent out to make the floor slippery, he heard the vent panel clang.

"Got it! Let's go!"

Jacey pulled herself up into the square hole and Deron ran over and started climbing the shelves. As he reached the top shelf, he heard the door swing open and bang into the mop buckets. He started to go up into the vent and felt a hand grab his ankle, pulling him back down.

## Thirty-five

Kathleen let her car drive her to the Anaheim Convention Center where she would meet Eric for their date, talking to him the whole way there and apologizing for being late.

"That's okay," he said. "I'm more interested in the after party more than the main event anyway."

"I've only seen the events on TV. I didn't know there was a party afterwards."

"You've been missing out on the best part."

Kathleen heard thunderous applause coming through Eric's communicator.

"Is it starting already?" she asked.

"Yeah, I can see one of the big screens from where I am. The Administrator just walked onto the stage."

She looked at her car's computer screen. "I'll be there in about seven minutes."

"No worries. You won't miss anything important."

By the time Kathleen arrived, met up with Eric and the pair had found their seats, the Administrator was midway through sharing the list of accomplishments that he said everyone should be proud of, because they were made possible by every citizen working to make Orange County and southern California in general the national leader it was rapidly turning into.

"You may be asking yourselves how we've become a national leader, or what I mean by that. I will have an announcement later that will be the best news we've all heard in a long time. But first, let's welcome my husband, the Assistant Administrator of Orange County, California, Mr. Steven Nguyen!"

The audience applauded loudly, Eric and Kathleen included, as Steven came down the walkway with crisscrossing spotlights lighting the way as he walked up to his husband, Phan Nguyen, and gave him a passionate kiss.

"Mr. Steven will share statistics for the recent quarter and then I will return to tell you where we need your help, and after that, ladies and gentlemen, and all other persons, I will give you the news that will make you most proud."

Kathleen gave Eric a questioning look, wondering if he knew what the special announcement was. He shrugged. No one had told his department anything about any special news or developments.

When the applause died down, Steven Nguyen, a white male who towered over his husband standing behind the podium with him began to speak.

"How is everyone tonight? Are we all good?"

The audience cheered, clapped, and whistled.

"Is the weather alright with everyone?" he joked. Again, the audience cheered. The perfect California weather made the Grand Plaza at the Convention Center a perfect venue for the night's events.

Steven smiled and waited. When the audience was quiet again, he began in earnest with his announcement. Crime statistics were down again, lower than the last quarter. Housing renovation completions were the same as the previous quarter. Skilled laborers were sorely needed and apprenticeship programs were actively recruiting. Deconstruction of abandoned quarters of the county had increased, as had the total number of tons of recycled materials. Those two stats always ran together since the houses and buildings that were deconstructed were naturally recycled. Megawatts of solar and wind power had gone up. Natural resources returned to nature was up, which was also a reflection of the deconstruction stats.

"I'm happy to announce that we've had an increase in the county population," Steven was interrupted as the audience cheered again. He gestured for them to let him finish. "But our numbers are not keeping up with our needs. We've made tremendous strides in reviving our county, but there is so much more work to be done. We need your help not only with increasing the population, but also with helping us even out the racial imbalance in our population. Please consider doing your part by making some babies!"

The audience went wild this time hearing the second most powerful man in local government urging them to have unprotected sex. The jumbo monitors around the plaza displayed the words, "Fuck for the Future!" and sent the crowd in a frenzy of celebration.

"Can you do that, Californians?"

They indicated that they could indeed.

"For those who want or need assisted fertilization, I have good news for you. The Birthing Center has received a wonderful gift from the brilliant minds at UC Irvine Medical Center. If you come in now for pregnancy assistance, you will be able to choose the characteristics of your future child. Height, hair color, eye color, build, and even pigmentation to some degree. So come on down and start designing your baby!"

More wild applause followed this medical breakthrough. Misters Nguyen smiled and kissed as they waited for the audience to simmer down a little.

Steven continued. "As you may know, our population is predominantly Vietnamese." The audience cheered as Phan Nguyen proudly smiled and bowed. "Followed by Hispanic, Caucasian, and then lastly, African American."

A Native American in the audience wondered about his race. Apparently they didn't matter. Some things never changed, he thought.

"We desperately need more African American citizens," Steven continued. "We will be working with other territories to locate them and invite them to live and work in Orange County. Steven's news will deal partly with these efforts. But before we get to that, I've saved the second best news for last."

When the crowd was quiet, the band played a musical piece that built up to a minor crescendo and when it stopped, Steven practically yelled into his microphone, "The number of officially registered and practicing churches has decreased another 17% since the last quarter and there are only three denominations left in all of Orange County with a total of forty-six churches," and yelling now to make himself heard over the thunderous applause, "and membership in those churches is declining rapidly!"

The audience was up and out of their seats, cheering, and dancing in the aisles. The band accommodated them by playing a funky dance beat for a few minutes. When the lights dimmed, Steven stepped aside and allowed Phan to take the microphone again and the crowd reluctantly and slowly returned to their seats and eventually the plaza went silent again.

"First, before I make this incredible announcement, I want to thank every one of you here tonight, and by extension, all of the citizens of this wonderful community. Without you, what I am about to say would not have been possible. We were lucky to suffer less devastation and massive loss of life during The War, unlike many other states. But aside from our relative good fortune, we were also lucky to have the greatest population in America," he held up his hand to subdue the applause that began, "with the willingness and determination to restore our cities. To make them better than they ever were before. And with my direction, we committed to safeguarding us against every social ill that contributed to the holocaust this country suffered. We've eliminated government abuse of power. Our police use non-lethal weapons. We employ as many people of color in positions of authority and law enforcement as we possibly can. We developed and staffed the Department of Equal Opportunity and the Equality Enforcement Corp who also use non-lethal weapons. We've given all of our citizens equal financial status. Poverty is a thing of the past. And we continue to work for equality in every way possible."

Again, the crowd started to cheer, whistling and clapping until Phan signaled for them to hold still just a bit longer.

"Because of our great successes in every sector of society that we've applied new solutions to with new and existing technologies and devoting our energies and our resources to advancements, we've succeeded in becoming the most advanced territory in the entire country."

This time he couldn't hold them back. The audience cheered again with wild abandon, celebrating their leader and themselves. Giving in to their overwhelming celebratory spirit, Phan and Steven danced for a moment as colored lights spontaneously swirled around them.

Phan returned to the podium and the crowd quieted, perhaps realizing that they still hadn't even gotten to the good part yet.

"Our success and leadership has not gone unnoticed. Our wealth has slowly but surely spread to other counties and states. And they always ask how we're doing it, and I always tell them. Recently however, another question has been asked by the acting heads of communities who have also attempted to rebuild themselves since the Wars."

He paused and looked out at the audience, trying to make eye contact with as many as he could. He looked down at his feet and took a deep breath.

"Seventeen former American territories have asked us to accept the position and responsibility of leading them into the future with our local form of governance, and have unanimously signed their allegiance to my administration and Orange County as the governing seat of the newly formed Equal States of America!"

Fireworks blasted into the sky. The band played a rockin' number. A new but familiar looking flag lit up on all of the jumbo monitors. Black, white, and blue balloons that matched the colors in the flag were dropped by drones carrying massive lightweight sacks over the crowd. The people cheered. Some of them cried. Children caught the balloons and threw them back up into the air.

Although no one could hear him, Phan wiped a tear from his eye and spoke into his microphone.

"Welcome to the E.S.A. Let the party begin!"

## Thirty-six

Charlie made his way to the government facility using a beaten and weathered Thomas Guide. Most of the street names hadn't changed and he had no trouble locating the place. The long parking lot was lined with a single row of spaces and he was a little surprised there weren't more cars there. The sun was going down and they'd be well into second shift now, but surely they'd need almost as many people at night as they did in the day.

He sat in his car for a moment before heading to the entrance of the large building. Anxiety struck him as he suddenly remembered that he still had his shotgun in the back of the car. He reached behind him and lowered it to the floor. That was the best he could do. It was still wrapped in the small blanket so it wasn't blatantly obvious what it was, but he wished he had something else to place over it to obscure the shape. He kept the interior of his old car spotless though so there was nothing in it he could use.

He assured himself that no one would be looking into his vehicle closely enough to even get suspicious, and besides, it was dark, so even someone walking by and glancing in probably wouldn't notice it. Now that he'd addressed that concern, he thought of the demand he was about to make to see his grandson. He took a few deep breaths and exited the vehicle.

He walked alongside a perfectly manicured row of bushes with ground lights every fifteen feet. The night air smelled pleasant. Despite being in a parking area the length and width of a regular street with cinderblock wall on his left, he could smell the scent of some type of flower which brought back pleasant memories. He couldn't recall anything specific about the memory; just a sense of some time in the past in which he'd been enjoying himself and had smelled this same fragrance.

Charlie approached the double-set of glass doors at the entrance. He thought for just a second of turning around and coming back some other time. He recognized this impulse as being one of irrational fear and he suppressed it, determined to carry out his intentions. He pulled the door open and walked forward with confidence and bravado like the young soldier he had once been long ago.

He approached a semi-circular front desk in the middle of the large lobby that was adorned with small palms on a reflective marble floor. He was slightly disturbed to see that the man behind the desk looked more like a police officer than a receptionist, which he'd been expecting.

"Can I help you, sir?" the guard asked, after watching Charlie cross the lobby.

"Yes, you can. I'd like to have a visit with my grandson, Deron Young, who I understand is receiving some type of treatment here."

"I'm afraid that won't be possible, sir."

"I'm certain that it's entirely possible. You simply bring him to a room and take me to that same room. Nothing impossible about it."

"Sir, we've only just begun the program here and a visiting schedule has yet to be established. If you'll leave your contact information, someone will contact you once visiting days and hours have been worked out."

"Bureaucratic oversight in failing to realize that people would wish to spend time with their loved ones is not going to prevent me from seeing him. I'm standing here now, and my grandson is here now. Protocol be damned. As a citizen whose taxes contribute to your salary as well as the operation of this facility, I insist on seeing my grandson. "

"Not that it makes a difference, but there haven't been taxes since before the war. But regardless, a visit cannot happen at this time."

"If you lack the ability to make that happen, get me one of your superiors who can."

Charlie watched gears turning in the guard's head. He could see that Charlie was not a complacent citizen who would be turned away simply because someone in "authority" denied him what he wanted. The guard clenched his teeth and started to slide back in his chair, about to get up when his phone rang simultaneous with a flashing red light on his desk. Charlie's peripheral vision picked up other flashing lights. He looked around the lobby and saw flashing red lights above many doors, including those at the entrance.

The guard hit a button on his phone console and listened to a voice in his ear. "Yes, sir!" he said. He stood up and approached Charlie. "We have a situation that demands my attention. You need to leave now, sir. I'm escorting you to the exit." He reached for Charlie's arm. Charlie stepped backwards, turning to avoid the guard's grasp.

"Don't you put your hands on me. I'm quite capable of making it to the exit unaided." He walked toward the door, then tried to open it but it couldn't. The guard stepped around him and unlocked the door.

"I'll be back. And I won't stop coming back until I see my grandson," Charlie declared as he went through the door.

"You'll be wasting your time. Deron Young isn't even here anymore," the guard said somewhat mysteriously, shutting the door and manually locking it.

***

When Drake awoke, he was angry and sexually frustrated. He felt as though he'd been robbed. He should've been enjoying the afterglow of a sexual experience, and yet he'd not only been denied that gratification, he'd been assaulted as well.

He went to the living room, sat on the couch, and fumed as he chain-smoked. It would be impossible to go after the prostitute since there was a record of his transaction with her. Revenge was not an option. But Drake was determined that someone should pay for what she'd done to him. The theft of his ABT funds, the humiliation, and the assault with her taser, all ate away at him as he thought about what to do.

Since he had not enjoyed the experience with the prostitute even before things turned disastrous, Drake's mind returned to the last thing that had really fueled his desire. He thought of his last cable install customer. He would love to pay a visit to Mitzi, but he realized a few reasons why that would be a bad idea, the main one being that she was a customer of his employer.

Next, he thought of the two coeds he'd watched the night before. Thoughts of them resonated with his current anger and frustration. He had also been denied any satisfaction with them. He decided that was where he'd go. In addition to still needing to get something out of his time and effort invested at their residence, the setup outside their house was fairly ideal.

Later, after the short drive, Drake stood outside the house, looking in the same window he'd looked through on his first visit. Both girls were home and moving around various parts of the house. He'd seen one of them when she came into the bedroom for a few minutes, but to his disappointment, she hadn't come in to change clothes or bathe. He was furious when the young woman left the room so soon after entering it. He silently cursed her and willed her to return and at least change clothes. When she had come into the room, his anticipation alone excited him far more than the naked blonde prostitute had. He didn't understand how that was possible, but he also didn't give it any thought beyond noticing it.

Once again, Drake felt a combination of anger and lust as he stood between the two houses, desperate for one of the young women to reveal herself to him. He wasn't sure if he'd be able to restrain himself if he got what he wanted. He was so angry, he felt like adrenaline was pumping through his veins laced with testosterone. These bitches need to be taught a lesson, he mentally repeated to himself, over and over.

As he stood there fantasizing about what he'd like to do to either of the college girls, and surprisingly, even to the prostitute from earlier, he was startled by the bedroom light switching on. He quickly ducked, controlled his excited breathing, then slowly raised his head just high enough to see the girl who had come into the room. He could barely contain his excitement when he saw her cross her arms, grab the bottom of her tee shirt and lift it up over her head and then toss it toward a clothes hamper by the closet. She wasn't wearing a bra.

He fondled himself briskly as he watched her walk over to her vanity mirror and brush her hair, change her earrings, then spritz herself with perfume. Then she went to her closet and after looking over several options, she selected a bright yellow top with spaghetti straps. She slipped it on, checked herself in the mirror one more time then left the room. And that was it. The house computer detected her departure from the bedroom and her subsequent departure from the house and it turned off her bedroom light. Drake wanted to punch the wall below her window. He wanted to punch it and punch it until all of his energy was expended.

He heard the car drive away and he also heard music playing somewhere inside. The other girl had stayed. That meant the night wasn't quite over yet. But he'd need to find another window now.

He started to move forward to go around the house to the other side when he saw someone walking down the sidewalk. He ducked back into the dark corner between the two houses and held still. Waiting. He was always waiting.

## Thirty-seven

Charlie walked to his car, wondering the whole way what the guard had meant by the last thing he'd said. He would've sat and pondered it for a few minutes, but whatever was going on inside had put the facility on some kind of lockdown. A security vehicle raced past him and he decided he'd better get away quickly before someone decided to question him and look inside his car.

He didn't know if Kathleen had lied to him about Deron being here, or if they'd transferred him to another location, or if maybe, considering the silent alarms and the sudden activity around the premises, Deron had escaped. He smiled as he drove away, hoping that's what had happened. It just might be that he'd taught his grandson well.

He drove to Kathleen's house to tell her what had happened with his attempt to visit Deron. But he found her house empty. Apparently she had decided to go out after all. He wasn't going to leave until after he'd spoken to her so he went inside and sat on the couch.

He brooded about her being out playing around while he was seemingly the only one concerned about Deron. The thought of losing Deron terrified him, especially after having just lost Feenix. Recent loss along with the fear of new loss put Charlie's mind into a morose state and suddenly he found himself thinking about Elizabeth and his last day with her.

*26 Years Earlier*

It was Kathleen's 7th birthday and Elizabeth wanted to do something special for her despite the turmoil, chaos, and violence rampaging through the city. A birthday party was not possible, and she had no ingredients for a cake, but she at least wanted to give her little girl a gift of some kind.

Charlie argued against it of course. Most businesses were closed, and those that remained open could only do so by employing many heavily armed guards to keep their stores from being looted and set on fire. With the high price of the guards, the cost of goods shot up. There was nothing they could afford to buy even if they were able to reach the store safely.

Once a week, a FEMA truck pulling a tractor trailer stationed itself at the corner of their street. National Guard troops stood guard while law-abiding citizens waited in line to collect a week's worth of basic food items. Even with the guards in place, it was a frightening and dangerous routine. Most of Charlie's and Elizabeth's neighbors were white and so their neighborhood was subject to frequent attacks, especially on the food distribution day. Food was not distributed to the lawless areas where armed and masked citizens ruled the streets and drove the law-abiding citizens away to other cities and FEMA refugee camps.

A delivery was expected on this day, but there would be nothing special in the food rations that could be used for a birthday celebration so Elizabeth got an idea. She wanted to go to a friend's house, two blocks over and ask if her friend had some flour and perhaps an egg. If she could make Kathleen a pancake it would at least be a cake of sorts.

Charlie said it was too dangerous. Especially on food day. Every week the lawless groups from the inner cities had gotten larger and tried harder to overcome the troops guarding the food trucks. You didn't need a clock to know when it was time to line up for food. You just had to wait for the gunfire to come to an end.

Elizabeth conceded that Charlie was right, but then when he went into Kathleen's room to play with her, she silently snuck out the door hoping to make it to Evelyn's house and back before Charlie noticed her absence. Her timing couldn't have been worse.

She had barely made it outside before the initial National Guard troops began to arrive, and as soon as they did, revolutionaries who had taken up positions between houses the night before attempted a surprise attack. As was usually the case, they were easily defeated, but it took time to ensure they'd gotten all of them and none were left hiding in bushes or under cars.

Kathleen wanted Elizabeth to join their tea party so Charlie called out to her. When she didn't respond, he went to the kitchen to get her. When found she wasn't there he quickly checked the rest of the house and panicked when he couldn't find her. He went outside and didn't see her anywhere. He only saw troopers checking the street for hidden raiders.

Charlie heard a shot to his left. He turned and saw a man with a bandanna covering his face fall to the ground several houses away. Then at the house just before that one, he saw a flash of blue as Elizabeth came running out from between two houses waving her arms. More shots rang out and she fell face down on the lawn beside a dead rose garden.

Charlie collapsed where he stood. As he went into shock at the loss of the love of his life, he asked why. Why would they shoot a white woman wearing a blue dress? She was unarmed and looked nothing at all like the gangsters from the inner cities they had just been fighting.


Charlie was startled when he heard the front door opening. It took him a few seconds to get his mind firmly back in present time and to push away the grief that always threatened to overcome him when he thought about Elizabeth's senseless death.

"Dad? What are you doing here?"

"I went to see Deron but he wasn't there."

"What are you talking about?" Kathleen was a little tipsy from the drinks she'd had, but her mind was starting to clear up. She put her purse and communicator on the coffee table and sat down next to her father.

"Kathleen, I want you to answer me and be completely honest." He spoke softly, with the memory of her as a little girl fresh in his mind. "Did you give me the correct address for where Deron is supposed to be?"

"Of course I did. What do you mean 'supposed to be'?"

"He wasn't there."

"He has to be there," she said, fighting the alcohol in her blood for control of her mind. "What makes you think he wasn't?"

"A security guard *told me* he wasn't there. They also had some situation that cut my attempted visit short, with red lights flashing all over the place and security vehicles racing around the property like maniacs. I'm entertaining the possibility that Deron may have escaped." Charlie smiled.

"Oh, no," Kathleen exclaimed.

"Oh, yes," Charlie countered. "And if you think there's something wrong with him, he's more than welcome to live with me. I happen to like him just the way he is."

"You don't understand." Kathleen got up from the couch and started walking toward the dining room, then abruptly turned back toward the living room, and thus she began pacing.

"What don't I understand?" Charlie began to feel the first glimmer of something new that wasn't quite right and he feared what he was about to hear. "What's going on?"

She stopped pacing long enough to give Charlie a worried look, then resumed. With her back to Charlie, she walked to where the living room carpet met the linoleum of the dining room and stopped.

"I'm afraid I didn't tell you as much as I could have about the reason Deron was selected for this therapy." She stood still, afraid to turn around and face the wrath she expected.

"I'm listening," he said, calmly.

She turned around and walked back to the couch, sat down and with her elbows on her knees put her face down in her palms. She exhaled a long, shaky breath into her hands, then lifted her head and bravely made eye contact with Charlie.

"If Deron ran away, and if he broke any laws while doing so, this could be bad. They were afraid that without intervention, Deron would turn into a criminal. And this... therapy program was meant to stop that from happening. It wasn't just a social skills thing like I told you it was." She braced herself for his response.

"Was his involvement voluntary? Or was that also a lie?"

"I didn't lie, Dad. And yes, they made out like it was completely voluntary, but..."

"But what, Kathleen? I need to know what's going on here and what we need to do to help Deron."

"It might be nothing. It's just the way they approached me. They didn't call or come to the house. I was out driving around, looking for Deron when they sort of pulled me over. I didn't really think much of it at the time. I mean, it was strange, and I knew that it was strange, but once I talked with them, I just didn't think about that part of it anymore."

Charlie turned without saying anything and headed for the door.

"Dad, where are you going?"

"To find Deron," he said. As he walked toward the door, the house phone rang. He stopped and turned around. Kathleen stood where she was, staring at him.

"You should get that. It could be about Deron."

Kathleen said, "Answer phone. Speaker," and the call came to life. "Hello?" she said.

"Ms. Young?" asked a voice she didn't recognize.

"Yes. Who's calling?"

"My name is Dr. Fielding. I'm the director of the research and therapy center that your son was a patient at until just a short while ago. Would he happen to be at home now?"

"No, he's not. Why wouldn't he still be there?"

"Apparently he was dissatisfied with some aspect of the program. Or maybe it was something as simple as teenage love. A young woman left the facility with him. Neither of them bothered with standard departure protocols, and they've both interrupted their therapy, which could result in them experiencing adverse side effects from the sudden cessation of their medication. It's important that they return to the facility at once. Has he contacted you?"

"I haven't seen him or heard from him since he left for school a few days ago." She was about to ask what medications Deron was on. She hadn't consented to any medicating.

"I didn't want to alarm you before, but Deron was involved in a serious assault shortly after his admission. We were going to leave it as a private matter as long as he remained in the program, but his sudden departure changes everything. Charges will be filed against him unless he returns immediately."

"Was Deron hurt?" Kathleen wrung her hands. Charlie glared at the wall speaker.

"Deron was fine. It was his victim who needed stitches. But as I said, we were willing to forgive and forget in the interest of helping Deron and proceeding with his therapy. But if he's out of the program, then I'm afraid to say that his behavior was just that of the criminal we hoped to prevent him from becoming. And he'll have to be treated accordingly, which means he will likely be charged with attempted murder. I hope I've made it clear how important it is that he return at once. Do you appreciate the seriousness of the situation we have here, Ms. Young?"

"Yes. Yes, I do. But I'm telling you, he's not here. I haven't seen him or heard from him."

"If you do, please bring him here, or call me at this number and we'll arrange for transportation. If I don't hear back from you before tomorrow, Deron will be a fugitive from the law. When he's caught, and he will be caught, his life will be as good as over. Good night, Ms. Young."

The line went dead and Kathleen heard the front door click shut. Charlie was gone.

## Thirty-eight

When Deron heard someone yelling at him and yanking on his leg, he pulled the weapon out of his pocket, aimed it at the man and fired. The man continued pulling but appeared a little nauseous. Deron looked at the weapon while holding on to the vent shaft with one hand. He saw five dots of gradually increasing size. The smallest dot was glowing. He let go of the shaft and quickly touched the largest dot, then aimed and pressed the trigger again. The man fell to the ground instantly. Another man entered the room and Deron shot him too with the same result.

He crawled up into the shaft and went to the left, the direction Jacey had gone. When he rounded the first corner, he found her there waiting for him. He was surprised. He thought she'd have continued without him. He started to tell her what had just happened – how he might've just killed two people, but she cut him off, saying they didn't have time. They had to go.

They crawled through the ventilation system as fast as they could. They made two random turns and then at the next juncture, Jacey suggested they split up so it would be harder to track them by sound, and to improve the chances that at least one of them would make it out.

Deron didn't like the fact that it also meant one of them could find the exterior vent they were seeking while the other continued searching in vain. But he couldn't refute her reasoning, and they had no time to debate strategy.

They went in opposite directions and Deron found that another benefit of their separation was his ability to go much faster than when she'd been in front of him. Ungoverned by her lead, he crawled like a toddler in a death race, only slowing to make turns, then increasing again to a speed that he would have found comical to watch under other circumstances.

At first he could hear the metallic pounding their knees made as they traveled, and then there was only the sound of his own knees and palms rapidly striking the metal shaft like pistons. By the time his knees began to hurt and he was entertaining thoughts of taking a break, he turned into a shaft with a slowly revolving fan blade at the end. On the other side of it he saw a square room with white walls and glowing digital numbers on several panels.

He stopped the slowly turning blade with his shoe and maneuvered himself safely around it and dropped several feet to the floor. There was a low ceiling, but it was high enough for him to run to the door without having to duck. The door was unlocked. He pulled it open and felt his stomach drop as he sucked in his breath. On the other side of the door there was open air and a long drop to the street below. A narrow path ran alongside the exterior wall of the room he'd just exited, ending at the corner of the room.

He couldn't believe there was nothing to keep a person from walking through that door and falling off the edge.

The path presumably led to a way down, but who would want to walk on it? Maybe they used some kind of safety line when they had to service the intake shaft room. Not having that luxury himself, Deron fought his fear of heights and hugged the wall as he walked its length and turned the corner. There he saw a half-tube safety ladder against the side of the building.

When he reached the bottom of the ladder, he looked around quickly. Jacey was nowhere in sight and he had no idea if she'd need to stumble onto the same room he'd found, or if there were possibly others. Whatever her odds were, he couldn't possibly wait around to find out if she was going to make it or not.

He ran across the asphalt toward a retaining wall with bushes planted in the elevated earth. Behind the bushes was a chain link fence with barbed razor wire at the top. Deron squeezed between two bushes and climbed the fence. At the top he carefully placed his hands between the evenly spaced razors and carefully lifted one leg over, then the other. He'd made it without hurting himself at all. As he climbed down the other side, he felt something tug at him. His shirt had caught on a razor and cut through it, releasing its grip as he descended.

When he reached the ground, he looked to his right and saw lights from the traffic on the boulevard a hundred yards away.

And now he was free and he was running. But he didn't know where to go. He couldn't go home. That was obvious. His next thought was that he could go to

Charlie's. There was no way his grandfather would turn him away. But the people looking for him would know that, so Charlie's was out. Where else could he go? He didn't know anyone else in town well enough to ask them to let him use their house as a hideout.

Then he thought of Michelle. Once upon a time, she'd have done anything for him. Back when they were best friends, which felt like a lifetime ago. He wondered what she'd do if he showed up at her house now. He was not only the social outcast who wasn't good enough for her new friends, he was also the guy who had been removed from the school by eeks.

He reached the front of the building he'd been running beside and turned right, away from the facility he'd just escaped. He crossed the parking lot just to get further distance between him and Fielding's goons but he still didn't know where he was going to go. Being adjacent to the rehabilitation center was too close for comfort so he started to cross the boulevard when he heard sirens approaching.

He turned back to the building, thankful that whatever business was they did here, it was closed this time of night. A police cruiser and an EEC patrol car raced past him and came to a stop a few doors down where a drone was aiming its spotlight at something on the ground. Deron creeped closer, keeping himself hidden while trying to get a better look at what was going on.

Two men were lying on the ground next to an outdoor table on the patio of a fast-food restaurant. A young woman was sitting at the table with two unfinished meals in front of her. The light from the drone aimed down at the men and a blue light pulsed below the camera. When the officers got out of their vehicles, one of them dismissed the drone. Its spotlight went off, and the red light dimmed out. A moment later the two men began to stir at the same time a news drone arrived on the scene with its red light on, broadcasting live.

Deron was relieved that the patrol drone and the police were not after him but he didn't want to draw attention to himself by crossing the boulevard so close to them. Especially not with a cop drone so nearby. The rehabilitation facility might've sent an alert out to law enforcement to be on the lookout for him and Jacey. Having crept to the end of the building, he was now close enough to hear what was going on with the people at the restaurant.

The man and woman who had been eating were dating each other. But the woman had also been secretly dating the other man. When he found out, he came to the restaurant and assaulted the other man. Several other patrons sent emergency alert signals with their comms thus summoning the nearest police drone to stop the fight by disabling both men with its sub-sonic frequency until police and equality officers arrived.

The man who started the fight was handcuffed and being placed into the back of the police cruiser. The other man turned his back to the police and put his hands on the back of his head, waiting to be arrested also. But an equality officer told the woman to get up from the table and put her hands behind her head.

"But I didn't do anything. I wasn't involved in the fight," she protested.

"If it wasn't for you there would have been no fight, and one of these men would not be losing his citizenship privilege," the EEC officer named Hernandez said.

"I didn't make Chuck attack Paul. How is that my fault?"

Hernandez looked at her with a weary gaze. They always had to explain the obvious to people. "You led each man to believe he was dating you exclusively, did you not?

"I didn't mean to get involved with Chuck. It's complicated."

"No," Hernandez said, "It's not complicated. You deceived them. You denied them their rights to equality in a relationship. Charles is responsible for the crime of assault, but you laid the foundation that made his crime possible. Without your deception, these men would have never met each other, nor ended up in custody. You're under arrest."

Deron stayed hidden until all three of them were hauled away and the police drone resumed its patrol elsewhere. He ran across the boulevard and into the neighborhood on the other side. He wasn't sure where he was headed yet, other than away from where he'd started. Having no other options, he found himself mentally mapping out a route to Michelle's house.

His only concern was to not be spotted by any drones. He wasn't chipped, so they couldn't scan him, and they couldn't use facial recognition unless they were in front of him, so he needed to look like an average citizen while trying to avoid their cameras. If he appeared normal, maybe they wouldn't come down for a closer look.

What if he looked like he was just getting some exercise? He wasn't dressed as a jogger, but he could change that a little. He pulled his shirt up over his head without stopping and then tucked part of it into his waistband behind him. He still didn't look like a typical jogger with his denim pants, but he was wearing running shoes and no shirt now, so that was at least a little bitter.

Deron slowed his pace to a casual jog. Not only did it look more innocent, he'd conserve energy. As he jogged, he contemplated how he'd gotten into this situation.

*All I ever wanted was to be left alone. How did this happen to me?*

He tried to remember what Dr. Fielding had said about why he had been chosen for this nightmare, but at the time, he hadn't been paying full attention as the doctor rambled on about changing the world. Something about ridding society of criminals so people could be happy. It made no sense. Deron wasn't a criminal. And being the loner that he was, he didn't see how he could have possibly affect anyone else's happiness.

He went to school. He read books. He wrote short stories. And he occasionally wrote love poems to Michelle that no one would ever know about; not even Michelle. He did his chores, and he watched TV once in a while. He led a pretty simple and boring life. He wasn't a threat to anyone.

If he could change anything in his life, he'd want to live with his grandfather, and his ultimate dream was to marry Michelle. How could the government, or anyone else have concluded that he was a threat to society?

Deron cleared his mind as he reached the end of a cul-de-sac that terminated with a brick wall separating it from the boulevard on the other side. He stopped running as he reached the wall and bent over, putting his hands on his knees and taking deep breaths. He looked at the wall in front of him and wondered who would design something so stupid. Why didn't they just leave the end of the street open so cars could drive through? Or at least leave an opening for pedestrians to get through. Maybe it was leftover from when police had to chase criminals in cars before they they had the ability to kill the engine wirelessly.

He walked to the wall and looked up. He judged that he could jump high enough to get a grip on the top. He looked behind him and was relieved to see that no one was coming after him and no one was outside who would remember seeing him scale the wall, which would probably be an unusual sight in this neighborhood.

He jumped up and grabbed the top of the wall and pulled himself up, swinging his left leg up, and then the rest of his body so that he was now lying on top of the wall. To his left, there was moderate traffic moving in both directions. He knew this looked suspicious and he needed to get down quickly and get on his way. But it felt so good to just lay there. He wanted to relax just a bit longer. He reminded himself that he was a fugitive now – and he didn't have time for the luxury of relaxation. At least not until he reached Michelle's house – and even then, nothing was certain. He didn't know how she'd react to him showing up, and he'd have to keep her parents from finding out he was there.

He maneuvered himself around until he was hanging down on the other side of the wall. He looked down, and then let go, landing straight down on his feet. The impact stung his soles and jarred his bones. He waited for an opening in the traffic and tried to appear casual. Then he bolted to the other side of the four-lane boulevard and thanked god that the next street on his route was not walled off. He entered the next neighborhood and slowed his pace once again to make it look like he was out for an evening jog.

## Thirty-nine

Squatting with his back against the corner where the wall of the house met the backyard fence, Drake watched the girl on the sidewalk cut across the lawn, heading for the house on his left. Shit. It had been perfect earlier when that house was completely dark. He had been safe here. But if this girl went into the ...

*Shit!*

The light came on in the one room he hoped she wouldn't go into. Now he'd end up stuck between houses until she left the room. Either that, or he'd have to get down on the ground and crawl past her window like a sniper. He was fairly certain he didn't have the strength to haul his body along with his elbows, and he really didn't want to get all dirty either.

He couldn't squat anymore because it was hurting his knees and his leg muscles were starting to spasm, so he sat on his ass in the sparse grass between the houses. He looked up at the window on his left. It also had venetian blinds, and they were raised halfway up the window. It suddenly occurred to him that he was looking at things the wrong way.

Rather than viewing this new development as trapping him between the houses, he could also see it as doubling his chances of seeing something good tonight. He silently stepped over to the wall of the other house, and now, ironically, he was hoping the coed who had stayed behind didn't go into her roommate's room and spot him looking in this other house.

The raised venetian blinds on the window gave him a clear view into the bedroom where he saw a beautiful, young brunette. The bag she had been carrying when he spotted her on the sidewalk was now sitting on her bed and she was removing items from it, admiring each of them as she placed them on her bed.

When the bag was empty, she stood there looking at several articles of clothing, smiling. She appeared to have made up her mind and selected one. She took off her top and threw it on the bed. Then she took off her bra and tossed it also.

*Holy shit!* Drake couldn't believe his sudden turn of luck. All this time he'd spent waiting for one of the coeds to enter the bedroom, and now, a girl far better looking than either of them was standing several feet away from him, topless. She picked up a long-sleeved purple top with a wavy, rippling water pattern and pulled it down over her head. She looked at herself in the mirror and smiled again. Then she yawned. She took the top back off, then gathered up the new clothes off the bed, made a stack and set them on top of her dresser.

Drake thought he had just broken a world-record for fastest erection without any physical stimulation. He watched her turn to a dresser and rummage through one of the drawers. Although she had a beautiful body from behind, slim, tan, and perfectly proportioned, Drake mentally urged her to turn around and face him again so he could get a good look at her from the front.

He could just barely see the sides of her breasts, sometimes swaying a little more into view and then out again as she moved items around in the drawer. She finally selected something and pulled it over her head. *Damn. Over already.* The show had just gotten started and now the damned girl was ending it. *FUCK!* Drake screamed inside his head.

The girl had pulled a grey sweatshirt over her head and was now stepping into matching sweatpants. *Oh, no you don't.* Drake couldn't take it anymore. He was tired of being fucked with by girls like her. He acted on an impulse born of lust and rage. He duck-walked away from the window and rounded the corner. The long, hanging leaves of the tree in the front yard concealed him as he walked to the front door. *For once, something in my favor.*

He quietly and quickly made his way onto the porch. The door wasn't even shut all the way. Again, he was in luck. This was meant to be. The gods were finally smiling on him. If only he had known – this is what they wanted him to do – take action. He wasn't meant to watch like some undeserving spectator. He was meant to act – to take! The gods were giving him a gift, and he'd damn well accept it.

***

Michelle was really pleased with the way her day had gone. She'd found a great new style of clothing, and possibly even made a friend. It felt a little weird thinking of someone Sara's age as a friend, but she really felt like one. Much more so than the people she had been calling friends lately.

She also planned on taking Sara's advice and talking to Deron. She hoped the woman was right in her belief that if she apologized, Deron would forgive her and their friendship would be restored. Michelle wasn't so sure it would be that easy, but Sara was convinced that true love was easily rekindled. With her mind at ease with the possibility of a new and improved life, Michelle relaxed and felt how tired she was. She was also thirsty from the long walk home.

She left her room and went down the hall, walking soundlessly in her bare feet on the plush carpet. She went through a doorway into the short hall that led into the kitchen. She saw the auto-host message indicator was blinking. Probably her parents. She'd play the messages later. First, she needed something to drink. She opened the refrigerator door and took stock of her options. Iced tea! Yes. That's just what she needed.

She leaned down and reached in for a bottle and felt a hand clamp over her mouth, then she was pulled backwards into the soft flesh of a strange man.

\*\*\*

Now that Charlie knew that Deron had definitely escaped, he was certain that what they had called "treatment" was definitely some type of brainwashing program. That weasel doctor had been experimenting on Deron, and the boy wouldn't have it. When he'd gotten a chance, he got out. Now Charlie just had to figure out where he'd gone.

Going home would be too obvious, as would going to Charlie's house. To Charlie's knowledge of Deron's associates, that left only one possibility that he was aware of: Michelle Granger.

He started driving toward the address he'd memorized the day before when he'd found the envelope addressed to her. As he drove, he imagined what he'd say when he got there. He didn't know if Deron would go to her house or not, and it would be extremely awkward to just show up there and ask if he was there.

He let up on the gas and let the car decelerate. He tried to think clearly. The last few days had really drained his energy and he was feeling the stress and fatigue of all the worrying he'd done. He wished he had a cup of coffee. Maybe he should just go to a 7-Eleven and have a cup and think this over. He knew he wasn't senile, but he also knew his mind wasn't as sharp as it once was. If it turned out that Deron was at Michelle's, then what?

## Forty

Michelle's scream was muffled by the palm of Drake's left hand. With his right, he pulled her backwards abruptly. She would have fallen if he hadn't been supporting her weight as he dragged her backwards, her feet sliding across the tile floor. She was still trying to scream and then she suddenly stopped and bit down on Drake's hand. He instantly let go of her and she fell to the floor. Michelle hit the tiles hard, first on her tailbone, then her head smacked down. She cried out in pain.

Drake yelled at her. "How do you like it, you little bitch? Hurts, don't it?"

Michelle curled up into a fetal position, crying and cradling her head. Drake reached down, grabbed her arms and resumed dragging her across the floor and then across the carpet as he walked backwards towards her room. With her mouth free of Drake's palm, Michelle realized she could scream for help. As soon as she did, she felt a sharp blow from one of Drake's shoes on the back of her head and she stopped screaming.

"Every time you do something like that, I'm gonna hurt you. Got that?"

She didn't answer. She only cried from the pain coming from two places on her head and from the terror of this maniac in her home. She was scared to death and couldn't believe that this was happening in the one place where she should be safe. All the way home from the club the night before, she feared people such as this looking at her and fantasizing about what they'd do to her.

She suddenly felt herself lifted up from the floor and then tossed into the air. She landed on her bed and immediately scooted backwards toward the headboard, away from the crazy man. She cowered against the headboard with her knees drawn up and her hair hanging in front of her face. She was crying and breathing rapidly, afraid of what was going to happen next. She figured he was definitely going to rape her, but she was more afraid that afterwards, he would kill her.

He grabbed a shirt from an open drawer in her dresser and threw it at her. "Wipe off your face," he said, sounding almost sane and gentle. "I don't like the black streaks running down your cheeks. I want you to look the way you did before. Pretty and sexy."

He saw something skimpy lying in the corner. It was black and furry. He remembered now that he'd passed this girl last night on the sidewalk as he was leaving. He picked up the two surprisingly small pieces of clothing and placed them on the foot of the bed. "Put this back on."

Michelle noticed that he didn't say, "Put this on." He wanted it "back on." He was one of the perverts on the street or on the bus that had seen her dressed in Jenny's slutty clothes. *Oh my god. This is all my fault.* She just stared blankly at the clothing, hating herself for having worn the clothes she believed made this happen.

"Put it on, *now*!"

She reached for the clothing absent-mindedly, moving slowly. She picked up the top and held it.

"I am running out of patience with you. You're going to do what I say and do it a fuck of a lot faster, or I'm going to do it, and I promise you, I won't be nice about it. Now get out of those clothes and put on the sexy ones, right now, dammit!"

Michelle didn't want to be here. She started to feel numb and could barely hear Drake's voice. She knew what he wanted her to do though, and she knew if she didn't obey, she was going to feel more pain. She pulled her shirt up over her head and tried to cover her bare breasts with one hand while reaching for the little top with her other hand.

"Yeah. That's it. You little bitch. Put it on!"

Drake began undressing as he watched Michelle on the bed. He intended to fuck her until his dick fell off. He couldn't believe he hadn't done this a long time ago. What a fool he had been limiting himself to merely watching. He had always held back because he couldn't think of how he could get away without a girl reporting him to the police. It was so obvious to him now what the solution was all along.

All he had to do was kill her when he was finished playing with her. He'd felt years of frustration because he'd never thought of that solution. But that was about to change, and he couldn't have started with a better piece of meat than the one in front of him. He started fondling himself as he walked to the side of the bed, closing the distance between himself and Michelle. She now had the tiny black top on but was still wearing her sweatpants.

"Look at me," he growled.

She turned to the right and looked at him. He looked back at her starting with her face, then down to her barely concealed breasts. He reached out and tore the top off of her with one hand. She started to back away from him and he quickly reached out and slapped her face.

"Stay right fucking there, you bitch." He handed the ripped top to her. "Wipe your goddamned face again. What're you crying for, anyway? Isn't this what all you bitches want? You don't get to choose who you're doing it with, but you're still going to have fun. You should be happy. I promise you're gonna enjoy this – maybe even as much as I am."

Again, Michelle tried to cover her breasts with one arm while wiping the tears from her face. She silently prayed inside her head. "Please help me, God. Please help me, God."

## Forty-one

Deron finally stopped running when he reached Michelle's front yard. He stopped under the tree with the long branches. He didn't see her parents' cars, but they could be in the garage. He needed a few minutes without being spotted so he could think. What would he say if her mom or dad opened the door when he knocked? What would he say if Michelle opened it? This was so bad.

There wasn't really anything appropriate to say in his situation. He'd possibly killed two men. He shouldn't be here. He should go to Charlie. Charlie would know what to do. Michelle was going to freak when he told her what he'd done. Charlie would just come up with a plan and help him. He was certain of it. That's the kind of man his grandpa was. He took things in stride and always responded to a crisis with a calm and rational mind.

But he couldn't go to Charlie's. They might have his house staked out, waiting for him to show up there. Michelle was the only person he could go to right now that they wouldn't know about. But he couldn't see what good she could do and he didn't know if she'd even be willing to help him. He needed to just get out of town. That's what he would do. He'd get on a bus and go as far away as he could.

But first, he had to tell Michelle he was leaving. He had to say goodbye. That he'd never see her again. And he had to tell her that he loved her. Still breathing hard from his run, he straightened up and walked to her porch and pushed the doorbell button.

Drake grabbed Michelle's legs, swung them to her right so she was fully facing him, then pulled her to the edge of the bed so she was now sitting and facing him as he kneeled on the carpet before the side of the bed. She had her arms crossed over her chest and he grabbed both of her wrists and pulled them away. He pushed her arms to her sides.

"Keep 'em there!"

First, he just stared at her, drinking in her beauty and marveling at the fact that she was all his. He could have her at the instant he decided to. She was amazing. He couldn't believe how perfect she was. He wanted this experience to last, but he couldn't stand not touching her anymore and he finally reached for her. First he squeezed one of her breasts gently a few times then he drew his hand back and slapped it. He smiled like a madman. His eyes glazed over.

"You think you're special, don't you? Too good for the likes of me! What do you think now?" He slapped her other breast, then squeezed both of them really hard and moved forward to bite her when the doorbell rang.

Michelle was freed from her spell of frozen terror and screamed as loud as she could. Drake backhanded her with all the force he could muster, cutting off her scream as he did so. Michelle flew across the width of the bed and toppled over onto the floor near the window. She did not get back up.

Deron heard the scream and tried the doorknob. Despite the events of the last hour and the long run to get here, his body still responded with an adrenaline rush. The door was unlocked. He shoved it open and called out as he ran toward her room, "Michelle!? Where are you?"

Just as Charlie pulled up in front of Michelle's house and looked at her porch, he saw what could have been Deron entering the house. But he couldn't be sure of what he saw because the front yard had a massive tree with long hanging branches that blocked most of the view. He could see feet running and the bottom of someone's legs, but that was it.

Drake stood just inside the doorway to Michelle's room, waiting. He heard the door open, and then he heard someone quickly coming toward him. He held a lamp that he took from the nightstand next to Michelle's bed. When Deron turned to enter the room, Drake swung the lamp down over the top of his head. Deron crumpled to the hallway floor.

Charlie put his car in Park and looked again at the stretch of hallway floor that he could see below the branches. The person he had seen running was now lying in the hall. And another person with bare legs was stepping over him and coming toward the door. Watching the person approach the front door, Charlie could just see enough through the branches to think that this man was possibly not wearing anything.

*What the fuck was going on in there?*

He didn't know if that was Deron or not, but he was sure as hell going to find out. If it was, there would be hell to pay. He reached into the backseat and slid his shotgun out from the blanket that was wrapped around it. He pushed the safety off and slid the action just enough to visually confirm that a shell was chambered. He knew it was, but he still wanted to be 100% certain of it - especially if Deron might be in danger. If that was Deron lying on the floor, someone was going to be very sorry. Charlie had experienced quite enough bullshit in his life, and someone harming Deron would really be the final straw for him. He opened his car door and heard the front door of the house slam shut. He got out and ran around the tree and up to the porch. Of course, the door was locked.

## Forty-two

Drake was getting extremely angry now. His head was throbbing, and his groin was throbbing even more. His hand was still bleeding. At least he wasn't bleeding as badly as the stupid kid in the hallway. He stepped over Deron and into Michelle's room. For a second he thought she'd gotten away when he saw the empty room, but then he remembered she had fallen off the bed.

He walked over to the other side of the room and saw her lying between the bed and the wall, below the window where he had first spotted her. He thought he should probably close the blinds since he was about to "get lucky." He laughed and decided there was no one that was going to see him through this window. The only window peeper around was already in the house. He laughed some more.

He bent over and slipped his hands under Michelle's torso and lifted her dead weight up onto the bed. He was glad she didn't weigh much. He looked at her lying there and felt like he needed to get back into the groove he had been in before he was interrupted. He didn't want her lying down. He wanted her sitting up. He tried to maneuver her into a sitting position against the headboard, but she kept sliding over one way or the other. He needed to wake her up.

Charlie was tempted to just shoot the lock right off the door, but there was still a tiny part of his mind that told him there could be an explanation for everything he'd seen so far. He needed to know what was actually going on inside. He rang the doorbell and waited. No one came. He rang it again.

Drake heard the doorbell and almost screamed in frustration and annoyance. *God, couldn't everyone just leave him the fuck alone?* How many people just had to come over to see this little bitch right when he was about to have the fuck of his life? *Just go the fuck away!* He waited, listening for the doorbell to ring again but it didn't. *Finally*, he thought.

But with all the action going on at this house, he knew he couldn't spend hours with the girl the way he wanted to. He needed to just get on with it, fuck her once, maybe twice, then get the hell out of here.

Drake slipped his fingers under the waistband of Michelle's sweatpants and pulled them all the way down and off of her, dropping them on the floor at the foot of the bed. Then he grabbed her feet and pulled her body toward him to better position her for what he was about to do.

He grabbed at her underwear and yanked it away. "You look so fucking sweet. And I'm gonna –"

Drake's body flew across the room as the shotgun blast sent pellets and pieces of glass into the side of his face and head. He hit Michelle's dresser and his nude body slid down to the floor just a few feet away from where Deron was lying.

Charlie crawled through the shattered window and put his shotgun down on the floor. He looked first at Michelle. Her lip was bleeding and her cheek was red as if she'd been hit. He looked at the rest of her, feeling uncomfortable as he did so, but needing to see if she was hurt anywhere else. She didn't appear to be. He looked at Drake. He seemed to be dead, or if not, at least close enough. He looked at the body in the hall and now he could see that it *was* Deron. He ran over to him, stepping over Drake's legs to get into the hall.

Deron was bleeding from his head. Charlie put his hand gently on Deron's head and patted lightly, trying to find the source of the blood. He found it on top of his skull. It was cool and sticky. It seemed to be clotting.

"Deron. Can you hear me? Can you hear me, son?"

Deron opened his eyes and looked at Charlie who appeared out of focus. His head hurt like hell and he wanted to cry and go to sleep and wake up later to discover that nothing hellish had actually happened to him the last few days. It was just a really long and really bad dream.

"Charlie?"

"I'm here, son. Just relax for a moment. You've been hurt, but you're going to be okay. I'll be right back."

Charlie went down the hall and found the main bathroom. He grabbed a washcloth and wet it with cold water, then went back to Deron and held the cloth gently to his wound.

"Ow!" Deron cried.

"Can you keep that there for a minute? Just relax and hold that."

He went back to Michelle's room and grabbed the naked man's ankles and dragged him away from the doorway over to the left side of the bed, leaving a trail of blood in the off-white carpet. He pulled the blanket off the bed and draped it over Drake's body. Then he left the room, going back to the bathroom off the hall where he wetted another washcloth and also grabbed a bath towel. Back in Michelle's room he covered her with the towel. He felt a little stupid covering her with a towel, but he needed to wake her up and he wanted her to awaken with some sense of dignity for whatever that was worth after what she'd just been through.

With the wet washcloth, he gently wiped away the blood around her mouth and on her cheek and spoke softly to her. "Michelle? Wake up, sweetheart. You're safe now. Come on, wake up."

Deron heard Charlie talking to Michelle and sat up abruptly. "Is Michelle—oh shit. My head!" His skull pulsed with pain from the sudden motion. "What's going on, Grampa?"

Michelle woke to the sound of the two voices and was utterly confused to see Deron's grandfather standing over her. *Oh God, was he the one who*

"What are you—" she started to ask, then looked down and saw she was covered by a towel and it seemed that she was forgetting something important and dangerous.

"It's okay. It's okay, now. No one is going to hurt you. Do you remember me?"

"Charlie. Deron's grandfather. I thought I heard Deron talking. Is he here?" And then suddenly remembering what had happened before she passed out, she yelled, "We have to get out of here. There's a crazy man here. He hurt me!" Michelle started crying and looking around, fearing that Drake would suddenly come back into the room.

"That man will never hurt you again. I promise. You're safe now. Deron's here, but he's hurt too. I'm going to take care of Deron and I need you to put some clothes on so I can call the police. Okay?"

Michelle nodded and continued to cry silently. Charlie stood up to leave the room, and then turned to Michelle. "Try not to look over here beside the bed on the floor. In fact, have you got a robe you can wear for a few minutes?"

Michelle pointed at the closet. Charlie walked over to it carefully to avoid stepping on Drake between the bed and the closet door. He slid the closet door open and saw a terrycloth robe on a hanger. He pulled it off and brought it over to Michelle.

"Here. I don't want you to have to see the man who hurt you, so I want you to get dressed in another room. Okay?"

Michelle nodded as she took the robe. Charlie turned around so she could put it on.

"That's good, sweetheart. Now let's walk to the living room and I want you to look straight ahead. Don't look to your right. Okay?"

"Okay."

Charlie walked beside Michelle to block her peripheral vision as he guided her out of the room. They reached the doorway and she saw Deron sitting in the hall holding a bloody washcloth to his head. "Oh my God, Deron! He hurt you too! Are you okay?"

She knelt down in front of him and put her hand on his cheek. She started to cry again as she looked into his eyes. "I'm so sorry!"

"Michelle, you have nothing to be sorry about. I'm okay. Are *you* alright?"

Charlie reached down to Deron. "Let's see if you can get up and walk. Slowly."

Deron took Charlie's hand and let his grandfather slowly pull him up to a standing position. He squeezed his eyes shut. "That hurts, but I'm okay. I can walk."

"Let's go into the living room. Both of you sit down and I'll get some clothes for Michelle."

The three of them walked slowly into the living room. Deron held one hand to his head and put the other around Michelle's waist. She put her arm around him and tried to keep him stable as he walked unsteadily. "I don't know what happened. How did you guys get here? You saved me, didn't you?"

Charlie went back into Michelle's room and came back a minute later with an armload of her clothes which he'd taken from her dresser drawers.

"Michelle, take some clothes and go get dressed in your parent's room, okay?"

Michelle took the bundle from Charlie, nodded, and began walking down the hall in a daze. Everything seemed crazy to her right now, but getting dressed gave her something simple to focus on, so she did what Charlie asked.

Charlie looked around the room and saw an autohost panel on the wall. He walked over to it and said. "I'm going to call the police now."

"No!" Deron shouted and jumped up from the couch, and immediately went back down, bringing his hand to his head and moaning in pain. Charlie turned around.

"What's the matter, Deron? I *have* to call the police. I killed a man!"

Deron looked up at his grandfather and said, "So did I. I think I killed *two* men actually. And they're after me. Uh, the police, not the dead men."

The two of them looked at each other in silence and then despite the gravity of the situation, they both laughed for a few seconds. "This isn't funny at all. Do you know what you're saying?"

"Yes, sir. Men from the government kidnapped me a few days ago. It's a long story, but I may have killed a few of them to escape. If you call the police, then we'll both be locked up. But we're not the bad guys, grandpa."

"You're right. But the only alternative is to run and hide. I don't mind doing that, but it's no life for a child. I don't think I can do that to you."

"I'd rather be on the run with you than in a jail, or that mind control hospital I was in."

"Okay. Then we need to get out of here fast. I just hate to leave Michelle like this. But I don't see that we have any choice."

"Don't leave me!" Michelle came walking into the living room fully dressed now in a pair of Levi's and her new long-sleeved purple shirt. "Where are you going?" She started to cry as she looked at Deron and his grandfather waiting for someone to answer her.

Before either of them could speak, they heard the distant sound of approaching sirens. Charlie made a snap decision. "Okay, you can come with us for now. Let's go!" He began running toward the front door. "Get in the car. I'll be right behind you!"

Deron and Michelle followed Charlie down the hall but kept going straight when he turned right, going into Michelle's bedroom. He picked up his shotgun and looked quickly around the room for something he could use to cover it. He didn't see anything, and the sirens were getting louder, so he said screw it and ran outside holding the shotgun vertically alongside his leg hoping to minimize its visibility to some degree.

The kids were in the backseat of his car so he entered the passenger side and slid across the bench seat to the driver's side. He jabbed at the On button to start the car and missed it. The sirens sounded only a block or two away. He did it again and the car started. He floored the gas pedal and the car lurched forward, pinning Deron and Michelle against the back of the rear seat. At the end of the street, he barely slowed down to make the turn. Tires squealed at both ends of the block as Charlie turned his corner and the first of several police cars turned theirs, passing Drake's car as they came around and raced the short distance to Michelle's house where they screeched to a stop.

## Forty-three

The police were responding to a report of shots fired with no additional information so they didn't know what type of situation they were facing. They feared the worst since they rarely received calls such as this since the Firearm Safety Act of 2020 which banned private ownership of non-sporting weapons. Confiscation had begun even before the Act during the riots of 2016 which eventually turned into the War.

Officer Kerrigan and Sergeant Adams were the first to arrive. They came to a stop in front of the house. Adams, who was driving, immediately got out of the driver's side, keeping low. He told his rookie partner to scoot over to the driver's side and join him, using their squad car as cover.

Adams called in a code to Command Central that would cause the doors and windows of every other house on the street to lock. Each house's Residential Computer System would announce that there was an emergency situation requiring all occupants to remain inside until further notice. Adams requested that live motion and heat data from the residential computer be relayed to his comm.

Kerrigan, who had only one year of experience on the force and hadn't ever responded to a "shots fired" before felt an adrenaline rush from fear and excitement. "What's the deal, Sergeant? You think it's a cop who lost his marbles?"

"It could be anyone, Mike. Why do you think it's a cop?" Adams answered, peering at the front of the house and relieved at the sound of two more squad cars taking up positions on either side of him.

"Who else could possibly have a gun?" Kerrigan asked, looking everywhere at once and willing his heart rate to slow down. He didn't want the sergeant to see that he was scared out of his wits. He knew there could be danger in his chosen career, but he had never thought that he might get shot – especially not so soon after getting his badge.

"Anyone can still have a gun, Mike. Never assume that they got them all. Some people buried 'em. Some still get smuggled in from Mexico, and some people probably still have the software to print them. We just don't hear about them because the fanatics who still have 'em are smart enough to keep them hidden. They know if they use 'em, they lose 'em."

His comm chimed. The relay with the Kolnick house was up. No motion. No heat sources. He tapped a speaker icon on the Residential Metrics app and listened to audio coming from the house. Adams radioed to the other officers on the scene that the house looked and sounded empty.

"Can we go in now?" Kerrigan asked.

"*You* can. I'll wait till we know the house is clear."

"But you just said it's empty."

"Listen, Kerrigan. You gotta pay more attention to words if you're gonna be a cop. It might save your life someday. I said the house *looks* empty."

"Res-Met says no heat and no motion. And we don't hear nothin'. If that ain't empty, I don't know what is."

Adams couldn't believe what little training new officers acquired in the academy. All procedure. Very little common sense.

"Where do you think the Res-Met software came from?"

Kerrigan didn't see what the sergeant was getting at and asked, "The geeks In E.D.?"

"Those guys are techs and analysts. Software is written by programmers. What if our perp is a programmer and he hacked the RCS feed? He could make it *look* like the house is empty. You wanna trust your life to what an app says?"

"Uh… no?" All of his recently departed fear came flooding back.

"Now listen. I'm going to pop the trunk. I want you to stay out of sight as much as possible while reaching in and grabbing the bullhorn. Can you do that?"

"Sure, Sarge." Kerrigan tried to sound casual. He slid his feet across the asphalt, doing a kind of squashed duck-walk to the rear of the car. Adams reached into the front of the car and touched a pictograph of an open trunk which caused the trunk latch to disengage and the trunk cover to rise a few inches.

Keeping his head below the level of the rear fender, Mike pushed the trunk lid up just enough to allow his arm to slip in to the opening. He felt around blindly for the bullhorn. "I don't feel it, Sarge. Are you sure we have one?"

Adams heard the panic starting to rise in his young partner's voice and told himself to be patient. He was just a rook and he was probably trying to keep from shitting his pants. "Okay. Get back over here and radio in that we haven't seen anything yet. We have no visual on the suspect. We don't want anyone coming into the line of fire."

Kerrigan, relieved to have a task he could accomplish without risk of getting shot, quickly complied. While Adams made his way around him toward the trunk, other officers responding to Kerrigan's report estimated the width of the street, plus the sidewalks and some of the yard space on each side of the street then tossed their holocade units toward the center of the street.

Adams heard the high-pitch whine as the units charged, then the subtle humming sound as they projected barricades, warning anyone who came along that this was an emergency situation and to stay back. He reached into the trunk and undid the strap holding the bullhorn. He went back to the front of the car where he had a direct line of sight to the open front door of the house.

Adams lifted the bullhorn slightly, gesturing to the other officers to indicate that he was going to talk to the suspect. Being the senior officer of the three units and the first on the scene, he was in charge of the situation.

"This is Sergeant Adams of the Orange County Police Force. Drop your weapon and come out with your hands up!" All of the officers stared at the front door, hoping to see the subject complying with the order. Adams could see red pinpoints of light dancing around slowly on the wall just inside the doorway. The police were ready to shoot to kill if the subject came out armed.

# Forty-four

Charlie rounded the corner and fought the urge to keep the gas pedal mashed to the floorboard. The cops were so close, but he reminded himself that the house would keep them busy for a while. If he drove like a sane person, they had a chance to get away. Now he just had to think of where to go. By default, he took turns that led him out of the neighborhood and then southeast toward the mountains without being consciously aware that he was doing so.

In the backseat, Michelle and Deron were silent. Deron wanted to ask where they were going but he figured Charlie might be still deciding that and would tell them when he knew. Deron turned and looked at Michelle. Even despite her recent trauma, he couldn't help but notice how beautiful she was. He wished that they were sitting together under entirely different circumstances.

"Are you okay?" he asked her so quietly he wasn't sure she had heard him.

She turned to him and nodded, then took hold of his hand in hers. She started to say something then decided against it, pursing her lips tightly together. She knew if she spoke, she'd cry, and for some reason she didn't know, she really didn't want to start crying. She wanted to hold on and not think and not talk and just see what happened next.

Charlie's mind was working feverishly. There was too much input. Too much going on to think calmly and clearly, but he had to force himself to slow his thoughts down. The rest of his life depended on what he thought right now and the decisions he made as a result of those thoughts. Before long, he and Deron would be wanted for murder and/or attempted murder. He was sure he would be exonerated once he explained why he had killed the man in Michelle's bedroom, but he didn't know enough about Deron's situation to say the same for him.

If there was any chance that Deron could claim self-defense, then Charlie thought he should drive them all to a police station and get the facts known before their flight from a crime scene brought them additional charges that they couldn't be excused from.

But if Deron had actually killed two people, or even injured them with intent to kill, especially government employees, then he needed to hide him and protect him. Charlie decided that he would tentatively head toward the mountains, but along the way he'd get more information and then decide if he should change course.

"Deron, I need you to tell me the short version of what happened to you as quickly as you can."

"Well, a few days ago two men came to my school and took me to a place that was like a hospital. A man there told me they were going to rewire my brain so I wouldn't become a criminal when I grew up. I hit him over the head when he wasn't looking so I could get away. They caught me and then started me on their therapy program to turn me into a compliant zombie or something. If the therapy didn't work, I would end up in their reject program where they experiment on your brain. The next day, me and this girl escaped and I shot two men with a weird sort of gun. I don't know if I just knocked them out or if I killed them. After I got away, I went to Michelle's, and the next thing I knew, you were waking me up."

Michelle turned toward Deron again. Her eyes widened in shock and disbelief as she looked at him questioningly, but she didn't let go of his hand.

"You said earlier you were kidnapped by these men?" Charlie asked. He couldn't believe how Deron's version of events was nothing at all like the story Kathleen had fed him.

"I guess. Yeah. I mean, I walked into the library and they were in there. The librarian pointed at me and they came over and said they wanted to ask me some questions. On the way to their car, I got scared and ran, and then later I woke up in that place."

"Were they police?"

"No. They were eeks. You know, the guys in black that patrol everywhere?"

"Equality Enforcement Corps," Charlie spat.

"Yeah. Those guys."

"You said the place they took you to was like a hospital, but not a hospital. What do you mean by that?" Charlie's eyes shifted continuously from the road in front of him to his rear-view mirror, then to the side mirrors and then back again to the front.

As Deron explained how he seemed to have woken up in a hospital room but then went to what looked like a regular office, they left Orange County behind and crossed into Riverside County. Charlie realized where they could hide – if they could make it that far.

## Forty-five

Every officer on the scene had his eyes trained on the doorway. The entire block was silent except for the humming of the holocades. In addition to the glow of the holographic barricades, the street was lit up with strobing blue lights from the patrol cars. With the report of shots fired, Adams had no intention of risking anyone's lives. He pressed a button on his lapel communicator.

"Orange County Dispatch," a female voice responded.

"This is Sergeant Adams. I have a possible armed and barricaded suspect inside a residence at 631 Maplewood. Request Hummingbird and EMS. Over."

"Copy, Adams. Requesting authorization for Hummingbird. Over."

Adams waited, hoping his commander didn't make a fuss over his request. Hummingbirds were rarely used anymore, but then again, they didn't often get calls regarding armed subjects.

"Authorization received. Hummingbird and EMS en route. Over."

"Thank you. Adams, out. Kerrigan, get me the floorplan on this place. We've got a Hummingbird on the way. We're not taking any chances."

Kerrigan put down his rifle and removed his pocket comm from a pouch on his utility belt and began tapping away at the screen. Adams called out to another officer to access video feeds from the street cams to see if anyone was seen leaving the residence. A few minutes later, Officer Paulson said, "I got somethin' here, but it's kinda messed up," and keeping his head low, he ran over to where Adams was still crouched behind his patrol car.

"Let me see it," he said. Paulson handed him his comm and Adams looked at the still image on the screen and tapped a button causing a recording to play backwards. The view was fully blocked in some places and in others it was just blurred. He watched as a green four-door moved backwards and came to a stop approximately in front of the house he was watching. Then a man got out of the passenger side of the car and ran backwards across the yard and into the house. Next, the rear passenger door opened and a person got out, followed by another person, then both of them ran backwards toward the front door of the house.

"What the fuck is this?" Adams said, looking at Paulson for an answer.

"I'm not sure. I think it's some kind of fat bug. Maybe a bumblebee?"

"This is great. How about the cam from the other end of the street?

"Uh. There's two. And they point east and west. There isn't one facing this direction."

"Goddammit. So our gunman may have just driven away and we can't even make out his plates. This is just beautiful." Adams watched the recording again in forward motion. "Aha! You're not that lucky, you son of a bitch. Paulson, I want you to beam this over to the geeks in the E.D. then I want you to drive over there and personally make sure they get on this and stay on it until they I.D. the make and model and do everything they can to clean up this image. There's a partial view of the license plate. We can at least get half of it. That's enough to nail this bastard."

Paulson took back his comm unit, tapped the screen a lot, then looked over at the front of the house to make sure he was still safe, ran to his patrol car and took off down the street. Adams thumbed his mic. "P743 to base."

"P743, this is base. Go ahead."

"Officer Paulson has just transmitted video surveillance evidence of a possibly armed and dangerous suspect. He'll be working with the Electronics Division on this. Can I get a replacement over to this location? Over."

"Copy that. Backup will be on the way."

Just then a police van rounded the corner by the convenience store, turned off its headlights and came slowly rolling down the street. Adams ran over to the driver's side of the van and spoke to the driver who was looking all around the street for signs of danger.

"Relax. If the shooter's still here, he's inside. No lights have gone on or off inside since we arrived, so if he's in there, he ain't doing anything. We just don't want to walk in and get shot. The RP said she heard gunshots, so we called you out just to be safe."

Officer Bryan Stevens from the Electronics Division smiled and said, "Hey, I'm glad I can help. It's not often I get to fly around a violent crime scene." He opened the door and got out. He looked over at the house with the open door. "Is that it?"

"Yeah. Just the way we found it. Street cam caught a guy and possibly two kids leaving the house. We don't know if that's him, or if they were escaping from a gunman inside or what."

"Well, did the guy leaving have a gun?"

"Can't tell. Some fucking bug or something was walking around on the lens at the time, so it's kind of fucked up. But we got a partial on the plate, so we'll find them." Adams talked as he followed Stevens around to the back of his van.

"At least you got the partial," he said, opening the rear doors all the way. "Sometimes the cams don't work at all and people just walk away." He reached in and opened another set of doors on a black, metal cabinet. He pulled out a large drawer from the cabinet, revealing what looked like a metal half-cylinder with two sets of wings and an oval-shaped head with cameras that looked like eyes.

"I can never get used to these things," Adams said, looking at the device as if it were alive.

"She probably ain't too hot on the idea of looking at you either," Stevens replied, laughing.

"She? Jesus. Don't give the fuckin' thing a gender. It's creepy enough as an *it*."

Stevens carefully lifted it from the drawer which had a foam tray with a shallow cut-out in the shape of the body. "You sure you don't wanna give her a kiss for good luck?" he said, swinging it toward Adams.

Adams took a step backwards and leaned back even further. "Just get that thing in the air so we can get the fuck out of here. The paperwork on this case is gonna be a nightmare and my shift ended twenty minutes ago. Whatever you find, or don't find, it's gonna be a long fucking night."

Stevens set it down carefully in front of the black cabinet and opened another drawer. He brought out a remote flight control unit and a tripod, extending its telescopic legs. Then he grabbed a pair of goggles with attached headphones. "Do you want video sync'd to your comm?"

"No," Adams replied. "Screens on comm units are too damned small to be of any use anyway."

"Sticky screens are in the top drawer. Grab one and I'll sync it real quick."

Adams took out a thick rolled tube and unrolled it against the inside of the opened back door. He pressed it and smoothed out the wrinkles as it unfurled.

"Got it," he said.

Stevens pressed a button on the control unit and a few seconds later an image of Michelle's empty driveway and garage door appeared on the screen. Next he put on a headset and pressed another button on the control unit and the small drone lit up. He pushed a few more buttons to activate the motor and the recording equipment then picked up the device and stepped back a few paces before very gently placing it on the ground in front of him. Stevens manipulated the controls again and Adams heard the buzzing sound from the top set of wings.

"All units on scene. Be alert for the perp. Dragonfly inbound."

All of the officers looked toward the van to watch the drone as it flew toward the front door where it stopped and hovered in the doorway. A ring of light lit up on the Dragonfly illuminating everything around it. The nose tilted down and the floor lit up.

"We've got blood. Do you want a sample now, or keep scouting?"

"Keep scouting. We'll come back to it."

"Okay, boss. I've got two doorways. One left and one right and the hall continues forward to a probable living room. Have you got a floorplan?"

Adams pulled out his comm and looked at the screen. "Yeah. Take the room on the right. Master bedroom."

"You got it," Stevens replied and sent the Dragonfly forward several feet and steered it into the master bedroom, leaving the hallway dark again.

Stevens described what he saw in a bored monotone. It was just an empty room with a bed and a dresser, lamps, etc. Adams told him to check the master bath. Another empty room. Stevens commented that the place looked pretty clean. Like a model house.

"Check the bedroom opposite this one."

Stevens flew back out of the master bedroom, crossed the hall and entered Michelle's room. "Looks like someone lives here after all."

Adams was startled. "Someone's in there??"

"No. Just looks lived in. Messy. Like a kid's room. And the window's busted up. Glass everywhere, like it was shot out."

"Any blood?"

Stevens spun the dragonfly around to face the way it had come in. "Yep! You got blood. Lots of it. And over here, this looks like a body under the blanket. You want me to uncover it, or keep scoping?"

"There's only two more rooms. He's either in the living room or the kitchen/dining-room, which is all practically one big room anyway. Go back out to the hall, turn left and there's a bathroom a few feet up on the left. Check that, then get to the rest of the house. I wanna get in there a.s.a.p."

Stevens checked the small bathroom then flew back out and went into the living room and kitchen. "It's clear. No one there unless you want me to check closets, attic, crawl space—"

"Fucker's long gone. We're going in. Give a warning to cover us with Legal and you can take off."

Stevens extended a microphone down from his headset. He cleared his throat and announced. "This is the Orange County Police Force!" The officers in the street heard his voice in a weird sort of stereo – live on the street, and amplified but distant coming from inside the house. "This house has been determined to be empty. If it is not, reveal yourself immediately. Anyone sighted after a five second countdown will be assumed to be hostile and WILL be shot. This is your only warning. 5, 4, 3, 2, 1."

As Stevens flew the dragonfly out of the house, Adams signaled for the officers to join him behind his car. "Okay, ladies. The house looks empty except for possibly one gunshot victim. There's blood in the entry hall and a possible homicide in the bedroom on the left. Put on your prophs before you enter and step carefully. Let's not fuck up our only homicide of the year."

The officers went to their trunks first for prophylactic gear then met up with Adams on the porch where he was already covering his shoes. He pulled a face mask out of a bag and before putting it on, said to Officer Nguyen, "Radio we're clear for EMS and get us an M.E. in case it's too late for EMS. Then keep the scene secure."

Nguyen frowned and said, "Got it," then walked back toward the patrol cars talking into his lapel mic.

Adams entered the house slowly with his right hand on his holster even though the house was believed to be empty. He wasn't taking any chances. Not when a citizen was running around with a gun. He aimed his flashlight at the floor and stepped carefully around the small pool of blood on the tile and looked into Michelle's room.

He saw the blasted window, glass shards, rumpled bedsheet, blood splatter, and wondered where the body was. Then he looked to his left where he saw a dresser. He aimed his flashlight down the length of the dresser, illuminating the shiny blood splatter. When the beam reached the floor he saw the body-shape under the blanket.

"Oh, there you are."

He reached down with a gloved hand and carefully lifted the blanket up and away, revealing the nude and bloody corpse of Drake Austin.

## Forty-six

Charlie looked at Michelle in the rear-view mirror. He didn't want to upset her by bringing up this subject, but he needed to get a grasp of what was going on.

"Michelle, do you know who the man in your house was?"

Michelle looked at the back of Charlie's head, then looked at his eyes in the rearview mirror and shook her head.

"Had you ever seen him before anywhere?"

"No... Wait. I think I saw him walking down my street a few days ago. I'm not sure."

"Did he say anything to you that would explain why he was there, other than..."

"No. He just called me names and was really mean and gross." Michelle started to cry and said something that Charlie didn't understand. Deron understood her.

"It was *not* your fault, Michelle. Don't ever say that. Don't even think it."

"But it is! I went to a club dressed like a total slut. People stared at me everywhere I went. I think he saw me when I was walking home. If I hadn't been dressed that way, maybe this wouldn't have happened." She covered her face with her hands as she cried harder. Deron put an arm around her and pulled her close to him.

He spoke softly to her as he stroked her hair. "It's not your fault some psycho attacked you, no matter what you were wearing. And I promise you no one will ever hurt you again."

He continued consoling her, wishing he could reverse time and protect her from what had happened. He'd give anything to go back just two days to when his biggest problems were occasional boredom and idiots at school. Now his life was complete chaos without even the next hour being predictable. But as bad as things were, he still felt thankful that he was with Michelle and Charlie. He just hoped things didn't get worse now.

Charlie wondered if the police could possibly determine that he had acted to protect Michelle without having him there to explain the situation. They would find a nude man, shot to death in a home where he had no connection to the residents and thus wasn't a guest. They should be able to figure out that he was an intruder, and his body was in a teenage girl's room. Surely they'd put the pieces together and realize that Charlie was a hero, not a villain. Thinking of the police reminded him of something.

"I need your communicators. Both of you."

They handed them over and Charlie lowered his window, stuck his hand out with all three of them in it and then tossed them upward as hard as he could. He looked in his rearview mirror and saw them shatter all over the street when they came down, reminding him of when he'd blown up model cars with firecrackers when he was a boy.

***

After Adams had inspected every room, he returned to Michelle's room and put his powers of observation on hold in exchange for his imagination. He tried to come up with a scenario that would fit the known facts. He needed to imagine a beginning and a middle that would fit the end. To do that, he needed to know more about the corpse.

He called for Kerrigan on his radio and he showed up a few seconds later.

"House is clean; nobody here, and nothing helpful in any room."

"Get me everything you can on this guy and any connection at all to the homeowners. And find the homeowners, while you're at it. I need to figure out what the fuck happened, and they might be able to fill in a lot of missing pieces."

"You bucking for Homicide, Sergeant?"

Adams just stared, not responding. It wasn't his job to investigate a homicide, but he wanted to know what had happened here. Why was there a dead guy with no clothes on in a young girl's room? Why was he shot from outside the house? Who the fuck stands outside and shoots a prowler inside? Why had an old man driven off with the two kids? Kidnapping?

Everything about this scene bothered him.

A short while later Adams was looking at the area outside Michelle's room, trying to figure out what someone who lived inside the house would be doing outside of it when Kerrigan found him. "Hey, Sarge. I got some info on the parents. Do you want it, or should I give it to McMannis?"

"That wingnut's on this case? Fuck. Me first, then him. What've you got?"

"Stanley and Barbara Kolnick. 42 and 48, respectively." Kerrigan looked up at Adams expectantly.

"Go on," Adams replied.

Kerrigan looked back down at his comm and continued reading. One child, Michelle Granger, age 16. I'm thinkin' that could be the girl in the video that got into the car."

"Anything's possible, except for the video getting into the car."

"Huh?" Kerrigan was confused.

"Nevermind. Continue."

"Parents in France on vacation. Child's location is unknown. I've got the phone number to the hotel they're staying at."

"Good work. Beam me that info. Anything on the stiff?"

Kerrigan focused on his comm, pressing and sliding his fingers on the glass surface, then he carefully aimed his unit at Adams' and tapped the screen.

Adams shook his head. They were standing two feet apart. He didn't need to *aim* for the data transfer.

Kerrigan tapped some more and said, "Drake Bernhard Austin. 54. Cable guy. Address in Garden Grove. I can't find any connection between him and the Grangers at all — unless maybe he worked on their cable."

"Gimme his data too."

"Already did, Sarge."

"Thanks. I'm gonna call the homeowners. What the fuck time is it in France?"

Adam's radio squawked. He thumbed the mic and said, "Adams."

"Hey Sarge! E.D. took the partial plate number we got from the video and found 17 matches. 6 of them in Westminster, so I started looking at—"

"Skip to the end, Paulson."

"I think the guy we're looking for is a Charles Young. He's got numerous infractions, but it's all piddly shit."

"Did you locate his car?"

"Yeah, he's heading southeast."

"Well, fuck, Paulson. Send an override command for his car to drive itself to the police station."

"We can't. He's driving a relic — a 2018 Ford Prescient. But we're in luck. It's got OBD III, so we can at least shut him down on the highway as soon as you give the word — unless Homicide has taken over…"

"Fuck McMannis. Stop the car and send me the coords. Get the closest local P.D. en route. I'm heading over now."

"You got it, Sarge. Can I head out too? I've never been on a homicide."

"Yeah. Meet you there." Adams yelled to the other officers, "We got him. Let's go." He got in his patrol car, followed shortly thereafter by Kerrigan. Adams held his finger on the starter sensor, impatiently waiting for the safety restraints to slide into position before the sensor would read his prints and allow him to start the vehicle.

"Should we tell McMannis we found the guy?

The engine hummed to life and Adams wished he was burning rubber as he pulled away but the car's computer controlled the acceleration rate of the vehicle and it was impossible to burn rubber in a new car.

"Fuck McMannis."

## Forty-seven

"I don't understand how people minding their own business can have so much shit rain down on them," Charlie said. "But the important thing is that you're both safe and no one is going to hurt you or brainwash you. Not if I can help it. Now we just need to—"

The engine went silent and Charlie had to force the steering-wheel to bring the car to the breakdown lane. He looked at the fuel gauge and saw that he had plenty of compressed natural gas.

"Why are we stopping?"

"I think we're in trouble. I hope you guys can run. When the car comes to a stop, get out and follow me – fast."

Deron and Michelle were roused out of their comfortable embrace and felt alarmed. They had no possessions except for Charlie's shotgun, so they were ready to run. The car came to a slow stop on the side of the freeway. Charlie opened his door.

"Let's go. We need to get as far from this car as fast as we can."

The three of them climbed over the guard rail and ran down a slight incline into an open grassy area. They were moving away from the lights of the freeway and toward a lighted neighborhood. At the end of the grass there was an embankment they'd have to climb up, but after that was a freeway sound barrier that was too high to climb over.

Charlie stopped and gestured to Deron and Michelle to stop with him. He saw a sewer pipe opening at the bottom of the embankment and he led them down to it. He told them to get inside and move forward as far as they could. If they reached an opening on the other end, then stop and wait. Deron went in first, followed by Michelle. Then Charlie entered. The weather had been warm and dry lately so the tunnel was dry. The three of them slowly crawled forward toward a circle of dim light far ahead.

Behind them they heard sirens and a helicopter approaching. Charlie hoped like hell no one would think to look inside the tunnel – at least not right away.


A local squad car arrived first and pulled over in front of Charlie's car. A minute later, Kerrigan and Adams arrived and blocked highway lanes with their car as they came to a stop near the other two cars. The police helicopter circled above, aiming its spotlight around the general area and sweeping the freeway, the grass, and nearby neighborhood streets.

McMannis pulled up in an unmarked detective's car and casually walked over to the other officers who were shining flashlights into the interior of Charlie's car.

"See anything?" he asked them.

"Possible blood spots in the back seat. I put a call in for crime scene techs," a Riverside uniform replied.

"Good man," McMannis said, then looked up to see Adams approaching him.

"I thought they'd have put you out to pasture by now," Adams said.

"Yeah, well you know. No matter how much happiness we bestow on the people, some of them just can't resist the primal urge to kill their fellow man once in a blue moon." McMannis grinned and stuck a toothpick in his mouth. He put a foot on the front bumper of the car and looked around the area.

Adams thought to himself, *Hasn't changed one bit.* "That's evidence related to a crime scene, McMannis. Mind not contaminating it with your goddamned shoe?"

"Sure. But that's *Detective* McMannis," he said, smiling and rubbing salt in an old wound.

"How could I forget?" Adams asked, and then they proceeded to argue over who would direct the investigation from this point on.

Adams claimed First on Scene prerogative. McMannis countered that this wasn't the crime scene. Adams said it was an extension of the crime scene. McMannis called bullshit and reminded Adams that this was a *homicide* investigation.

"I think it's been so long since you've had a homicide, you don't even know how to handle one. Why don't you just stand down and let a real cop with experience handle this?" Adams asked.

"If you had the necessary experience and qualifications, you'd be a *homicide detective* instead of *still* wearing a uniform. So I've got this, *Sergeant*."

Adams felt years of held back anger from having been stabbed in the back by McMannis, costing him his promotion to homicide, and he swung at the detective. McMannis dodged and the two law enforcement officers brawled on the interstate which was lit up like a stage by the helicopter spotlight.

The co-pilot said, "I don't believe this shit."

"Fuck 'em," the pilot said. "Drop some search drones. We need to get over to Avalon. They've got a shit-storm brewing over there."

The co-pilot tapped some controls on the panel in front of him causing small bays on the bottom of the craft to open and release three drones. They would begin searching for pedestrians as they flew in ever-widening circles, one working its way east, and the other two going north and south. Any subjects spotted would be relayed to the OCPF officers.

The co-pilot radioed to the cops on the ground that they'd dropped drones and were headed out to an all air-units call off the coast and would be unavailable indefinitely.

Two hundred yards away to the west, Deron stopped when he reached the other end of the tunnel. Charlie was surprised and relieved that he hadn't heard anyone enter the pipe behind them.

The three of them crawled out and stood up, each of them wiping their dirty hands on their clothes. Charlie looked around and thought about what to do next. He could hear the helicopter but he couldn't see it. It sounded like it was heading away from them, but he figured it was circling and would be back momentarily.

Since they had been fleeing to the east in his car, Charlie reasoned that their pursuers would expect them to continue in that direction. He grabbed the hands of the teenagers, pulling them further west, and said, "This way."

They ran beside the sound barrier wall until they saw another drain tunnel half a mile down from the one they'd emerged from. This time, Charlie went in first, gesturing for Darren and Michelle to follow him and to remain silent. He led them to the other end of the tunnel and stopped about fifty feet from the end.

"I think we might be safe here until they leave," he told them.

"But won't they check all the tunnels?" Deron asked.

"I don't think so. At least not the ones west of my car. They're more likely to assume we continued east, or south."

It turned out that Charlie was right. After the captain of the Westminster Division of the OCPF came to the scene to oversee the search and suspended Adams and McMannis without pay, he directed officers to search in a wide fan pointing east radiating out to the southeast and northeast.

The drones searched in ever-widening circles around the area. They detected the officers but ignored them as their chips identified them as law enforcement. One of the drones flew over the fugitives, but they were not visible from the air and only the helicopter had thermal imaging capabilities.

After several hours when they could hear nothing but the occasional freeway traffic passing, Charlie crept out of the culvert and snuck up to the highway, staying as low as he could while still getting a look to the east. His car was gone, as were those of the officers.

## Forty-eight

"You can come out now. I think everyone's gone."

Deron and Michelle crawled out of the dirty tunnel, and again, tried to wipe dirt and algae off their hands onto their pants. They looked tired and dirty and Charlie didn't feel entirely certain he was doing the right thing by taking them on the run. But the alternatives were for Deron to be locked up in a "treatment" facility where he'd lose the spirit of who he was, and for Michelle to return to the crime scene she called home.

"Michelle, do you have any family you can call? Someone you can stay with instead of running with two fugitives?"

She bit her lip and shook her head, clinging to Deron as a buoy for the stormy sea of emotions in which she was still adrift.

"You don't have any relatives in Orange County, or anywhere in California?" Charlie would be relieved if he could be unburdened of the traumatized girl.

"Grandpa, she doesn't have anyone but her parents, and if they cared about her, she wouldn't be here right now. She has to stay with us."

Charlie came close to her and gently brushed away some dirt on her cheek. "Are you sure this is what you want to do?"

She nodded meekly and Charlie wondered if she even had the mental faculty right now to decide her own fate.

"Okay. We'll keep going, but if you find yourself thinking that you want to go home, or call someone, just let me know. I won't be angry. I think it would be best for you to see a crisis counselor and a doctor after what you've been through."

Michelle turned away, not wanting to mentally go there. Not yet, anyway. The horror of it was too fresh, like wet paint.

"Okay, I'm going to cross the freeway to see if there's a tunnel we can use on the other side. If I'm not back in five minutes, that means I found something and you two should cross over and meet up with me."

"Couldn't it also mean you got caught?" Deron asked.

"If that happens, you might as well come over anyway. You won't be able to survive on your own out here. None of us will actually, unless we're able to reach an old friend of mine. And even then, there's no guarantee he'll be able to help us. But let's take things one at a time. If you hear a helicopter, get back in the tunnel. I'm guessing you have one of those microchips in you, right?" Charlie asked, looking at Michelle.

"An Identi-Chip?" she replied, holding up her left wrist.

"I was afraid of that. Do not come out of the tunnel if you hear anything – a car, helicopter, drone – anything at all. That type of chip requires line of sight to be scanned, so just stay out of sight of anything and you should be fine."

"Should be?" Deron asked, alarmed.

"Yes. We used to have chips on our car windshields so we could pay highway tolls without stopping. I'm sure they have new scanners on the freeway now, but I don't know what they look like. We're well between light posts though so she'll probably be fine crossing here."

Deron and Michelle looked around, fearfully trying to spot anything that might support a scanning device.

"Try not to worry. I'll be right back..."


Charlie took off jogging toward the freeway, slowing as the terrain inclined. He looked around for cameras and wasn't sure if he could make one out in the distance to the west. If it was a camera and if it was being monitored, he was definitely going to attract attention, running across the freeway. Traffic was sparse and crossing would be easy so he decided to walk across so as not to look like someone who was literally running from something or someone.

There wasn't a tunnel on the other side where he expected one to be, but there was one further east, forty or so yards away. He made his way to it slowly, wanting the kids to cross to this side and easily spot where he'd gone. He walked backwards, mentally urging the kids to appear at the guardrail.

He reached the tunnel entrance and they still hadn't appeared, so he peaked inside the tunnel, not entering it all the way. He did not see any light on the far end as he had hoped he would. Not even a glimmer of streetlight illuminating an opening. Maybe this tunnel curves more, he thought.

As he sat down to wait, he tried to estimate where he was and how to get to his old friend's house from here. He hadn't spoken to Emile in a few years, but if he was still living in the same place, Charlie had no doubt that Emile would do what he could to assist. He didn't plan on asking him for much. The last thing he wanted was to cause trouble for yet another innocent person, but if he could borrow some money, they might make it out of the state. And maybe they could get a lead on the location of one of the anti-government free zones that were rumored to exist.

*There they are!* He saw Deron and Michelle carefully straddle the guardrail as they climbed over it, then make their way down the embankment, changing course diagonally to head toward him. He felt terrible looking at them as they approached. They were dirty, tired, injured, bloodstained, and probably starving.

"This tunnel looks dark. We'll have to go slow and be careful. Do you two need to rest before we go in?"

"I'm okay," Deron said, then looked at Michelle who nodded, indicating she was good to go. Charlie felt an urge to hug them and apologize and tell them that he was proud of them. They were exhibiting so much strength in such adverse conditions. *These kids deserve so much better than this.*

"I'll go first. Try not to let the dark bother you."

Charlie felt a tap on his shoulder as he lowered himself to his knees. He turned and saw Deron handing him a lighter. Charlie smiled.

Using the lighter every several feet, they reached the end of the tunnel and found that it did curve, and it sloped downward as it turned to the right. After the plane leveled out again, Charlie flicked on the lighter briefly and found a handle on the wall. He gripped and pulled but nothing happened. Then he tried swiveling it and it turned. He opened what turned out to be a door in the wall with a ladder leading down to another level that was much larger than the tunnel, so he decided to explore, even though it meant leaving the kids in complete darkness.

"I'll be right back," he said before descending.

Deron felt for Michelle by waving his hand around slowly until he made contact with her. She felt his touch and moved toward him. His hand followed the trail of her arm down to her hand, which he took in his, then they sat in the dark silence, gripping each other's hands tightly as they listened to the sound of Charlie's shoes on each rung.

As soon as Charlie reached the bottom, he glanced around and saw dim lights lining a tall and wide sewer system. He went back up quickly. He lit the lighter again at the top and told Deron and Michelle to come toward him. They were going to travel upright for a while, with light.

## Forty-nine

Charlie estimated that if they had an approximate pace of three or four miles per hour, and they'd been walking for just over three hours, they could be roughly in the vicinity of Emile's house, give or take a couple miles. Now he just needed an exit ladder.

When they came to one, Charlie climbed it but couldn't get the hatch door to open. He climbed back down the ladder thought he heard something. He spread his arms out and stopped. Deron and Michelle stopped walking and looked at Charlie. He held a finger up in front of his nose and mouth.

They all heard it now. Footsteps, getting louder; coming toward them from around a bend in the sewer. He motioned for them to get behind him, and stay close to the wall. He took a few steps to put some distance between them.

Suddenly Charlie saw something he hadn't seen since before the post-war reconstruction: Thugs. Typical, lowlife thugs. They stopped as soon as they made eye contact. The taller, meaner looking one on the left pulled out a knife. The smaller guy looked around, either for an escape route, or for something to use as a weapon. Charlie was guessing escape. He looked startled rather than aggressive.

Charlie assessed the threat potential in seconds. They both looked like they'd been deprived of food and sleep for some time. The tall guy's face was gaunt. Greasy hair hanging down over desperate eyes. Clothes that hung on his bones. His partner was no better off, but didn't appear eager for combat like his buddy.

"We're just passing through," Charlie said. "I won't give you any trouble, but I won't stand for any either."

"Give us your money and food, old man, and I won't have to cut you." He brandished a knife and tried to see past Charlie to where the Deron and Michelle were huddled together. Charlie stared at the young man's eyes without moving or speaking.

The punk turned to his friend and said, "Go take what they got, Scrab."

The unarmed smaller man who had hair that might've been blond if it hadn't been so dirty started to walk, curving to the right to make a wide berth around Charlie who sidestepped to his left, blocking the younger man's advance while keeping his eye on the other man. Scrab stopped when Charlie blocked his way.

"You got the knife, Mick. I ain't got nothin'."

The tall one lunged forward one step, knife hand extended. Not quite attacking yet, but trying to intimidate. Now that Charlie was further to the right, the knifeman had a better view of Deron and Michelle. "I'll make you a deal, old-timer. Give us your money and the girl and we'll let you and the boy go."

"We have nothing, and you're getting nothing. And if one of you even touches that girl, I'll kill both of you with my bare fucking hands. How's that for a deal?"

The one called Mick charged forward with his knife out in front. Charlie would've shaken his head in disgust at the lack of tactical combat skill if he wasn't already countering the lame offensive. He pivoted, turning to face Mick from the side, reaching for his extended right arm while stepping in close to him and spinning back out around Mick's other side, easily breaking his arm as he rotated.

Mick spun around without a choice, following his arm and trying to reduce the excruciating pain. Charlie looped his left leg behind Mick's legs and shot his right hand forward, palm out into Mick's chest, following through with the motion to not only send him to the ground, but to ensure the impact was maximized.

Mick struggled to breathe and Charlie turned to Scrab who had backed against the far wall with his hands in the air, shaking his head. He had no beef with Charlie.

"I'm sorry, man. I'm sorry!"

Charlie spotted the knife on the ground and carefully bent to pick it up, looking at Scrab as he did so to make sure he wasn't going to have a change of heart as he briefly put himself in a vulnerable position. He shifted the knife to his left hand, then bent down again and grabbed one of Mick's feet and dragged him backwards around the bend and out of sight. There was a barely audible thump and Mick's screaming stopped.

Charlie quickly re-appeared, relieved to see that his estimation of Scrab was correct. He hadn't moved a bit. Charlie had taken a risk when he dragged Mick away, leaving Deron and Michelle to fend for themselves. He was glad to know that his mind was still sharp enough for an accurate threat assessment. *Old-timer my ass*, he thought.

"Did you... did you kill 'im?"

"No, but I will if he asks for it again. How about you? Do you wanna take your chances with an 'old-timer'?"

"No, sir. I don't want any trouble. We're just hungry, and Mick... I think taking is the only way he knows."

"How is that possible when the government will pay for a comfortable living and provide everyone with just about anything they could want, including sex. Why would anyone need to take anything from another person in this society?"

"Um... well, we're not from here. We grew up on the island."

"What are you talking about? What island?"

"You know, from the Purge?"

"No, I don't know. What purge? Why don't you fill me in?"

"I don't know the details cuz I wasn't born then, but my ma told me her and my dad were brung to the island on the second wave of the Purge on account of their criminal records and stuff. The first wave got the ones that were in prisons. The second one got the ones who already did their time and got out."

Charlie remembered now that there was a penal colony established some time ago. But he hadn't known that they also colonized people with previous records who weren't incarcerated at the time. But it explained a lot; the drastic drop in the crime rate and the later focus on what would've been considered very trivial crimes; and the disappearances of people that the police never seemed to follow up on.

"You came here from Avalon?"

"Yeah. We grew up on the island, always thinking of a way to escape, and then a few weeks ago, we finally did it."

"How?"

"Mick had a plan for us to see the medical officer. He's real smart, Mick is. We ate soap and leaves and got real sick. When we were being transported, Mick stabbed the guard and after he got our handcuffs off with the guard's keys, he shoved him overboard. He took cuffs off a bunch of other guys and then we took off. The last time I looked back, I saw smoke on the island. We mighta started a revolt. I don't know. We reached the mainland and just kept on going. Till now."

"So you came to California and now you're traveling in the sewer. What for?"

"We heard there's a place where people live with no government."

"A free zone?" Charlie couldn't believe that the rumors had made it as far as the penal colony.

"Yeah. That's what they called it. You know where it is?"

"No. But I've heard of it," Charlie said.

If the free zone was real, and if Charlie could actually find it and get the kids there safely, he figured the price they'd have to pay for living in a completely free society would be to co-exist with the likes of Scrab and Mick. He wondered how crime was handled in such a place – if it existed.

"How come you guys are in the tunnel when you have the life of luxury up above? They say you can buy anything you want, even if you don't have no money. Everybody's rich now. That true?"

"Essentially. As long as you work you can get a subsidy on just about anything. If you don't mind being forever indebted, I suppose you feel like you were rich."

"Then why are you guys down here when it's paradise up there?"

"I wouldn't call it paradise, but whatever. We're looking for something, and we're gonna move on. If we run into you again and your friend hasn't learned his lesson, he won't get a second chance. Do you believe me?"

"Yes, sir. I saw your moves. I know you coulda kilt 'im."

"Come on, kids."

Deron and Michelle got up and stayed close to the wall as they caught up with Charlie. Scrab couldn't take his eyes off Michelle as she walked past him. That cleared away the brief thought Charlie had of inviting him to join them, if he would've been willing to leave Mick behind to fend for himself. But seeing the predatory trance Scrab went into at his first good look at Michelle brought him back to his senses.

They rounded the corner and saw Mick still unconscious lying on the ground. Deron noticed the big knot on the side of his forehead and figured Charlie must've kicked him and knocked him out. As they continued to walk, they remained silent, which was good since Charlie was in a hyper alert state, listening to see if Mick was going to wake up and stupidly try for revenge.

Charlie kept an eye out for a ladder and when he found one, he had better luck than the last time, popping his head into the opening at the top and finding a dark tunnel.

"Back in black," he said aloud, thinking of an old song. He called the kids over and told them to follow him. He'd wait inside the tunnel with the lighter burning.

After crawling again for what felt like nearly an hour, this time through damp muck, they finally emerged into an old industrial park in an abandoned part of town that hadn't been deconstructed yet as part of the effort to centralize all residences and businesses. It was still dark out, but not as dark as before, so they had to hurry. The sun would be up soon and Charlie wanted to be off the street before then.

They walked past buildings with old, faded signs still legible on some of them. *Joe's Paint & Body. Elite Binding. Los Angeles Times.* That one brought back memories. On the wall of the LA Times building, someone had spray-painted, "fuck equality" in green jagged letters. So they weren't the first to pass this way on their way out of town. Charlie noticed that the glass door to the Times building was busted out and he got an idea. He went up to the building and looked inside. It would do.

"I want you guys to wait here while I try to find an exit so I can get an idea of where we are and where we need to go from here."

He went in first and they followed him. He used the lighter to guide them to the nearest long table. Deron turned his back to it and hopped up and Michelle copied him. Charlie gave Deron the lighter, said he'd be back as quick as he could and slowly stepped back to the broken glass door.

Michelle scooted backwards until her back was against the wall. Something touched her forehead and she screamed. Deron instantly lit the lighter and saw that an electrical plug at the end of a dangling power cord from an old radio rested at the same height as her head. He grabbed the end and threw it to the side. It swung back and hit her on the side of the head.

"Ow!"

"Sorry. Sorry! That was really dumb," he said, getting into a standing position, feeling the wall as he rose. He took the offending radio and threw the whole thing this time. It crashed and broke into multiple pieces and then there was silence.

"I'm so tired, Deron. I wish I could just go to bed and forget this night ever happened."

"Me too. I want my old life back. Not that it was all that great or anything, but you know..."

"Yeah. My life wasn't as good as I thought it was either."

"I used to think my life was great, but then everything changed."

"You mean when they took you from the library?"

"Uh... before that, actually."

She didn't ask for further clarification, and he didn't offer any. She just inched over until their sides were touching and said, "Can you flick the light for a second?" He did and she used it to find his hand with hers as she lay against him, silently mouthing the words, "I'm sorry." She wanted to say them out loud, and she would later, but if she did it now, it would be like opening up another wound and she lacked what she needed inside to face that one on top of the others she was already trying to manage.

Charlie was back in twenty minutes, hoping they'd stayed awake. He stopped when he reached the door and called out. "It's me. Are you guys awake?"

"Yeah, Grampa." Deron lit the lighter long enough for Charlie to make it over to the table.

"I've figured out where we are, but now I need to know if you two will be alright waiting here for a few hours. If Emile's willing to help us, I'll send him back to pick you up."

Michelle asked, "Can't we go with you?"

"Well, you could, but the police are looking for three people. I'm less conspicuous by myself, and you guys could probably use some rest."

Deron's yawn said that he concurred. "I could probably sleep for a bit if I can ignore my growling stomach."

"Good. How 'bout you, Michelle? Can you try to take a nap? It'll be good for you and the time will pass without you knowing it."

"Okay."

"Grampa, what if your friend won't help us?"

"I don't know, Deron. We'll have to figure things out as they come. But I'm pretty sure he will, so just think positive and try not to worry. I can be at his house within an hour, and then he can be back here in less than that. So it won't be long."

They watched Charlie take off at a brisk pace. When they couldn't see him anymore, Darren said, "I'm exhausted, but I don't think I can sleep right now.

"I feel the same way. My mind is still trying to figure everything out, but I just wish it would stop. I'm so tired."

Darren sighed and looked around, then he hopped off the table and walked toward the darker part of the building.

Michelle was mildly anxious about being left alone, but he wasn't walking toward the door so she told herself to relax. She heard blow really hard then start coughing in the dust cloud he created. He came back with a stack of papers which he divided into two stacks and put them on the table a foot apart.

"Pillows," he announced. "I'm going to lay down. You're welcome to join me."

A minute later, lying on their backs with their eyes closed, their hands found each other again.

"Deron."

"Yeah?"

"I'm so glad you're here." She tightened her grip on his hand as she spoke.

"I'm glad we're here together," he replied, wishing he could think of something more meaningful to say.

"Really?"

"Really. There's nowhere I'd rather be."

"You're not mad at me for…everything, or anything?"

"Michelle, I don't think I could ever be mad at you."

"But I was so awful to you. I betrayed our friendship and...what might've came after...if..."

"Shh. It's okay. That's in the past, and you didn't do anything wrong. You just had to find your way. And now here we are. So I'm happy."

She sniffed and wiped her eyes with her free arm.

"Michelle, please don't cry. I swear I'm not mad at you. Please don't be upset."

"I'm not upset," she said, crying even more now.

"Then what's wrong?"

"Nothing. I just... I love you, Deron!"

He rolled over to face her and then he kissed her very gently on her mouth as he looked into her eyes.

"I love you, Michelle. I will always love you. No matter what."

Tears rolled down her face as she silently cried with relief and the rekindling of something like joy in her heart.

Deron kissed away her tears and put an arm around her. She put an arm around him and they held each other as they drifted off to sleep, exhausted and in love.

\*\*\*

Forty minutes later, Charlie approached Emile's house as the sun rose and birds chirped. He wished it was still dark, but at least there was a better chance of Emile being awake now. He whistled as he walked down the street, attempting to give the impression that he was out for a morning stroll, enjoying the weather before the sun got too high.

As he approached Emile's door, it opened and a shadow behind the screen door said, "Why if it ain't Corporal–" Charlie shook his head just a little. Emile got the signal and finished, "—Sonofabitch. Come on in and tell me what I can do you for."

The screen door opened and a shaft of light turned the shadow into Emile. Charlie went in and waited for Emile to close the door then he pointed at his ear and then gestured around the room.

"How about some coffee out on the patio, neighbor?"

Charlie raised the pitch of his voice and altered his manner of speech. "That sounds like a fine idea. Don't mind if I do."

"Well, come on in to the kitchen. I'll let you add the cream and sugar. I always forget how much you take, though Lord knows I should have it memorized by now."

Charlie loved how smart Emile was. He picked up immediately that Charlie needed to keep his identity a secret. Odds were against anyone monitoring the audio feed from Emile's house computer, but old Special Forces soldiers never left anything to chance. Charlie mentally relaxed with the certainty that he was in good hands – even if there was nothing Emile could do to help, it lifted his spirits just being in the presence of his old friend. He looked just like he always had, except there were more lines at the corner of his bright eyes, and the color grey had begun a battle with his close-cropped black hair, capturing the territory around his temples. His big welcoming smile hadn't changed a bit though.

On the back patio, Emile whispered that it was safe to talk, but quietly, just in case. Charlie gave him a condensed version of the events of the past twelve hours, skipping most of the details but including enough to make it clear that he was on the run, and he wasn't guilty of committing any actual crimes according to the standards they lived by. He also told Emile about Deron and Michelle and where they were hidden away. Emile said he'd pick them up and have them back in no time.

"There's just one problem," Charlie said. "Michelle has a microchip in her arm and I'm guessing she can be easily scanned on the roads."

"Not a problem," Emile said.

"Are you sure? RFID had over a sixty foot range in the old days. I'm sure it's farther now."

"It is. A lot. But it's also easily blocked."

Emile signaled for Charlie to follow him back inside. He went to a kitchen cabinet and took out a roll of aluminum foil and extracted a long sheet. He folded it into a small square and put it in his back pocket and smiled at Charlie before walking over to the front door.

"Well, thanks for stopping by, neighbor. If you need any help following my instructions on fixing that joist, just let me know and I'll come over and help ya with it."

"Thank you again, Emile. I'll let you know if I need any assistance. See you later."

Emile gestured toward the back door and Charlie headed back to the patio as Emile opened the front door and the screen door, held them for a second, then closed them. He then went back to the patio door and indicated to Charlie that he'd be back in one minute. He went to the hallway leading to the bedrooms and pulled a string down from the ceiling which caused a folded ladder to descend. He lowered it and quietly went up into the attic and came back down a few minutes later and reversed the process.

He returned to the patio carrying a large brimmed floppy hat with a flower on the front and a blue tarp. He gave Charlie a hand signal that no one else would've understood if they'd seen it. Charlie nodded. Emile went back inside and Charlie tiptoed over to a chaise lounge and rested his tired old body. He figured he had time for a twenty or thirty minute nap. Another flashback to his old military days: sleep when you can.

Emile drove to the industrial complex, found the LA Times building and announced himself as a friend of Charlie's as he approached. No one answered, so he came up to the door and knocked on the metal frame causing pieces of broken glass to fall on the concrete floor. He heard motion inside but couldn't see anyone in the light shining through the doorway.

"Hello? It's Emile. Charlie's friend."

"We're in here," Deron replied.

The sleep teens quickly introduced themselves and then Emile told them how he wanted Deron to lie down on the backseat of his SUV and he'd brought a hat for Michelle to wear. Not a great disguise, but enough for the circumstances. He also told them not to talk on the way back or in the house, but to wait until they reached the back patio. And even then to only speak in a whisper.

He unfolded the aluminum foil and wrapped it around Michelle's arm close to her wrist. Deron got in the back of the SUV and Emile covered him with the tarp. He and Michelle got in the front and Emile turned on the stereo, singing along with turn-of-the-century oldies as he drove.

Several minutes later Emile parked in his garage and led them through the house and out onto the patio. They smiled when they saw Charlie asleep on the lounge chair. Emile walked over to him and gently lifted Charlie's hand that was hanging over the side of the chair.

Charlie's eyes flew open, but then he relaxed when he saw Emile, Deron, and Michelle smiling at him.

## Fifty

The four of them sat around the patio table eating breakfast while Charlie filled Emile in on the rest of what had happened to all of them and the predicaments they were in.

"So, what are you planning now?" Emile asked.

Charlie hesitated to answer. He felt like what he wanted to ask was possibly going to make him look foolish. But he had no options, so he went for it.

"Have you heard anything about free zones?"

Keeping his voice just above a whisper, Emile said that he had.

"Well, finding one is about our only hope."

"You've always been lucky, Charlie, and once again, your luck is in. I know for a fact that there's one nearby. They're literally underground, so I don't know exactly where it's at, but I can get you close."

"So they *are* real."

"You bet your ass. There are some people who just can't live under the government's thumb. If I knew right where to go, I'd be on my way, but I guess it's easier to live with material comfort than it is to give up everything for a dream – especially if there's no certainty of making it come true."

"I know what you mean. I would've gladly dumped everything I have to live free if I had known they were real and where to go. But I couldn't have left Deron behind. Now that he's in the same boat with me, we have nothing to lose."

"Hey, where's Feenix?"

Charlie dropped the slice of bacon he had just picked up and looked at his friend. Then he looked over Deron and lowered his eyes.

"She passed away a few days ago."

"I'm sorry, man. I thought that dog would live forever."

"She seemed like she was going to. She went way past the average for her breed. But I guess it's best that she did, considering everything that's happened."

Deron struggled not to cry at this news, which on top of everything else was just too much for him to take. To his surprise, he found himself thinking about his mom and missing her too. He pressed his lips together, trying to keep control, but he lost it when Michelle went to comfort him by reaching for his hand.

Everyone was silent for a moment as Deron struggled to regain his composure. He squeezed his eyes shut for a few seconds, swallowed, then said, "I'm going to miss Feenix. She was the best."

Charlie nodded. Emile wanted to change the subject. This was too depressing. He glanced around the table to see everyone's progress with their breakfast.

"Anyone need more to eat?"

Deron and Michelle declined and thanked him for the offer. Charlie said he was just about stuffed as he finished off his scrambled eggs.

Emile got up and took his coffee with him as he walked onto the lawn and lit a cigarette away from the kids who were still eating. Deron told Michelle he'd be back in a few minutes and followed Emile, asking the older man if he could spare a smoke.

Michelle looked at Charlie with a measure of hope in her eyes and asked, "Will your friend take us to this free zone place, Mr. Young?"

"I think he'll take us as close as he can. And then it's up to us. I can't promise we'll even find it, but we can sure as hell try. Deron and I don't have any other options at this point. But you still do. Say the word and I'm sure Emile will drive you back home."

Michelle pushed the food around on her plate, thinking. Then she said, "There are things I'll miss in my life, but I feel like I'm where I belong and this is the right thing to do."

"What about your parents?"

"Honestly? I think they'll act like they're all concerned but they'll be secretly pleased to be free of the burden I am to them."

"I can't imagine anyone thinking of you as a burden, Michelle."

"I can," she said, looking down at her hands in her lap.

Charlie's heart felt like it was breaking for the poor girl. Looking at the crusted blood on her face made it even worse. She and Deron were good kids and were entitled to have good lives. He vowed that they would never feel unloved or unworthy. He would die if that's what it took to prevent anyone from ever harming either of them again.

Emile came back to the patio with Deron trailing behind him, looking tired but hopeful.

"Charlie, I don't know if the cops will find a link between us, but we should assume that they will, and that they'll do it quickly. I think everyone should take a very quick shower, and in the meantime, I'll pull my truck into the garage and act like I'm detailing it. Then we'll slip you guys into the back and I'll drive you as far as I can into the mountains without being too suspicious."

"Sounds like a plan. I can't thank you enough for everything you're doing. You know if our roles were reversed..."

"Don't mention it, amigo. You saved my life in the riots. This is nothing."

"Maybe so, but I wasn't risking anything at the time. I just came up behind them."

"But still," Emile said, thinking back to one of the ugliest events in American history.

***

Adams couldn't believe he'd been fucked over again by McMannis. All he had to do was catch an old man and two kids. It should've been a piece of cake. With the old man being armed, it would have made for a great arrest. He would've been the top story on the news. He might've gotten his long overdue promotion.

There was really nowhere for them to run. They had to have been heading for the free zone, and it would've been easy to intercept them if he'd been allowed to do his job. But the captain had ordered a search of the neighborhoods only to the south of the freeway. When they failed to locate them, the captain declared the search over. Adams had been sent home and told to forget about it.

If they had been able to catch them, they would have exiled them. As it was, they had probably gone to the mountains and were as good as self-exiled. But Adams couldn't let it go and he was still thinking of a way to catch the armed bastard that had eluded him.

Even if he was immediately allowed back on the job and if there was a chance to catch the fugitives, he would not be given approval to take a taskforce into the wilderness. The last time the police tried that, they lost too many officers. The drones were unable to provide air support and the free-zoners were scattered throughout the woods, and were extremely proficient with their weapons. It had been like going up against an invisible army.

His only hope would be to catch them before they got too far into the mountains. But how could he do that? He'd have to go in on his own, driving his own vehicle and hoping to find them just walking down the street, unescorted by the armed anti-government radicals.

Adams got an idea. He jumped up and ran to his car. He got inside, shut the door and said, "City Hall." As the car drove him to work, he made several phone calls.

## Fifty-one

Deron and Charlie had both fallen asleep. Michelle would have liked to also, but she lay next to Deron with her eyes wide open. She watched as the view outside one of the back windows changed from all blue sky to tree tops and leaves. Endless leaves. She'd never been so far away from the city before and she was entranced by the sight of so many trees. To her, it was like they were entering an enchanted wonderland.

After a while, the hum of the tires on the road and the unchanging scenery lulled her into a relaxed and sleepy state. As she started to drift off, she scratched at her wrist where the edge of the aluminum foil made it itch.

Charlie had changed into some of Emile's clothes before they left. Deron could only take advantage of a shirt since Emile's pants were too short in length and large in the waist. Michelle was still wearing the outfit she'd left her house in, with the dirt and grime from the sewers etched into her knees.

As far as Emile could tell, they were far enough out of the city that there were no more cameras, nor were there any light or power poles to attach them to. He considered that there could be cameras hidden in the trees, but he hadn't spotted any yet, and he was constantly looking for them whenever he could take his eyes off the winding road that took them up into the San Bernardino National Forest.

Although the government formally denied the existence of free zones, they knew they were out there, but Emile assumed they must not care too much about them because they didn't go all out to find them and eradicate them. Maybe they'd figured that anyone who wanted to live off the land so badly was better off not having to be monitored in the cities. He wondered what the authorities thought of him driving this far out of town, past the last monitoring camera.

The more he thought about it, the more nervous he became. He was anxious to offload his passengers, grab some plants, and head back. As an amateur horticulturist, he intended to explain his brief trip to the forest as a plant gathering excursion if he was stopped on the way back, or questioned about it later.

He finally pulled over, justifying his actions by telling himself he had no idea how far into the woods they needed to go to find a path to the free zone, so it would be better to drop them off too soon rather than too late. The rumor was, if you walked through the mountains, they'd find you – if they wanted to.

One story went that a group of five had hiked through the mountains and at some point were knocked out somehow. When they awoke, there were only three of them in their group. They traveled all the way to Big Bear Lake where they tried to survive in the ruins of the old resort town until eventually they gave up and returned to the Orange County metropolis between the mountains and the Pacific ocean. It was assumed that the two missing members were somehow granted membership in the free zone community since they were never heard from again.

No one knew for sure if the story was true. It might have been made up and spread around just to see if anyone would try heading for the mountains; a government ruse to detect malcontents who hadn't already been spotted by database records and behavior analysis.

Charlie woke when the vehicle slowed down and left the pavement. He shook Deron's shoulder. "Wake up, son. I think this is our stop."

Emile had pulled off the road and driven a few yards into the forest floor where a group of wildflowers swayed in the breeze. He went around to the rear of the vehicle and opened the back door. Charlie and Deron crawled out with the backpacks Emile had loaded up for them.

"Oh no," Michelle cried.

Everyone turned to look at her and saw her pulling the aluminum foil back into place. "Do you think...?"

"Don't worry," Charlie said. "Nothing out here can scan you. Look around," he said, smiling.

Rays of light beamed down between the branches and leaves. Michelle thought it looked magical. She was tired of sitting in the car, and tired overall, but she was smiling as she looked at the forest and stretched her back muscles. She took deep breaths through her nose, relishing the scent.

Emile reached into the back of the SUV and pulled out the small duffel bag he'd packed for Michelle. He had almost nothing to offer her in the way of clothes, so it was loaded with some toiletries, snacks, and some light camping supplies.

He wished he could've provided them with a handgun. They might've been able to use it for hunting as well as self-defense, but Emile had officially turned over all of his guns when they began enforcement of the firearms ban. He couldn't risk getting pulled over with a gun in the vehicle.

"Anything special about this spot, like a hidden trail or anything?" Charlie asked him.

"No. As far as I know, you just stick to the road. I don't know if they have cameras or humans watching, but apparently, they'll see you, and if they like what they see, they'll make themselves known – one way or another." Emile didn't mention that an encounter might include being knocked unconscious if it went well, and being killed if it didn't. Maybe Charlie had heard the same story he had.

"Well, unless you decide to join us someday, I guess this is it."

"I think I'll be along after I finish a few projects. Sure would be nice if you could call though."

"If there's any chance at all, you know I will."

"I'm sure there's no chance. They're not connected to the communications network, and a radio signal would be picked up."

"Yeah, I guess you're right," Charlie conceded. "Hey, thanks again, for everything, Emile."

The two men shook hands then came together for a hug. Watching them, Deron and Michelle grasped each other's hands.

"I gotta grab some plants and get outta here. You guys should get movin'. Driving past the last highway camera probably triggered some kind of alert. If someone shows up, we want them to think I was alone."

"Thanks again, bud!" Charlie picked up the duffel bag from the ground near the back of the truck. "Let's go, kids!"

***

Getting Jacey out of jail was easier than Adams thought it would be. All he had to do was enter into the computer that he had taken custody of her and after that, he had no trouble getting her past every sensor in the jail and right out into the parking lot. Apparently his suspended status didn't block his access at all. They'd probably change that later, after they found out what he'd done.

The next phase of his plan went easily too. He took Jacey over to the Electronics Department and had one of the E.D. techs embed a GPS tracker in her underwear.

Getting her to part with her underwear was a little difficult, but when presented with the option of staying out of her cell without even knowing why, or going back to it, she liked being out better.

The last part involved lying, and it was the only hard part of the plan. Jacey was completely unwilling to be the bait that would help Adams catch Deron's grandfather. At first he tried reasoning with her. Charlie Young was a murderer. Did she really want a murderer running free?

She didn't know if that was true though, and if she had to put her trust in something she didn't know personally, she was not inclined to believe a cop. And if it *was* true? Well, that wasn't her responsibility. Deron had done everything she'd asked to help her get free, so her loyalty was with him.

Failing that approach, that's when Adams decided he needed to lie. While it was true that Jacey had been kicked out of the rehabilitation program and had been charged as an accessory to an assault on federal employees, he didn't know what they had planned for her. But he told her she would be convicted and sent to Avalon where she probably wouldn't last long since every violent person the Orange County Police Force had ever encountered was now at Avalon. Every violent offender that had once been in prison was there. There were very few guards, and the ones who were assigned rotation there really didn't care what the prisoners did to each other. That part was true at least.

He didn't tell her that women were housed separately from men. And when he told her the murder rate among prisoners, that's when he knew he'd gotten her attention.

"You probably won't be killed though. At least not on purpose."

"Will I be in protective custody or something?"

"No. You'll be a sex toy. Come to think of it, I guess you *will* have some protection. Whoever ends up owning you will protect you from those who want to own you. But they'll probably rent you out as well." He let that sink in for a few minutes and then she spoke up.

"What is it exactly you need me to do?"

"I just need you to find Deron. If you find him, then you'll find his grandfather. I'll give you a chip scanner and all you have to do is walk down the road. If you pick up a signal, you alert me by pressing on the tracker in your waistband."

"That's it? If you find Deron's grandfather, will you let Deron go free?"

"Can't do that. He's a fugitive from the law."

"But he's just like me. He never did anything except for daring to be himself. Why is that such a crime?"

"It's not about that. I don't care what the feds do in their mind control labs. I want Deron because he's an accessory to kidnapping."

"I don't believe you."

"If you find him, you'll see for yourself. I'm sure they still have the girl with them."

As Jacey thought about what Adams was saying and tried to figure out how she could help him catch Charlie while coming up with a way for Deron to get away, Adams brought the car to a stop.

"Why are we stopping?" she asked, a little bit alarmed.

"We need one more person on our team — if he'll agree to help. I'll be back shortly. Sit tight."

Adams got out of the car and locked it to respond to his voice only. He walked up a residential driveway, following the sidewalk that led to the front door. He knew he'd have already been seen on the security cam and the house would've announced his arrival, but he announced himself anyway.

"Sergeant McKenzie Adams. Orange County Police Force. I need to speak to Jim right away."

"Please wait while the occupant is summoned," the autohost responded.

Ten seconds later Jim McMannis opened the door and asked, "What the hell do you want?"

"A fresh start and a Hail Mary. Can we talk?"

Twenty minutes later, Adams, McMannis, and Jacey were headed toward the San Bernardino mountains at sixty-five miles per hour which was the maximum speed electronically governed by highway sensors.

"You realize they might not even be in the mountains and this could be a huge waste of time."

"I told you, the girl's last known location was at the last sensor before the end of the county line heading up into the hills."

"They could already be long gone for all we know."

"Could be. Or we'll catch 'em and come back to town as heroes. Like cops in the old days, going out and arresting real live criminals who are actually dangerous."

"Even better if we snatch them right out of the fuckin' free zone. We'll be legends. That's the only reason I'm agreeing to this."

The unlikely partners looked at each other, then Adams said, "I don't want a run-in with those crazy fuckers, but if that's the way the story goes in the news, I won't bother correcting 'em."

"How do we know where to drop the bait?" McMannis asked.

"I did a lot of math based on the last scan of the Granger kid, the time the same vehicle was spotted heading back into the city, and the approximate speed three people would be walking. The impossible part is estimating how long they woulda walked before calling it a night. So it's an extremely rough estimate."

"That's putting it mildly."

"Worst case, we enjoy some nature and go back saying we worked out our differences and try to get our jobs back."

"That'd be worth it," McMannis said.

The two of fell silent and Jacey stared out the window, determined to find a way out of this new trap she found herself in.

A short while later, they pulled in to a scenic turnout and parked the car as far off the mountain highway as possible. Adams booted up his slate and launched the tracker software. A blue dot sat right on top of a small black square on the display. He had Jacey locate the tracker and press it. When she did, the blue dot turned red and radiated outward before turning back to a blue dot again. He repeated his earlier instructions and asked if she understood what she needed to do.

"Walk down the road, and send a signal when I see them. A retard could do this," she spat.

"Then get going. And if you find them, you better not be a retard, or it's your ass, in more ways than one," McMannis said.

## Fifty-two

They had been walking for hours, only taking a short break once in a while to have a few sips of water. When the sun went down, it was much colder than they had expected, but Emile knew it would be cold and he'd packed the best he could – one hooded long-sleeved sweater for each of them.

Charlie began looking for a place to sleep when it started getting dark, but he didn't know what he was looking for exactly. Some place far enough from the road, but not so far into the woods that they could get lost, or be in danger from wild animals.

When he spotted a clearing to the right, they walked over for a closer look. It was visible from the road, but far enough away that anyone would have a hard time spotting them at night unless they knew what they were looking for.

They ate a meal of beef jerky and more water than they'd allowed themselves during the day since they could hear a stream nearby and knew they could refill their canteens in the morning. They did not build a fire for warmth, and all three of them were too exhausted for much conversation.

Charlie showed them how to unfold their space blanket sleeping bags, spread them out, and carefully slip inside without tearing them. They all fell asleep quickly despite the lack of comfort lying on the forest floor without even a bed of leaves.

Just before dawn, Charlie awoke to the sound of footsteps and couldn't believe his eyes when he saw a teenaged girl walking toward their camp. His mind wanted to say that it could only be Michelle, but there was no way in hell that she could've cut her hair, dyed it purple, and arranged it in spikes while he had slept.

He was surprised to the point of being speechless and was grateful that she spoke first.

"Hi. I'm sorry to wake you, but is that Deron?" she asked, pointing at a sleeping form under the shiny silver material.

"Who are you, and how did you possibly know to look for him here?"

Charlie felt a surge of alarm ripple through his frame. Deron couldn't have told her in advance about coming here because he hadn't even known.

"I didn't know – but I hoped," she said.

Deron and Michelle awoke from the conversation and Deron sat up, startled.

"Jacey!? What are you doing here?"

"Who's Jacey?" Michelle asked innocently, but afraid of the answer she might receive.

"She helped me escape from the center we were in, but we split up in the air vents and I haven't seen her since. How did you get here?"

"I hitched a ride for most of the way, and I've been walking since then. I'm glad I found you. It'll be nice to have some company. Walking alone through the woods really sucks."

Charlie slid out of his bag and quickly folded it back into a five inch square and tucked it into his backpack.

"You asked for Deron by name as if you expected to find him here. How is that possible? No one knew he'd be here, including him."

"I was on the run going in this direction so I thought there was a chance he might have also. People escaping the city usually come this way hoping to find the free zone. That's what I'm doing anyway. Aren't you?"

Again, Charlie felt ill at ease with the coincidence and he wasn't sure if he was able to think objectively or if he was being paranoid. When people talked about the free zone in southern California, reference was always made to "the mountains." Charlie had never heard anything specific regarding the road they were on that led toward Big Bear Lake until Emile told him this was the best intel he'd picked up over the years. And now, someone who Deron met in a government facility had met up with them on the same road they were on. But if it wasn't just a coincidence, he didn't know what else it could be. If the police knew their location and brought Jacey to them, why wouldn't they have just arrested them and taken Michelle home?

Charlie felt that it was impossible to tackle this mystery so early in the morning without the benefit of some coffee. He told the kids to find a tree to take care of their business, then they'd fill up their canteens and be on their way. He welcomed Jacey to their group but the mystery of her arrival wouldn't stop gnawing at him.

As they walked that day, the three teens engaged in conversations about their former concerns, goals, and problems. They speculated on what it would be like to live without electricity and they listed the things they'd miss from their former lives.

Charlie tossed ideas around in his mind and tried to come up with explanations for Jacey's appearance – other than the one she gave. He finally decided that when they went to sleep, he'd go through her backpack and look for anything suspicious like a communicator. He knew if he found something like that, particularly a sat-com which was the only thing that would work out here, he'd know she was a plant. But if she was, what would he do about it? What could he do?

At the end of another long day of walking through the trees and listening to the birds and the teens, Charlie began seeking a place to stop for the night. He was concerned that there might not be any water nearby. He hadn't heard the sound of any streams since the one they'd left this morning.

He tried looking past what he could easily see at the sides of the roads, looking deeper into the woods for any clearings when suddenly Michelle cried out and stopped walking. He went toward her just as she began to fall, then he felt a stinging sensation in his neck and as he went to lower her to the ground, he collapsed to his knees. The last thing he saw as he toppled over was Deron crumpling to the ground as if he'd suddenly decided he was going to sit down on his butt in the middle of the street.

Eight dark figures dressed head to toe in black emerged from the woods onto the road. They lifted the bodies in pairs and flitted back into the woods with them like thieving shadows.

# Fifty-three

Deron was the first to wake up. He felt like he was floating and he heard the sound of water and the smell of kerosene. He opened his eyes and saw a rocky surface all around him. Orange flame flickered to his left. He turned and saw a figure in black holding a torch. Other dark figures sat silently. Charlie and Michelle were lying beside him.

He slid his hand to the right along a wooden surface that only extended a few inches. He lowered his hand and felt water. He was at the back end of a wooden raft. It occurred to him that he could easily fall off into the water. What the hell was going on? He sat up.

"Where am I? Who are you?"

One of the dark figures looked at Deron and said, "Let me ask you a question first. Where was your group headed?"

Deron didn't know at first if he should answer. He wished Charlie was awake to deal with this. He was sure Charlie would know what to do. He tried to analyze the situation the way he assumed that Charlie would have. They were on a raft, inside something that looked like a river in a long cave-like tunnel. If these were cops, they would've loaded them into police vehicles or maybe even a helicopter. He concluded that there'd be no harm in telling the truth.

"We were traveling away from the city hoping to find the free zone."

"Congratulations. You've found it. Sort of.

"What does that mean?

"That means you're as close as you can get without actually being there. But the good news is, you might make it the rest of the way."

"Does that also mean that I might not?"

"We don't grant access to just anybody who comes along. When we saw you, we figured you might be looking for us, so we're bringing you in for a screening. We're in constant need of new members."

"I can't say I like your welcoming committee," Michelle said, surprising everyone that she had been awake and listening. "Where's Jacey? That girl that was with us."

The man with the torch answered. "That's an odd way to describe her – 'that girl.' How long have you known her?"

"We just met her yesterday. Well, except for Deron. He knew her a few days before that."

"So she just showed up suddenly in the middle of the forest and introduced herself?" the man asked.

"Yes. She literally did."

"That makes sense. She had a GPS tracker sewed into her underwear."

"What the hell?" Deron couldn't believe it. "What does that mean?"

"It means the feds put her onto you, probably hoping to find us."

"But how could they... I don't understand. Where is she now?"

"We'll talk about that later. For now, let's get off this raft and talk about you guys."

Deron felt the raft suddenly tug to his right. He tilted left into Michelle who toppled over onto Charlie, waking the old man with an oomph as her hand came down on his stomach. Charlie jolted up and asked what was going on, thinking he must be in a dream. A crazy dream brought on by exhaustion.

"These are free zone people, Grampa. They want to talk to us."

Charlie tried to shake the sleep out of his head and saw a black gloved hand reaching for him to help him up and off of the raft. He took the hand, and stepped into shallow water, then onto sand. Several torches lit up a large cave with orange fire light that cast dancing shadows. In addition to Deron and Michelle, he counted ten other people sitting in various places on the sand. Dressed all in black, they almost blended into the cave walls with only their hands and faces visible.

"This is it? The free zone is ten guys in a cave?" Charlie asked in disbelief.

A few of the men laughed and one said, "We'll be twelve guys and a girl if we admit you to the club." More of them joined in the laughter.

Charlie wasn't seeing the humor in the situation. He looked around, needing to get away and collect his thoughts. He could make sense of nothing. Passing out on the road, then waking up in a river, and now sitting in a cave with these men. Too much was happening too quickly.

"Would anyone happen to have a cigarette?" he asked. It had been some time since he'd had one, but if ever there was a time to resurrect an old bad habit, he felt this was it.

One of the men pulled a small bag out of an inner breast pocket, loosened the tie string, then put a pinch of tobacco into a small strip of paper and rolled a cigarette. He stretched his hand toward Charlie who walked over and gratefully took it.

Another man offered Charlie his torch. When he took it and lit it, he saw that the cigarette was covered with small words. *Beareth all things, believeth all things, hopeth all things, endureth all things.* The tobacco had been rolled into a strip cut from a page out of a bible. He lit the cigarette and handed the torch back.

"Thank you," he said and sat down, anticipating a head rush.

Deron asked if he could also have one and the friendly man in black rolled another. As Deron and Charlie enjoyed the unusual tobacco one of the men came over and sat near them, introducing himself.

"I'm Victor M.," he said, extending his hand.

"Charles Young. Charlie. And this is my grandson Deron, and his friend, Michelle."

"It's nice to meet all of you, and I'm sorry about the way we approached you, but it's a necessary precaution. The government would prefer to have absolute control over everyone, so our existence is a slap in the face to their authority and dominion. Officially, they claim we don't exist. But unofficially, they'd love to eradicate us. We're fortunate that they don't try too hard. The majority of their resources are reserved for controlling the population within their borders, so we're something of a wishlist item for them."

"Is this why they haven't found you yet — because you live in a cave?"

"Partly, yes. We're actually spread out all across the state. All over the forest around Big Bear Lake and further east in a variety of places. There's not one central location where we're gathered."

"Not even a central governing committee?"

"Some things we can't reveal to you. You're still outsiders at the present moment, and that brings us to the purpose of this rendezvous. Deron says you were looking to join us. Tell us your story — how you ended up in a position to leave civilization behind and seek out a legend."

Charlie told them the whole story, leaving out none of their crimes. A society based on fugitives and outcasts was bound to have its fair share of people who had run afoul of the law, so he didn't fear exclusion on those grounds. He was more concerned about what contribution the three of them would be able to make. And that's exactly what Victor wanted to know after hearing Charlie's story.

"What can your group do for ours if you were to become members?"

Charlie considered this a moment. "I don't know how valuable it would be, but Deron is really good at reading and writing. He'd be good at studying a subject if you have books on it, and then sharing what he learned with others in an easy to understand way. He's really good with words. I've only just recently met Michelle, so she'll have to let you know what skills she has. As for myself, I'm ex Special Forces with plenty of weapons training, some rusty wilderness survival skills, and I have experience in masonry, carpentry, plumbing and general handyman work."

"Charlie," Victor said, "I think your skillset alone will cover your small group."

The word "group" reminded Charlie of something he'd been curious about since he got off the raft.

"Where's Jacey? The purple-haired girl who was traveling with us."

"She was taken to another location."

Charlie just looked at him confused and waited for a more detailed answer.

"She was bugged, Grandpa."

Charlie looked at Victor. "Is that true?"

"Yes, she may not have known it but she was wearing a tracker. We removed it and took her to another location where she'll wake up and be questioned extensively to determine if she was knowingly working for the government or not."

"We woke up this morning and she just appeared at our campsite. Are you saying the government knew where we were all along and put her onto us?"

"That's very possible, and sounds most likely but I don't have any details at this time. Considering that she and Deron escaped this new program they're using to brainwash children, it would seem that she was caught, recruited, then brought right to you. I'd like to think she was coerced and isn't a willing rat."

"What if she is?" Charlie couldn't help but ask.

"Then she'll be exterminated," Victor said plainly.

"So, what about us?" Michelle wanted to know, not really concerned about whether or not Deron would get his purple-haired friend back.

"That depends on you. We have to assume you were tracked before your friend with the hair arrived. Are any of you chipped?"

Charlie and Deron shook their heads. Michelle turned white and nodded.

"Oh, shit. Emile and I didn't even think of that. We've probably led them right here to you. You should all get out of here while you still can." Charlie had lost hope for him and the kids.

"Relax, Charlie," Victor said. "The signal range in Identi-Chips is very short. They were never designed for long-range tracking. Personal Communicators on the other hand, were. So we're safe, depending on how far away they've been tracking your friend from."

"So I'm okay then?" Michelle asked hopefully.

"Presumably, but we still can't take chances. We're willing to bring you in, but it will require the removal of your chip. I wish I could say it won't hurt, but it will. And we have to do it here. We don't have hospitals or clinics."

"Forget it, Michelle. We'll find somewhere else to live. I won't—"

"Do it," she said. "I've been through worse already this week, and this is actually my choice and it's for a good cause."

"Michelle," Deron started to protest.

"It's okay, Deron. I want it out of me anyway. I never wanted it in the first place, but my parents said it would make me safer." She looked at Victor. "I'm ready."

Victor nodded at a young man named Alex who walked over to the water and dipped his knife into it, rubbing it on both sides. He came back, picked up a torch and held the knife in the flame, turning it from side to side.

"Come over here and lie down." He held the blade in the flame.

After a minute, Alex laid her arm out at a forty-five degree angle from her body, with her wrist close to the torch sticking out of the sand. He pressed his fingertips in the flesh at the base of her palm and slid them slowly up her arm. After two such passes, he said, "Got it," and kept one finger on the spot. He held his knife over the spot and said, "It won't be too bad, but it'll hurt like a bitch for a while. Are you ready?"

She nodded and closed her eyes as tight as she could. "Go ahead."

Deron came over and held her free hand. When the knife tip punctured her skin, she winced and gripped Deron's hand tightly. Alex pushed the tip in another eighth of an inch and got it behind the microchip, lifting it up and pushing it out through the incision. He quickly placed his thumb over the cut.

"Michelle, you're gonna want to put your thumb where mine is and hold it there until the bleeding stops."

She let go of Deron's hand and put her thumb next to Alex's. "Okay." He removed his, and hers took its place. "That wasn't as bad as I thought it was going to be."

"Most things aren't," Alex said and went away to wash his knife.

"Now what?" Charlie asked.

Victor smiled. "Now I think you'll make a fine addition to the group. If you'll just agree to the few but vital rules we have, we'll take you to one of our residential dens and setup temporary quarters."

The rules were pretty simple. For the sake of the group's survival in all California locations, a man named Harrison Smith was essentially their dictator. But he was benevolent and not at all power-hungry. He had to exercise total authority because there just wasn't the time or practical ability to have a democratic underground society. Harrison gave orders, and everyone followed them. If they didn't understand them, or didn't agree with them at the time, the rule was to obey first, and ask questions later. Smith could grant temporary proxy powers to anyone at any time and that person spoke with the same authority as he did.

Otherwise, the rest was easy. Everyone made a contribution in whatever way they could. Contact with anyone outside the group was forbidden except for missions such as this one, which only a select few engaged in. And then there was the primary directive: Do Not Be Seen.

They had camps and enclaves underground, in caves, and in canopied forests. Victor assured them that life wasn't spent entirely in artificial light in dark places. They were slowly building cabins under tree canopies, and they swam in lakes, rode sleds in the snow, played in the forest, and so on, but at all times, they were vigilant. During outdoor activities, there were always a few people assigned to guard duty. If they gave a signal, everyone instantly obeyed no matter what.

"If you're in the middle of takin' a piss in the sun and you hear a particular bird call, you take cover, even if that means pissing all over the place while you run."

Deron and Michelle laughed. Some of the men smiled. One said, "It's happened."

Victor continued. "It's funny, but it's also dead serious. The penalty for disobedience that could result in the discovery of any residential group is dire."

"Is that penalty the same one Jacey will have if she was working for the government?" Deron asked.

"It is," Victor replied. "We don't like it any more than you do, but it's for the survival of every one of us – you included, if you agree to the rules."

Charlie looked at Deron and Michelle. They nodded. He turned back to Victor.

"We're in. Thank you for having us."

"Welcome to the underground, Charlie, Deron, and Michelle. We're glad to have you among us."

The men got up, came over to them, introduced themselves and shook their hands. As they did so, each of them removed their hoods so their faces could be seen more clearly. One of the men turned out to be a woman. Michelle smiled when she saw her long blonde hair in a ponytail when the hood came off.

## Fifty-four

They all rode out of the river tunnel on two rafts back into the moonlight. Some of the men connected the rafts to ropes that were part of a pulley system so they could be pulled back to the other end of the tunnel.

"From here we walk," Victor said.

"About how far?" Charlie asked.

"It's about a mile back to the road, then we'll cross it, go over the guard rail and rappel down to a tunnel that goes in about a half mile before it opens up into a cavern."

"Like the one you questioned us in?" Deron asked.

Victor and several of the other men laughed.

"This one's more like Grand Central Station."

Deron and Michelle had no idea what that meant. Charlie couldn't believe it was true, but he knew they had no reason to lie, and they'd definitely been living somewhere unnoticed all these years.

The walk through the mountain forest went slowly and it was still dark when they reached the highway. Victor looked both ways through binoculars, then held up one hand signaling for the others to wait. He crossed the highway quickly by himself first, then on the other side standing in front of the guardrail he pulled his binoculars out again to scan from his new vantage point. He gave the

All Clear signal for the others to join him then part of his head flew off and he toppled backwards over the guardrail and down a few hundred feet into a ravine.

Someone yelled, "Down!" and most of them hit the ground, rolled and came up with their pistols drawn. Charlie, Deron and Michelle ran back to the woods they'd just emerged from. The team on the ground had no targets and didn't know where the shot that killed Victor had come from.

They started to sniper crawl backwards toward cover when one of them men cried out. "I'm hit!" Several of the men saw the suppressed muzzle flash and began shooting into the trees to the west. Two men grabbed the man who was hit and carried him to the woods where Charlie was standing in the open.

"Where's your gun?" Charlie asked.

"In the street," the wounded man replied.

Charlie ran for the street. Deron yelled for him to come back. Charlie ran behind the men who were now backing into the cover of trees, still firing to the west as they did so. He dropped when he reached the asphalt and shots were fired at him. He rolled a few times before coming to a stop on his side with a pistol in his hand and one leg sticking out at an odd angle.

Deron screamed, "Nooo!" and a hand clamped over his mouth.

"You're giving us away, kid!" a man hissed at him from behind, then pulled him deeper into the woods, following the rest of the retreating team.

McMannis had been grazed by a shot that scraped the top of his head. Blood was steadily rolling into his eyes and down his face.

"Goddamn this stings like a motherfucker."

"You should try this," Adams said, holding one hand over a wound high on his chest near his shoulder.

"At least we got the old fucker. And I bet a few of them freezoners are hurtin' too."

"I've always heard what badasses they're supposed to be, but they all just turned rabbit against two little old cops."

"Let's roll that bastard out of the street. If someone runs him over, we might have trouble proving that the roadkill was our fugitive. Then let's get us a fucking ambulance so we can go home and be heroes, all blood-covered and everything."

"Fuck you, I'm really wounded. Look at this," Adams said as he started unbuttoning his shirt to get a better look at his wound. McMannis stopped to look and that was the moment Charlie had been waiting for. Neither man was looking at him as he fired six shots in three seconds. Two to each man's chest, and one to their heads.

Charlie got up, ran over to them and grabbed their guns, ammo, and communicators then ran toward the woods to catch up with the others.

# Epilogue

Fourteen months later, Michelle had a baby. There were no drugs or medicines, but the midwife knew methods that made birthing easier than it typically was in hospitals. She named her baby girl Novata Young and couldn't wait to dress her in clothes that she had learned to make for her.

Charlie worked at various jobs in multiple camps in California and Nevada. He wasn't present for the birth of Novata as he was currently on an assignment near Lake Tahoe and wasn't expected back for months. His skills in hand-to-hand combat and wilderness survival were in high demand and he hadn't felt so productive or valued in a long time.

Kathleen suspected that Deron, Charlie and Michelle were together, but she couldn't imagine how such a thing was possible. When she first saw the news reports of Charlie being wanted for murder, she didn't believe it. Charlie was bad, but not that kind of bad. It made no sense. Why would Charlie kill someone at Michelle's house?

Eric stopped calling her, saying it was a conflict of interest and new agents came to her house weekly, asking if she'd seen or heard from Deron. They believed her when she said she hadn't, and stopped coming after a few months. She missed her son, but resigned herself to the fact that he was like her father, and was probably happy with him, wherever they were.

Stanley and Barbara Kolnick returned from France immediately upon being informed of their daughter's disappearance. However, as far as their friends and associates could tell, they were far more obsessed with the fact that a man was killed inside their home than with their missing daughter. They were constantly expressing their fear that someone must've been targeting them and said they feared for their safety. Such fears did not however put a damper on their social schedule. They rarely mentioned Michelle, to each other, or anyone else.

Jacey's GPS tracker was removed and embedded in a small chunk of ground venison which was fed to a crow which was then shot at with a BB gun sending it off in panicked flight.

When the police captain found out from E.D. what Adams had done, he called the surveillance officer who was monitoring Jacey's whereabouts and asked for an update.

"She was last seen flying over the San Bernardino National Forest, possibly heading toward San Diego, sir."

After an extensive interview with Jacey, she was told she was free to go. When she left the men who had held her, she began making her way further east, not knowing where she was going. Another team three miles away encountered her and granted her admission to the community, convinced that she was not working for the government. She later became a hair stylist, eventually learning how to dye hair naturally. She also formed a close friendship with Deron and Michelle who forgave her for her coerced betrayal.

Emile came through the mountains two years later driving a small moving van. He had parked it as deep into the woods as he could, then made his way back to the road and walked for a day before he was taken at night. When he awoke in the cave by the river and gained Alex's trust and thus admission to the free zone, he told them where his truck was, and what was in it. He'd been hoarding supplies for years. Among them were alcohol, coffee, cigarettes, chocolate bars, firearms with thousands of rounds of homemade ammo for each type, batteries, kerosene, stick matches, and the list went on.

Alex wondered if it was a trap, but he felt that Emile was telling the truth. He gave himself the job of scouting the area and looking inside the back of the truck. He wouldn't delegate the risk to anyone else. When he returned the following day, he instructed as many men as he could to retrieve the supplies. It was like Christmas for the free zone.

Deron became a teacher, responsible for teaching children how to read and write. The free zone community had very few traditional books, but their library was growing slowly with homemade books with ink and parchment they had learned to make. The production of materials was slow, and each time Deron obtained more, he wrote in a journal that he planned to add to the group's library one day. He also wrote stories based on books he had read, with as much detail as he could recall.

He was in love with the rustic life he lived with his beautiful wife Michelle, and now he was thrilled that he had a family of his own. He missed his mother at times, but he missed Charlie even more and couldn't wait for him to come back and meet his great-granddaughter.

As for his old life in Westminster, he only missed the abundance of books he'd had at his disposal, and he missed Feenix. A couple who had recently joined the community had come with a pregnant Shetland Sheepdog and had promised Deron and Michelle one of the puppies in exchange for a small book and some clothing which the two of them would make by hand.

Deron and Michelle didn't know how well a dog would do living in underground caverns and caves with occasional time in the woods, but they agreed it would be the perfect addition to their new family.

Charlie named the puppy Liberty.

*The End*

Also by Edward M Wolfe

In The End

Reaching Kendra

To purchase these titles, please visit the author's Amazon page at: http://amazon.com/author/edwolfe

To be informed of new releases, sign up for the author's mailing list at http://edwardmwolfe.com

## About the author

Edward M Wolfe was a low-paid field reporter for one of the first independent news websites in the late 90's, and also as a city beat reporter on the Oregon coast.

He now enjoys poverty as an author living in Tulsa with two human children and two canine children. All of them write stories, play musical instruments, and compose music. Except for the dogs.

Made in the USA
Charleston, SC
07 July 2015